"I alread

Maya had been playing with some petunias and had somehow sensed Rob's presence. She'd turned her head to look at him and raced over to where he was standing.

"Um...I know you do. What are you doing with the flowers?"

She gave him a serious look. He wasn't sure she was going to answer him. "Playing dress-up," she finally said.

"Really? How do you do that?"

She let out a put-upon sigh. "Come on, I'll show you." She led him to where she'd been playing. "Sit down." She handed him a flower. "You can be Holly. I'm P'tunia."

Rob accepted the flower Maya held out to him. "I see. Holly as in Hollyhock."

Maya nodded. "Hock is her last name. *My* last name is Grant. That's my *daddy's* name."

Dear Reader,

"Prophecies? What prophecies?"

That was my response when my editor asked, "We know Grace's prophecy—'You'll marry a prince, but you'll have to save him first.' What's Kate's?" Grace Radonovic, the heroine of my first single-title release, *Betting on Grace* (Signature Select Saga, 11/05), is the youngest of four sisters. The family's Romani, or Gypsy, background added an intriguing dimension to my heroines' lives and their relationships. All four acknowledged their mother's ability to see into the future. If Grace had a prophecy, wouldn't Kate, Liz and Alex, as well?

Umm...of course. But what happens if Kate hates her prophecy and does her best to ignore it?

Kate is like a lot of young women I know. She isn't afraid to lean on her family for help, but is wary of reaching out to a stranger. Especially a man who is too young, too cute and too single. She can't picture anyone wanting to take on the burdens she bears, but she doesn't know Rob Brighten.

There's a scene in this book that involves teaching children how to swim. Having lived through an accidental drowning in my family, I feel especially passionate about this topic. In April, May and June of this year, I'm giving away a book and CD as part of my Web site contest. The book is called *Stewie the Duck Learns to Swim, a Child's First Guide to Water Safety*. If you're around young children and water, please visit www.debrasalonen.com to find a link to the Stewie the Duck site. In no time at all you, too, will be humming, "Don't jump in till you learn to swim...."

I hope you'll look for Liz's and Alex's books later this year. Talk about fateful prophecies!

Have a safe and wonderful summer!

Debra

ONE DADDY
TOO MANY
Debra Salonen

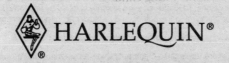

TORONTO • NEW YORK • LONDON
AMSTERDAM • PARIS • SYDNEY • HAMBURG
STOCKHOLM • ATHENS • TOKYO • MILAN • MADRID
PRAGUE • WARSAW • BUDAPEST • AUCKLAND

ISBN 0-373-75118-4

ONE DADDY TOO MANY

To Laura Shin, the most prophetic of editors

Books by Debra Salonen

HARLEQUIN SUPERROMANCE

SIGNATURE SELECT SAGA

Don't miss any of our special offers. Write to us at the
following address for information on our newest releases.

Harlequin Reader Service
U.S.: 3010 Walden Ave., P.O. Box 1325, Buffalo, NY 14269
Canadian: P.O. Box 609, Fort Erie, Ont. L2A 5X3

Chapter One

"You're fired."

Kate Radonovic Grant glanced around the empty parking lot, glad she'd tested the words aloud before actually saying them to the man who was meeting her here.

Thanks to television and a certain real-estate tycoon, the phrase had turned into a cliché. Kate needed to find a different way of telling Rob Brighten that he wasn't her lawyer anymore.

"Your services are no longer needed." *Yeah, right!* Rob had met her family—and had defended several members. If anyone needed an attorney on retainer, it was the Radonovic clan.

"Rob, this isn't working out," she tried.

No, too relationship-ish.

The fact was she liked Rob. And she appreciated everything he'd done for her family, but this was about Maya. And she couldn't take any chances where her daughter's future was concerned.

She walked back to her ten-year-old Subaru wagon and turned around to face Romantique, the restaurant she owned with her sister, Grace. Sighing, she rested her butt

on the faded silver fender. The day was already heating up
and the wind—a constant in Las Vegas—whipped her hair
about her face.

She parted the curly mop with her fingers and pushed
as much of it as she could behind her ears. She'd left the
house in such a hurry she'd forgotten her visor and sunglasses. The bright morning sun was already giving her a
headache, but as soon as she'd resolved this matter with
Rob, she'd escape into Romantique.

March had been a lion of a month for Kate and her family.
Four long weeks of stress. First, they'd found out Nikolai
Sarna, houseguest and distant relative, wasn't an out-of-
work ex-con at all. He was really a cop investigating Charles
Harmon, the man Grace had planned to go into business
with. Then Grace managed to get shot, and Charles, who'd
been arrested for insurance fraud and a bunch of other
charges, had directed his fury at the Radonovic family.
Using his many connections, he'd created havoc, including
the E. coli firestorm that had closed Romantique.

But that had only been part of Kate's ordeal. Ian Grant,
her ex-husband, had somehow managed to convince the
State of Nevada parole board that he was fully rehabilitated
and should be released early after serving just two years
of his six-year sentence for embezzlement. She'd hired
Rob to argue against parole at the hearing, but apparently
her fear that Ian might take their daughter and disappear—
as only a Gypsy can—didn't impress them.

Ian was being released soon. And he wanted shared
custody. Rob had failed her.

He was a nice guy but new to the area—and young. He'd
handled her family's legal troubles with finesse but hadn't
been able to block Ian's bid for freedom. Why? Was it be-

cause he didn't believe her when she told him Ian was a threat? Or was he not that interested in child custody cases? He hadn't even handled the case himself.

Maybe Maya is right, Kate thought. Although only four and a half, her daughter was quite astute when it came to reading people. "He doesn't like kids," she'd told Kate not long after being introduced to Rob.

Kate hadn't given the charge much credence because, at that point, price and expediency had been her main criteria for picking a lawyer. Besides, Maya usually managed to find something wrong with every man of dating age that her mother came into contact with. Kate knew why. Maya's most cherished dream was having a mommy and daddy who lived together. "Like a real family," as Maya put it.

Which was never going to happen.

Ian was a charming con man who couldn't be trusted. Period. And Kate would do whatever it took to make sure her ex didn't have easy access to his daughter. Even if that meant firing her current lawyer and going into debt to hire the toughest family attorney in Las Vegas.

Pushing off from the car, she resumed her pacing. She'd called Rob's cell phone on her way to work, thinking she might be able to handle the matter on the phone—or even better, leave a message. But he'd answered on the second ring and had immediately offered to stop by the restaurant, as if the detour weren't miles out of the way.

She walked to the back door of the building. She loved this place almost as much as she loved her daughter. She'd poured her heart and soul into the restaurant after her marriage failed.

The burnt sienna stucco walls and dark green canvas canopies, which required replacing twice a year thanks to the beating they took from the Las Vegas sun, had been her idea. "I want to create a Tuscan flavor," she'd told Grace.

Her fingers closed around the greasy yellow caution tape and ripped it away. Her anger simmered at the undeserved, malicious charge. The blow to Romantique's reputation had been disastrous, perhaps even fatal. They wouldn't know until they reopened. *If* they reopened.

With Grace out of the picture—and Kate distracted by the threat Ian posed, Romantique's future looked shaky at best.

The distinctive sound of a sports car engine intruded into her thoughts. Seconds later, a sleek silver status symbol pulled into the parking lot her restaurant shared with an upscale strip mall in northwest Las Vegas.

Her heart rate sped up a notch. Because of what she had to do, not because of Rob's presence, she told herself. Unsuccessfully.

Robert James Brighten.

Rob.

If she were honest, she'd admit that part of the reason she needed to let him go was the disturbing attraction she felt toward him. Which was crazy. Not that he wasn't damn appealing, but the timing couldn't have been worse—even if he weren't all wrong for her. Single. Never been married. Childless. Four years her junior. Not to mention, the son of her friend and right hand in the kitchen, Jo Grant.

Thank goodness he'd never given her any indication that he was attracted to her, she thought, bracing herself for what she had to do.

The Lexus purred to a stop. Kate waited on the sidewalk as the driver's side door opened. Rob unfolded his long legs and rose with the amazing fluidity of the young and fit. Once standing, he leaned over to retrieve something and her gaze zeroed in on his derriere. Elegantly sculpted in a tailored pinstripe suit. She tried not to ogle, but a person who had been without sex for as long as she had been could only muster so much willpower.

As usual, he was dressed conservatively. "His ex-fiancée brainwashed him into believing that dull and boring made him look older and more lawyerlike," his mother had complained one time. Jo's antipathy for the woman her only son had planned to marry had been obvious.

Kate couldn't help smiling when he turned to face her. A pale plum shirt rested beneath a red-and-silver tie. Maybe his ex-fiancée's influence was wearing off.

"'Morning, Kate," he hailed. "I'm glad you caught me before I got to the office—or should I say the Black Hole?"

The wind attacked his thick brown hair, which was long enough to graze his collar. She recalled thinking the first time she met Rob, when Jo had brought him to Romantique for lunch, that he possessed a hint of renegade under the guise of his staid suit. A touch of Gypsy, she'd privately called it.

After Ian, who was Romani, Kate had vowed that if she ever got involved with another man, he wouldn't carry a drop of Rom blood in his veins. Rob fit that criterion. Too bad he was wrong for her in every other way.

"Thanks for coming. We need to talk."

He nodded, pausing to toss his expensive-looking sunglasses on the seat of his car before he locked the door. "You heard about the parole hearing, I take it."

He stepped closer, squinting against the bright light. His eye color had intrigued her from the first. An odd combination of gold and green that reminded her of a desert shrub she couldn't name.

His smile was friendly, concerned. His demeanor that

of a person you could trust. *If* Kate had any trust left. Which she didn't.

Ian had made sure of that.

"What went wrong? I thought you were filing a motion or something. Don't victims have some say when a convicted felon comes up for parole?" she asked, trying to keep her emotions from showing in her voice.

"In the past, yes. But nowadays the bottom line is money. The state of Nevada has more prisoners than it wants to feed, clothe and provide medical care for. White-collar criminals like your ex-husband are deemed a low threat to the community at large. Plus, he has health issues. They couldn't wait to get him off their books."

"What kind of health issues?"

"Apparently, he has hepatitis C. As I understand it, hepatitis involves an inflammation of the liver and spreads through contact with infected blood, like AIDS, but the recovery rate is better, with proper treatment."

She'd heard of hepatitis in a vague way. "Are they absolutely sure? Ian is a consummate liar. If there was a way to fake some illness to play on the parole board's sympathies, he'd do it."

Rob shook his head. "No, his illness is legit. And he had a young, idealistic law student helping make sure his paperwork was in order. He did everything right at the hearing, and I didn't."

Kate blinked, shocked to hear such a bald confession.

"I blew it, Kate. In California, the process would have been handled differently. We'd have had more time to present our case. But that's no excuse. I should have gone to the hearing myself, instead of sending my associate."

"Why didn't you?"

He met her gaze, his green eyes truly troubled. "I honestly felt a woman would hold more sway with the board, since she was reading your letter. I gambled...and lost. But my gut says nothing we argued would have made a difference. They based their decision on economics."

Money. That Kate understood. Her savings account was just about depleted, and she still hadn't gotten a bill from Rob's firm.

"You won't be billed for this, by the way," he said as if reading her mind.

"I beg your pardon?"

"I failed, Kate. I sure as hell don't plan on charging you. Talk about adding insult to injury."

Pride made her say, "I'm not a charity case, Rob."

"I know. You're a businesswoman. And you know the importance of maintaining positive customer relations, right? Bad PR can kill you when you're just starting out— or, in my case, just starting over."

According to Jo, Rob had had mixed emotions about being assigned to the Las Vegas branch of the law firm he'd worked for since passing the bar. He claimed to welcome the challenge and was delighted to be living closer to his mother, but Jo said he still had one foot in the Bay area. Whether that meant property-wise or emotionally, Kate hadn't asked. She knew he'd made an offer on a house here but the negotiations had fallen apart. Jo claimed that whole thing had been for the benefit of his bosses—to show he was a team player and in for the count.

"He hates the desert and can't wait to get back home," Jo had said. "But he also knows that buying property is a good thing, especially in this kind of market."

Kate wanted a house so bad she sometimes dreamed of floor plans.

"So where does this leave me?" she asked, forcing her mind back to her most immediate problem. "Ian is definitely getting out of prison, right?"

"Correct. According to the state of Nevada, he's paid his debt to society and deserves a chance to start life fresh, although he'll be on parole for the next two years."

Debt to society, she silently fumed. What about his debt to her? To their daughter? "I don't care what he does as long as he leaves us alone, but that isn't going to happen, is it?"

His frown made him look older. "He's Maya's father. He's petitioned the court for joint custody. There isn't a hearing date set up yet, but you and Ian will both meet with a court-appointed mediator who will evaluate the situation and make a recommendation."

Kate's heart rate sped up recalling the dream she'd had the night before. A nightmare, actually. Her daughter being carried away on the back of a giant white spider. A spider with Ian's eyes. "He'll take her and run. I know he will."

Rob didn't appear to question her assertion. "If you can prove that he's unstable or prone to flee, you can request that all visits are monitored."

"Proof? Do dreams count?"

His smile seemed steeped in sympathy. "I told you when you and I talked in my office that family law isn't my strong point, which is why I'm going to find you a new lawyer. Someone with more experience in these matters. I'm not going to risk failing you again."

"You're quitting?" She didn't have to fire him? This was good, right? Then why her sudden sense of panic? "Rob, I understand economics. If Ian's release was inevitable, you're hardly to blame. I just wish I'd had more warning." Although how that would have changed things, she didn't know. She was up to her eyes in debt and responsibilities. Instinct said: run. But with Grace in Detroit, the fate of their restaurant—and Romantique's employees—rested squarely on Kate's shoulders.

Rob looked at the woman standing an arm's length away; the serious frown on her beautiful face told him she was deep in thought. Ian Grant probably would have made parole no matter what Rob did or didn't do, but he still felt guilty. He hoped what he was about to tell her would make up for his bungling of the case.

"I know nothing is going to excuse this blunder, but I do have some interesting news that could, potentially, mean a lot to Romantique."

"Really? What's that?" she asked, brushing a wind-whipped hunk of hair out of her eyes. Her gorgeous mocha brown eyes.

Rob liked Kate. He admired her. She'd been through hell the past couple of weeks. *Make that the past couple of years.* He didn't know anyone—except maybe his mother—who managed to rebound with as much class after the kind of blow her ex-husband dealt her. Ian Grant embezzled hundreds of thousands of dollars from his investment clients, a list that included Kate's recently-widowed mother, then tried to leave the country with another woman. Kate had been left behind to pay the price. According to his mother, she'd sold everything she owned, including their home and cars, to pay back those she could. She'd moved in with her mother and had buried herself in her work, spending sixty to seventy hours a week to make Romantique a success.

Now, the restaurant was in jeopardy. But what Rob had in mind might help.

"Mom said you've been given the green light to reopen, right?"

She nodded, the look in her eyes weary. "Unless the rumors have scared away all our customers. People are fickle. Who knows what will happen?"

"Um…isn't that an odd thing for someone with your background to say?" he asked, keeping his tone light. Kate's heritage was Romani, or Gypsy, as he would have said before his mother educated him. Even before Rob moved to Vegas, his mother had filled him in on her employer's large and…unusual family.

Her lips turned up in one corner, acknowledging his jest. "Unfortunately, the ability to see into the future didn't make it into my genes. Now, Maya, on the other hand…" She didn't go on, but Rob understood. He'd only met Kate's daughter a couple of times, but he'd sensed something uncanny about the child. She seemed to look at him with ancient eyes that could see to the bottom of his soul.

"Well, even though I'm not Rom, I predict this will bring favorable PR and hordes of customers back to Romantique."

She stared at him.

"Here," he said, extending the hardcover book he'd been hiding behind his back. "This is for you."

She recoiled slightly at first, as if any gift came with strings attached, he guessed, but then her expression turned curious. "A book?" She took it from him, turning it so the front jacket cover was legible. Out loud, she murmured, "Prowess: Loving The Older Man."

Her lips puckered for a moment, then curved in a smile. She glanced up, a grin threatening to burst into a laugh. "I don't see how my reading this will benefit the restaurant, but um…thanks?"

Rob's heart double-thudded and he had to step back to keep from touching her. He knew Kate wasn't an effusive person like other members of her family. She ran a kitchen like a submarine commander, but she didn't hug.

"You're welcome. But don't worry. You don't have to read it. Just glance at the face on the back."

Her elegant brows flickered. She flipped the book over. "Adam Brighten. Your father?"

Rob nodded. "It's his new bestseller. He sent a copy by courier yesterday. He's going to be here in Vegas the week after next for a book signing and…he's getting married. And," he beamed at her. "The celebration could be at Romantique."

Instead of looking happy, she frowned. "Does your mom know?"

Rob was touched that her first concern was for his mother. "Yes. He called her before he called me."

His parents divorced—officially—just weeks after Rob graduated from high school, but he'd known for years that they'd only stayed together because of him. But even after going their separate ways, they'd remained friends. This had bugged his ex-fiancée to no end. "People who are so radically different shouldn't like each other so much," Serena had maintained. "It's not natural."

What wasn't natural was how long it had taken him to realize he and Serena were doomed as a couple. Unfortunately, her father, Jordan Ames, who was a senior partner of the firm where Rob worked, hadn't seen the wisdom in Rob's decision. In retribution—from Rob's point of view, at least—Rob had been "offered" a new assignment. A chance to manage the Vegas branch. A law office filled with a bunch of misfits who weren't thrilled to have someone Rob's age running the show.

If Kate's case was any indication—the transcript of the hearing would give him a clearer picture of what happened—he had an uphill battle ahead. He was, undoubtedly, in over his head, but he wasn't his mother's son for nothing. He'd whip this office into shape, then return home to the Bay area triumphant. But, first, his father needed his help, which, coincidentally, might prove fortuitous to Kate.

"Is Jo okay with this?" Kate asked, drawing him back to the present. "I mean, I know she's moved on and probably wants the best for him, but…marriage. Wow. That's a big deal, right?"

"For my dad? Absolutely. If you'd have asked me yesterday, I would have said he's a confirmed bachelor. But apparently once he met Haley it was love at first sight. Two months later he proposed."

"Whoa," she said, her look telling him a great deal even though all she said was, "That's quick."

Rob agreed, although he'd refrained from saying so to his father. "I think Dad's been lonely and dissatisfied with his life for a long time." Not that Rob talked to his father often. When the two got together, they golfed. Period.

"Dad said they met at a photo shoot for a magazine that was interviewing him. She's a model. My age or a little younger."

"Oh." She handed him back the book. "Well, um, congratulations. I'll give your mom a call—"

He interrupted. "Don't bother. She's on her way here. Should be arriving any minute."

"Jo's coming here?" Kate looked toward the street, as if expecting Jo to pull up right that instant. But Rob knew what 8:00 a.m. traffic was like in Vegas. Even more prone to bottlenecks and accidents than in Oakland, where he'd grown up, or San Francisco where he'd graduated from college and first practiced law.

"You know Mom. She hates to miss out on work." He motioned toward the building. "Have you gone inside yet? It's too bad you didn't have proof that the complaint was bogus *before* the health department got involved."

Rob had been pleased to hear that Charles Harmon had admitted faking the E. coli claim. Unfortunately, his confession couldn't undo the damage to Romantique's reputation.

She took a key from the pocket of her snug, faded jeans. Her gray University of Nevada Las Vegas sweatshirt had seen better days, but on Kate, it looked stylish. Her running shoes were thick-soled and functional, albeit slightly tattered.

He followed her inside, standing close enough to get a hint of her fragrance. Not perfume. Just soap and a crisp, citrus-scented shampoo.

"I have a professional cleaning crew coming this afternoon. I'm just here to take inventory so I can give Grace some idea of when we'll be ready to reopen. She's going to put together a press release."

Rob cleared his throat. "Didn't you hear what I said? I think my news might make any additional advertising redundant."

He watched her shoulders rise as she inhaled a breath of chilly, stale air. "What do you mean?" she asked on the exhale.

Her breathlessness was so sexy it produced a humming sensation perilously close to the place that would reveal how he felt if she turned around and glanced down. He'd made it a point to keep the attraction he felt toward her to himself—for propriety's sake. Plus, she really wasn't his type.

He forced his attention back to the topic at hand. "How would you like to reopen on a high note? Reporters. Photographers. A crew from *Entertainment Central.*"

She gave him a questioning look. "Have you been snorting the dust from too many old law books?"

Playfully, he tapped her on the nose with the corner of the book she'd handed back to him. "As best man at my father's wedding, I get to pick the place for the reception. Where better than Romantique? A hundred guests. Celebrities. Paparazzi. TV coverage."

She swayed slightly as if the possibility made her knees weak. They bumped body parts. Mostly elbows and forearms, but a little skin. A little warmth. Enough to make his throat dry up.

"Here? You want to hold the reception here?" She sounded shocked, as if good fortune were so alien a concept she couldn't get her mind around it.

"Where else? Mom's even promised to bake an appropriately spectacular cake."

Kate stared at him, her brown eyes so wide and fathomless he felt momentarily lost in them. He saw her embrace the possibilities. "This could be big."

"Did I mention Dad's bride-to-be was on the cover of *InStyle* a few months back?" He knew nothing about the magazine, but his mother had sounded impressed when she'd called.

"The bounce we get from this might make people forget the rumors," she said, motioning him to follow. She walked inside, turning on lights as she led the way to the main kitchen.

He hesitated, reminded of the fact she'd summoned him this morning. "Before I forget, you're the one who called me, remember? I sort of blew past that point without letting you speak. Sorry."

She stopped dead in her tracks and turned to face him. A rosy hue inched up her neck. A second later, her chin lifted. "I'd planned to fire you," she said softly. "But maybe I was a bit hasty."

Chapter Two

"No, you were looking out for yourself and Maya. Just what a good mother should do."

His cheerful tone wasn't what Kate had expected.

"But I'd like the chance to make amends," he continued. "If you want me to get a restraining order in place or hire a bodyguard, I'd be happy to do it."

A bodyguard? Who could protect her daughter from someone like Ian, who outwardly was as unthreatening and docile as that mild-mannered neighbor who suddenly, for no reason, shoots his family? In her dream, Ian had carried Maya away while everyone watched. What good would a bodyguard do—even if she could afford one?

"You don't think I'm overreacting? My sisters were quick to point out that Ian has never shown much interest in our daughter in the past, so maybe this is just an attempt to rattle me."

"That could be. Or he saw the light while he was inside."

She thought she detected a hint of sarcasm in his voice. "Either way, I don't plan to make this easy for him. He was too busy to be a real dad to her when he lived with us, so this sudden concern for Maya doesn't ring true. He wants something, and I have a hard time believing it's his daughter's love. And if he thinks he's going to take her away, he's in for the fight of his life."

Rob nodded as if he was totally convinced. "I have the name of a retired lawyer who does consulting for free. Let me call my office and get his number. We can give him a call and see what he suggests. Okay?"

Free is good.

While Rob used his cell phone, Kate reviewed the conversation she'd had with her mother over breakfast. Yetta seemed to think the only way Kate was going to be able to move forward in her life was to make peace with the past, which included coming to grips with Ian's betrayal. Kate didn't know how that was possible, but she knew it was useless to pretend that he didn't exist—the way she had while he was incarcerated. Ian was Maya's father. He would always be a part of her life—unless she killed him. Which would be a distinct possibility if he tried to take Maya away.

"Read this and tell me what you think," Yetta had said, giving Kate a letter she'd received from Ian the day before. In it, he'd pleaded for Yetta's forgiveness, vowing to make back the money he'd stolen and to do everything in his power to rebuild her family's trust.

He'd also mentioned his poor health and belief that Western medicine had failed him. *"I know you could help me recover my health, Yetta,"* he'd written. *"You are Puri Dye—keeper of the old ways. Your herbs would surely be my salvation if you could find it in your heart to help a weak, lost soul."*

Clever as always, Ian had appealed to her mother's humanity, plus he'd shown his respect for his ancestry.

"You're not thinking about helping him, are you?" Kate had asked, appalled.

"I haven't decided," Yetta had answered. "But you can't avoid this collision with the past, Katherine. It's your destiny."

Kate had refused to discuss "the prophecy." In the past, everyone in their Romani clan had put a great deal of stock in Yetta's power of precognition. Each of her four daughters knew from a very young age what their mother had foreseen in their futures. In Kate's opinion, hers read like a bad fortune cookie: *You can't escape your destiny nor avoid the past when the two intersect.* Baloney.

Kate's faith in her mother's prophetic abilities had been tested—and broken—more than once. First, Yetta had had no warning of her husband's stroke. Then, after his death, she'd put her trust—and the money from Ernst's life insurance policy—in Ian's hands without telling anyone. And when he disappeared, Yetta had seemed truly mystified by Ian's betrayal, as if she'd had no warning whatsoever.

No, Kate didn't give a crap about her so-called destiny, but she did care about Maya's future. And she'd do everything in her power to keep her daughter safe.

To that end, she brought her attention back to the present when she heard Rob say to the person on the other end of the phone, "Great. I'll tell her. Thanks a lot."

He closed his phone and looked at her. "Okay. He'll meet with you tomorrow morning. If you like him and feel comfortable with his representation, my secretary will hand-deliver the files that I have on the case."

"You're giving up on me, huh?" She wanted to take back the question the minute it came out. She sounded needy and pathetic.

Rob gave her a stern look that made him appear much older. "Absolutely not. I'm putting my ego aside and letting the more experienced litigator take over."

"That's very noble."

"Noble." He snickered softly. "Yeah, right. I don't think nobility is in my genes. Unlike Nick. The prince."

His comment told her Rob had heard the gossip about Grace and her future husband, Nick Lightner. Unlike Kate, Grace's prophecy was cut and dried: You will marry a prince, but you will have to save him first. Grace had done just that—both by taking a bullet that might have been meant for him and by convincing him that he was worthy of love.

"You know, I don't think I've ever heard your prophecy."

"For good reason. It's nonsense. Now, what were you telling me about your father's party?"

Rob let the blatant change of topic go without comment because he sensed an undercurrent of emotion in her voice. "Maybe we should wait for Mom to get here. She'll certainly have an opinion on the subject. Meanwhile fill me in on Grace. Have she and Nick set a date?"

"I don't think she's decided on the exact day. Nikolai's still waiting to hear about his promotion, but most likely they'll make Detroit their home."

Her tone sounded resigned.

"That's really wild. She's marrying the undercover cop who was responsible for getting three Romani family members arrested. What happens here? Mom says Grace is going to continue handling the bookkeeping by fax and Internet."

"Right. And I get to hire a new hostess. You can't exactly telecommute that."

He didn't buy her flippant tone. "This has got to be tough, Kate. I'm sorry."

She made a halfhearted attempt at a smile. "Me, too. But I don't have a lot of say in the matter. My sister has the right to fall in love and marry her Prince Charming. Maybe if Romantique was still making money and our reputation was intact, I'd sell the place and move. So far away Ian would never find us. But since most of my savings went to pay the bills while we've been closed…." She winced. "Sorry. More information than you wanted, right?"

She looked so disconsolate Rob was tempted to hug her. "Not at all. I'm just sorry I added to your worries."

She shrugged. "Maybe this is the way things are supposed to work out. Mom says Ian is a part of our lives for a reason—it's up to us to figure out why."

He was surprised by her fatalistic attitude. He'd always been impressed by her take-charge mentality. Rolling over and accepting fate's whims didn't seem like her.

"That might be true, but it still pays to be prepared. Prison can change a person. And not necessarily for the better. Grant is sick. My associate said he looked like death warmed over at the parole hearing, but that doesn't mean he couldn't do a lot of damage—"

"Yoo-hoo, I'm here," a loud, raspy voice called, cutting off his train of thought. A smoker's voice. His mother's. "Oh, good. You've got the book."

The woman hurrying toward them was short and stocky with closely cropped silver hair. "I didn't want to run out and buy a copy. Adam and I were married seventeen years. Would it hurt him to give me one?"

Rob handed the book to her. "Here you go. It's all yours, but I suggest you double up on your blood pressure medicine before you start it," he said, sending a wink Kate's way.

"Oh, pooh, you know this is just commercial blather. Adam doesn't actually believe any of this malarkey."

"Then why'd he write it?" Kate asked.

"To make money, of course. And to prove he could."

Rob wasn't sure either of those explanations was true. As he'd read the words his father wrote, Rob heard excuses. Clever, cerebral excuses for a self-indulgent life that had wounded many and left some, his son for instance, baffled and uneasy.

Kate looked at him as if sensing his ambivalence. "Well, I'm glad his publishing career is working out. Especially since he wants to drop a little of that cash here."

As Kate filled his mother in on the plan, Rob watched the two interact. His mother was a flake, according to Serena, but Kate treated Jo with respect and what appeared to be genuine affection. His mother had never seemed happier.

Another reason why Rob needed to ignore the attraction he felt toward Kate. Besides, she broke all his rules.

Rule No. 1: the women he dated had to be single, never been married. He didn't need someone else's emotional baggage—he had enough of his own.

Rule No. 2: no kids. This point was nonnegotiable. Not even when the kid was as cute and smart as Maya.

Rule No. 3: career-minded, but not obsessed with her work. According to his mother, Kate lived and breathed Romantique. He was still young. He wanted the freedom to dash off to the islands for a romantic weekend on a whim. Spend his money foolishly. Indulge in long Sunday mornings spent on breakfast in bed and crossword puzzles.

So what if that sounded totally hedonistic? He was living out of a suitcase at a long-term-residence hotel. That didn't exactly make him daddy material, right? Especially for someone who'd been burned as badly as Kate had.

Nope. He had to do the right thing. The noble thing. He'd help her settle her custody issues, throw her restaurant some business while making his dad happy, then get the heck out of her life. And Vegas. Who in their right mind thought living on the desert twenty-four/seven was a good idea? He missed the Bay area more than he ever thought possible. *What I wouldn't give for a little fog…*

He started, realizing the two women were waiting for him to reply to some question. "Huh?"

His mother gave him a look that said she knew what he was thinking. He couldn't read Kate's face as easily. "Jo asked if there was a wedding planner involved."

Rob didn't have a clue. But he'd find out.

He pulled out a checkbook from the inside pocket of his suit coat and quickly scribbled an amount and his signature. "At the moment, all I'm concerned about is making sure we have a place. Will this work as a deposit?" He handed her the check.

Her gasp told him she was surprised. And pleased.

"Dad gave me carte blanche," he told her. "He wants the best. I know I can trust you to deliver that."

Kate managed to keep her emotions together until Rob left. She stared at the zeroes neatly scribed on the amount line of the check until tears clouded her eyes.

"Honey girl, don't cry. I've been telling you all along, good things happen to good people. Sometimes, it just takes a while to prime the pump," Jo told her, giving Kate's shoulders a robust squeeze.

Jo was the one person, aside from Kate's sisters and her daughter, who could hug her and get away with it.

"This is too much," Kate said. "Your son must think I'm a charity case."

"My son is infatuated. He just won't admit it."

The check Kate had been drooling over slipped from her suddenly numb fingers and fluttered to the tile floor, which was covered in white dust and foot tracks. "He…you… no…don't kid about something like that, Jo," she said when her power of speech returned. "Rob's a great guy. The best. But no way in the world would he be interested in someone like me."

Jo, who'd grabbed a broom from the utility closet, leaned on it and said, "*Someone like you?* You mean someone who puts family first, who works twenty hours a day and still manages to be a great mom and fabulous boss? And would look like a model, if she ever wore anything but jeans and a chef's uniform?"

Kate laughed out loud. "Very funny. I'm skinny, burnt-out and emotionally bankrupt. But even if I were a gorgeous young supermodel, Rob and I wouldn't stand a chance."

"Why?"

"Because I'm a mother, and I get the distinct impression he doesn't like children."

"Oh, pooh," Jo said. "He used to love kids. In high school, he spent every summer working at our community pool. He just comes off a little stiff because he's been around law books and stuffed suits too much. Maya could whip him into shape quick enough."

Kate doubted that. Maya, who was the most intuitive four-year-old Kate had ever known, wasn't smitten with Rob, either. "He's icky. And his shoes squeak," her daughter had declared after meeting Rob at Romantique one evening when he dropped by to pick up his mother.

Kate didn't think either point was true, but she hadn't pressed the issue, other than to reprimand her daughter for her use of the word *icky.*

"Well, this is a moot point," Kate said. "He's your son. And a client. And my soon-to-be ex-lawyer. That's all."

Jo resumed sweeping. "Yeah, sure. Only you two are going to be working very closely over the next two weeks. Some might regard that as fate lending a matchmaking hand." She used her broom to tap out the beat to "Here Comes the Bride."

Kate laughed, even as a shiver ran down her spine. "Stop. I did the bride thing once. And believe me, once was enough. I learned my lesson. From now on, I only say, 'I don't.'"

Chapter Three

"What will you do, Katherine?"

"Murder sounds appealing. If only my future brother-in-law really had been a hit man," Kate said with a sigh. She kept her voice down so as not to alert Maya to her return. Her daughter was in the living room watching a DVD.

It was only three o'clock in the afternoon, but Kate was exhausted. She'd put in six long, grueling hours cleaning Romantique. Even with a professional crew and Jo's help, the job had been more difficult than she'd expected. Physically and emotionally draining.

Her mother's kitchen smelled of ginger snap cookies and lentil soup. Warm and welcoming. But Kate was consumed by a restless energy. Something was going to happen. Good or bad, she couldn't say.

"There must be other options, dear," her mother said, her tone sardonic. "You don't even know where Ian will be staying, do you? A halfway house. Or a hospital. There's no reason to think he'll be anywhere nearby."

Kate stepped closer to her mother and lowered her voice. "Anywhere in Clark County is too close for my comfort. He's not only a liar and a thief, but he's sick.

Maybe contagious. What if he gives this disease to Maya?"

Yetta dropped the spoon she was using to stir her stew. "Is that what you think will happen?"

Kate rolled her shoulders trying to work out a few knots. "I don't know. For the first time in my life, I wish I could see into the future. My gut says run, but do you know how much all this stuff around my neck weighs?"

Yetta wiped her hands on a towel and put her arms around Kate. "Yes, dear, I think I do."

Kate tried to keep herself rigid, but her mother's scent—comforting and familiar—filled her nostrils and made her relax—just a tiny bit.

"Why is this happening now, Mom? Nobody made Ian steal that money. What he did was his choice, but Maya and I had to pay for it. I sold our house, cars, boat and all the toys Ian couldn't live without. I emptied my trust fund to repay people. We moved in with you. I'm thirty-two years old and living with my mother," she said shaking her head.

"Not because you needed me, but because I was lonely and miserable until you and Maya brought me back to life," Yetta said firmly.

The words were nice to hear—and deep down Kate knew her mother meant what she said, but nothing could erase the sense of failure Kate felt. She'd finally started rebuilding her life. She'd had a flourishing business and money saved for the deposit on a new place of their own—until this E. coli fiasco. And now, her ex suddenly decides he wants to be a daddy.

Kate stepped back and resumed pacing. "I just don't get it. Ian signed the divorce papers without a word. Ever since, I've had to make all the decisions about our daughter's welfare, and he never once asked to see her. Not once. Now, he wants to share custody. Why? Does he think he can do better?"

Yetta returned to the stove and picked up the spoon she'd used to stir the soup. "Katherine, no one in their right mind would question your parenting skills. Your daughter is an absolute delight—wise, generous and kind. But Ian is her father. Not a good one, I agree, but he exists. And there will come a time when she'll resent the fact that you kept her from seeing him. She might even run away to be with him. That could be disastrous."

Kate closed her eyes. Suddenly, she had a clear image of a young teen with flowing brown curls on the side of the road. Hitchhiking. Alone. Vulnerable.

"I didn't say I'd never let her meet Ian," she said, shaking her head. "Maybe after he gets well…is this something you can recover from? Liz would know. I'm going to call her."

"She isn't home. She had some kind of hearing with those two poor women from Charles's hotel. They're asking to be allowed to stay in the United States, and Elizabeth is trying to help."

Kate had been too distracted by her own troubles to pay much attention to her sister's latest humanitarian effort. "Well, the lawyer Rob set me up with said he'll schedule an appointment with a family mediator once Ian gets released. I only hope it's later rather than sooner. With this wedding coming up in a hurry, I'm going to be swamped."

She filled her mother in on the job Rob had tossed her way then asked, "Do you need my help? I've been so busy worrying about Ian I just stood here and let you do all the cooking."

"Heavens no. The soup just needs to simmer a bit longer."

Simmer—pretty much all Kate had been doing lately. And she was sick of it. She walked to the doorway that connected to the living room. "Hey, poops, let's go fly the kite you got for your birthday from Auntie Liz. It's still light outside and we both need the exercise."

Twenty minutes later, at Lorenzi Park, Maya called out in a high-pitched squeal, "Run, Mommy, run fast."

Ironic, Kate thought as she gamely fought to keep the kite aloft. Her daughter was urging her to do exactly what her sixth sense said to do. Run. But which way? And for how long? Would distance alone be sufficient to avoid this upcoming confrontation with her own failure?

She'd loved Ian, but he'd lied to her, along with everyone else. *I was a gullible fool once, but I'm through letting him control my life—even in absentia.*

Her goals were clear-cut and simple: rebuild her restaurant's reputation, care for her daughter and, when she could afford it, move into a place of her own. She knew she couldn't rely on anyone else to make these things happen. Not her family, not Ian and certainly not Rob.

The fine string pulled taut beneath her fingers as breeze and kite connected. "Okay, Miss M, let go of the tail."

The exotic blue-and-gold parrot-shaped kite shot skyward, nearly ripping the plastic spool from Kate's left hand.

"Ooh, pretty," Maya said, clapping and jumping up as if to touch the dancing yellow ribbons. "You're good, Mommy."

The praise was sweet, but it turned out to be premature. A minute later, the wind died. The kite drifted back to the ground faster than Kate could rewind the string. She ended up surrounded by an unraveled mess.

The image fit her life perfectly, she decided. She and Ian had been flying high—briefly, dazzlingly. But then everything crashed. And she couldn't get over her anger. Even now, she wanted to punish Ian for ruining their perfect life. But her mother was right. Someday, Maya would hold Kate accountable for the decisions she made today.

"Don't worry, Mommy. We can try again."

Kate sat down and pulled her daughter into her lap. "Maya, love, we need to talk. Remember how I told you your father didn't live with us because he did something wrong and had to go away?"

"Uh-huh."

"Well, now he's coming back."

"When?"

"I don't know exactly. Soon, I think."

"Will he move into Grandma's house with us?"

"No."

"Will he live in an apartment? Like Jo?"

Kate had taken Maya to visit Jo, who lived in a gated senior complex for active adults. The place had three pools, tennis courts and two gyms. And nearly everyone they met had a dog. Maya had been enthralled.

"I don't know. But since he's younger than Jo, I'd guess not. You have to be a certain age to live in that kind of place."

"Oh. How come Daddy isn't coming to live with us? Like Gemilla's daddy?"

Gemilla, Kate's cousin's daughter, was Maya's best friend.

She focused on rewinding the loose string, her hands trembling. Not from the chill in the air, she knew. This was a talk she'd put off for too long. "Gregor and MaryAnn are married, honey. You know that. Mommy and Daddy are divorced. Divorced people live apart but they still share

their children. Sometimes the dad spends a lot of time with
his kids and sometimes not so much."

"When can I see him?"

Every cell in her body cried, "Never," but Kate forced
herself to smile and answer, "I don't know. We'll work out
a schedule once he gets…settled." She'd almost said well,
but she didn't want to worry Maya until she had all the facts.

Maya nodded and jumped to her feet. "Okay. My turn,"
she said, grabbing the spool of string.

Kate was just about to reprimand her for being rude
when her cell phone rang. She didn't recognize the number
but since it was local, she took the call, as she stood up.

"Hi, Kate, it's Rob. I know it's bold of me to ask, but I
need a favor."

Rob. She'd spent way too much time thinking about
him this afternoon as she was cleaning the grill. Fantasiz-
ing about the impossible. A different her. A different him.
A different time in their lives.

She shook her head to chase away the silly dreams.
"What kind of favor?"

"The shopping kind. Mom and I are at Rosemary's
having dinner and I realized I need a gift for my dad.
She told me you decorated Romantique almost single-
handedly. You know where to shop in Vegas. And you have
excellent taste. Is there any way you could spare a couple
of hours some day this week? I know you're going to have
your hands full with this party, but, believe me, I'm shopping challenged."

Interior design was Kate's private passion. While married
to Ian, she'd had seemingly unlimited funds to indulge her
hobby. But, aside from outfitting Romantique, she hadn't
even stepped foot in a store except to buy things for Maya.

The wind gusted hard. Maya ran gamely trying to keep the kite aloft, but the parrot flapped just once or twice before making a spectacular spiral straight to earth.

"Oh," Maya said with a sigh of disgust, then she trudged over to the fallen bird and started winding up the string again.

Kate wondered briefly if Rob had somehow sensed this hidden passion of hers, but did that matter? He'd brought her a huge party. She owed him a favor—and if his request involved something she enjoyed… "Okay."

ROB CLOSED HIS PHONE with a smile. She'd agreed to take him shopping. He wasn't sure what had made him ask. Need—definitely. Serena once said that Rob had the worst taste of any person she'd ever met. She'd never allowed him to pick out a thing—clothing, items for the condo, the color of his car. She'd undermined his self-confidence—department-storewise—so completely, he actually suffered a slight panic attack when called upon to buy a gift for someone.

He looked toward the bar where his mother was having a smoke with her brandy. His mother thought that was the funniest thing she'd ever heard. When he'd brought up the subject over dinner, Jo had suggested he ask for Kate's help.

"You're not trying to fix us up, are you?" he'd asked.

"Of course not. You're not her type."

He agreed, but it still irked him to hear her say so. "What makes you so sure?"

"She's a single mom, and you've never exactly gone out of your way to cozy up to her kid."

Rob hadn't bothered to deny the charge, but neither was he ready to explain—to his mother, at least—why he'd avoided having much contact with Maya. She was a beautiful little girl. The few times they'd met, a part of him had wanted to squat down and find out what was going on behind those big, intensely observant brown eyes, but he hadn't let himself.

As he sipped his coffee, he brought to mind a memory that still haunted him. It was the moment Rob fully understood the word *affair*. He had been nine or ten at the time. The latest woman his father had been seeing—a beautiful young coed who'd returned to college after her marriage failed—showed up one night at their door. She'd come to confront Adam, to convince him to leave his wife. She'd brought her six-year-old daughter with her. Rob would never forget the anguish and confusion on that child's face. The little girl might not have understood everything that was going on, but she knew her mother was in pain, and she knew that another man was rejecting them. Again. Just as her father had.

Rob had vowed never to date women with children. Relationships were tricky, ephemeral. He refused to risk contributing pain to some kid's life. The longest he'd ever dated a girl—prior to his two-year relationship with Serena—had been eight months. With that kind of track record, someone like Kate, no matter how great she was, was off-limits.

But that didn't mean they couldn't be friends. And business associates. Right?

"Well, what'd she say?" a voice asked.

Rob's nose twitched at the familiar scent of cigarette smoke. He'd given up hassling his mother about her bad habit. Instead, he smiled and said, "Yes. She said she would help me find just the right gift for Dad and…" For a second, he couldn't remember his future stepmother's name.

"Haley."

He snapped his fingers. "Right. You're lucky. You don't have to shop. The cake you're making will be the perfect gift."

He stood up, checking his pocket for his keys and sunglasses. "Are you ready? I have some briefs to read. I swear the lawyers in this office are the laziest bunch of miscreants I've ever worked with. All they want to do is golf and take two-hour lunches."

His mother shouldered her purse strap. "Isn't that why you went to law school—because Tiger Woods beat you out of a spot on the pro tour?"

He laughed. They both knew he wasn't anywhere close to Tiger's standard. Golf was a hobby. An excuse for Rob and his father to spend time together without really talking. But the law—Rob loved being a lawyer. Well, he had until his ex-fiancée's father sent him to Las Vegas as punishment for breaking his daughter's heart.

He ushered Jo toward the door, nodding goodbye to the hostess, a beautiful blonde who'd flirted with Rob when they first came in. In the past, he might have asked for her number, but tonight his mind was still on Kate's laugh.

"You know what you need, don't you?" his mother asked, as he held the door for her.

Thinking she was talking about the gift he was going to buy, he said, "No. What?"

"A family."

Rob's heart made a funny skip in his chest. "And which store sells those? Only the top-of-the-line, of course. No bargain basement families for me, you know."

She shook her finger at him. "You're joking now, but when you're my age. And all alone. You'll be sorry."

Once outside, Rob took his mother by the shoulders and

gave her a gentle squeeze. "Don't get all mushy on me, Mom. I was only kidding. I plan on having a wife and kids. Someday," he added pointedly.

"Well, someday has a way of disappearing, like potato chips. You reach in for one, then another, always looking for the very best. Then suddenly the bag is empty, and you're fat and old and out of shape."

Rob fought to keep from laughing. He could tell she was serious and he didn't want to hurt her feelings. "Well, that's a theory of life I haven't heard before."

She made a skeptical snort. "You're smug, Rob. Albeit with good reason. You're young and handsome. You have a high-paying career and a great deal of ambition. But you're also short-sighted."

He pressed his finger to the bridge of his nose. "I am?"

"Yes. You are. Because sometimes you're so concerned about what's on that silly list of requirements for the perfect mate, you don't see what's right in front of your face."

He knew she was referring to Kate. And Maya.

"I see my car," he said, opening the passenger door. "And if you don't get in, I might leave you here." He kept his tone light, so she'd know he was teasing. But her comments got to him.

He'd always been candid about the qualities he wanted in the person he married. Was that wrong? He'd often heard that the best way to make sure something happened was to visualize it. He had the list memorized. And his mother was right—Kate didn't fit the list.

But that was okay. He wasn't asking her to marry him— he only wanted her help shopping.

Chapter Four

"Did not."

"Did so."

Hands on hips, Rob stared down at his adversary. She was one tough, single-minded opponent. Her oratory skills left a little to be desired, but what did he expect of a four-year-old?

"Rob. Maya. If you two don't quit bickering, I'm sending you both to time-out chairs."

Rob looked at Kate, who was openly grinning. When she'd called that morning to tell him she had a few hours free if he wanted to go shopping, he'd immediately instructed his secretary to rearrange his schedule. No easy task, but once the juggling was complete he had an open block of time to spend with Kate. And Maya, it turned out.

"Just try to get along for a few more minutes. Mom promised to call as soon as Alex got back from her doctor's appointment." Apparently the eldest Radonovic sister had some kind of ongoing gynecological problems. Kate had explained that since the Dancing Hippo, Alex's child-care center, was short-handed at the moment, she'd felt she should keep Maya with her until Alex returned.

No problem, Rob had thought. Until Maya started pushing buttons Rob didn't even know he had.

"Sorry, Kate. I don't know what's wrong with me. I'm not usually this defensive about my shoes." He glanced down at the demon cherub with the innocent smile. "But they don't squeak. They cost an arm and a leg."

"Then you'd only need one," Maya said.

Her mother made a sound somewhere between a snort and a giggle. Rob reluctantly grinned. The kid was smart. He respected that.

"Can we get back to the business at hand?" Kate asked.

She had her hair pulled off her neck with a silver and turquoise clip that matched her slim-fitting capri pants. Her black V-neck top exposed a patch of skin where a matching necklace hung. He'd wanted to compliment her but Maya's scrutiny had stopped him.

"Until you narrow down the field, I can't even tell you which store we should be looking in. Do you want something personal? Something for their home? Practical? Memorable?"

Rob had no idea.

He reviewed her choices but nothing jumped out at him. Outside of golfing apparel and equipment, he didn't know his father's taste well—and he had yet to meet Haley, the future Mrs. Brighten. "I assume they're going to live in Palo Alto—Dad has a house there, but I could be wrong. Should I call and ask?"

Maya grabbed the hem of his suit coat and tugged.

"What?"

She motioned for him to bend down.

He did.

"Sexy," she whispered, her voice ringing in his ear.

He shot upright. "I beg your pardon."

She put her hands on her hips and sighed. "My Auntie Grace is getting married and I heard Mommy tell Auntie Liz not to waste her money on pots and pans 'cause the best gifts are sexy."

He looked at Kate whose cheeks were decidedly pink.

"Really? Well, I'll take that under advisement."

Maya's eyes narrowed. "You talk funny."

The kid in him had a reply: "You smell funny." But he was mature enough to keep it to himself.

Maya suddenly pointed to Rob and broke out laughing. Rob looked at Kate, who appeared baffled by her daughter's display of hilarity. It was almost as if Maya had read his mind. But that wasn't possible. Was it?

Good Lord, he hoped not.

Kate heard a familiar jingle and reached into her purse. The word on the display of her phone read: Mom.

"I…um…think I have a copy of Haley's bridal registry around here somewhere," Rob said looking as if he welcomed the excuse to escape.

"Good. That might give us a place to start," she said.

"It's in my bedroom-slash-office-slash-storeroom. I'll be right back," he said, hurrying across the suite.

They'd met at his place since it was centrally located. As he walked away, Kate fought back a smile. Listening to him argue with Maya had been a revelation. Apparently she wasn't the only adult who got sucked into her daughter's challenges.

Kate put the phone to her ear. "Hi, Mom. How's Alex?"

She only half listened as Yetta explained about Alex's test results. All normal. That was good. With her other ear, Kate took in Maya's litany of complaints.

"This place is too brown, Mommy. It smells funny. Do you think he's going to change shoes. They do, too, squeak. Can we go now?"

Kate bid her mother goodbye then closed the phone. She tried to stifle her irritation as she squatted down to deal with Maya. Normally, her daughter was up for any kind of adventure, but the little girl had been cross and contrary all morning. Or rather, ever since she found out about this stop at Rob's.

"Maya, what's wrong? I told you why we're here."

"I don't like him."

"You don't even know Rob. He's Jo's son. You like her, don't you?"

Her eyes went big. "I love Jo. When she's working, you can do things with me."

Kate's heart melted. She'd been so busy making a success of Romantique she'd missed out on a lot of time with her daughter. "That's right. And, thanks to Rob, I'm going to be able to get the restaurant open again. He brought us a big job, so helping him buy a present for his father is my way of thanking him."

Maya's lips puckered in a serious look for a minute. "All right. But I don't like it here."

"Well, I'm sure Rob doesn't plan to stay here forever. Do you, Rob?"

She'd heard his return—even without squeaky shoes.

He glanced around. "No. Of course not. I actually had a place in escrow but it fell through."

Kate had heard that. His mother claimed the deal went sour because Rob didn't truly want to be here. That he was only going through the motions to impress his bosses.

"You might like The Lakes. It's in Henderson. Not far

from where Liz lives. Jo said you golf, and they have several nice courses."

"I'll remember that. At the moment, I'm so busy, I can't even get back to my Realtor." He shrugged.

"I like Grandma's house," Maya said.

"I know you do, honey, but we're not going to live there forever. Someday we'll move into a place of our own."

"With Daddy?"

Oh, Ian, thanks for putting me in this position. "No, sweetie, not with your dad. We talked about this, remember?"

"But…maybe—"

"Crystal."

Kate and Maya looked at each other then at Rob, who was pointing at the paper he'd brought in with him. "The list says, 'Anything crystal.' That covers a lot of areas, doesn't it? Both housewares and artsy-far…" His mumble sort of faded away.

Kate felt a serious tenderness touch her heart.

Maya tightened her grip on Kate's hand. "Where's your swimming pool?"

Rob appeared baffled by the sudden change in topic, but he pointed over his shoulder, kindly choosing to ignore her daughter's petulant tone. "In the courtyard opposite the lobby. It's not very big, but they keep it nice and cool. Wanna see?"

He motioned for her to follow him to the pair of windows on the opposite side of the room. Kate watched them.

They looked charming together. Almost like a daddy and his little girl.

She tried to ignore the totally unwelcome thought. Rob wasn't the daddy type and she needed to remember that.

"Our swimming pool is round," Maya stated. "Not square, like that one."

That one. There was no missing her daughter's critical tone. Kate looked at Rob and blushed. "Um, we'd better go. I told Jo I'd meet her at Romantique later to go over the updates your dad's wedding planner faxed."

"You bet. The sooner we get this over with, the sooner I can breathe easy. I told my secretary if we couldn't find anything, I was putting her in charge of the task. She said she'd quit first."

Kate could tell he was joking. He didn't seem the type to be a bully in the workplace. If her hunch was right, he was a softhearted boss.

"Ready, ladies?" He fished a set of keys out of his pocket and said, "Why don't I follow you in my truck?"

"You have a truck?" Kate asked. "I've never seen you drive anything but the Lexus."

He led the way through the pleasantly landscaped grounds to the parking lot. "I usually keep it at Mom's, but she asked me to pick up a new patio umbrella that she bought, so I drove it home last night. It belonged to my uncle. My dad's brother. He passed away four years ago. Since he and my dad didn't get along—the result of something that happened when they were younger, I was Uncle Pete's only heir."

He paused at the curb, looking for Kate's car. She'd parked a few stalls down from the late-model navy-blue, four-door pickup truck that he pointed his remote key at.

"Ian had one similar to this," she said, pausing to get her keys out of her purse. "We used it to pull our boat."

"We had a boat?" Maya chirped.

Kate nodded. The toys. The expense. The arguments. *Maybe if I'd paid more attention to the checkbook...* She pushed the thought aside. She'd been slightly preoccupied at the time with her infant daughter, her father's stroke and opening a new business. Plus, Ian had always demanded total control over their mutual finances. "I'll take care of the money, you run the house," he'd insisted.

"You were just a tiny babe, sweetie," Kate said, grabbing Maya's hand to lead her toward their car. "We'll meet you at the Hippo, okay?" she called over her shoulder to Rob. "Then, I'm thinking Caesar's Palace. They have several shops with amazing crystal pieces."

She didn't wait for an answer. The day was heating up fast. The car was stifling. She'd locked it out of habit and had forgotten to crack open the windows. She heard Rob's truck engine roar to life as she checked to make sure Maya's seat belt was fastened, then she hurried around to the driver's side and got in. She turned the key.

Nothing happened.

"Oh, no. Not today," she groaned. Her starter had been acting temperamental all week. She jiggled the key and tried again. Not even a spark. Another unplanned expense she couldn't afford.

"What's wrong, Mommy?"

Everything, honey. Pretty much everything.

KATE LOOKED but didn't touch.

She'd never been a huge fan of art glass. She was more of a tactile person. Leather. Wool. Silk. Pottery. Those interested her far more than crystal, which was too cold for her taste. But she could admire any art from afar.

Especially at these prices.

"Wow. This place is really something," Rob said, stepping beside her. He'd been a fabulous sport about her car trouble and her ornery daughter—even though Maya had pestered him the whole time he was attempting to install her booster seat in his vehicle. Kate had been distracted, contacting family members about borrowing alternative transportation—with no luck.

"Thank God we dropped Maya at the Hippo."

Kate probably should have been offended by the relief she read in his tone, but she wasn't. Maya would have needed to touch everything. Especially the delicate little crystal animals that were set about on shelves right at a child's eye level. What were these people thinking?

"Look at this one. Right up Maya's alley, isn't it?" he asked, bending down to peer at a smooth green-and-red frog that seemed to have been captured in glass midjump.

"She loves frogs."

"Should I get it for her?"

The question took Kate by surprise. "Why would you do that? Her birthday isn't until February."

He looked sheepish. "I don't know. I guess I wanted to apologize for being such a putz earlier. I'm usually not that argumentative."

"You're a lawyer. Isn't that your job?"

He snickered softly. "Okay. You got me there. But I can usually pick my fights, and I rarely test wits—and lose—with an opponent who is under the age of five."

Kate leaned down and picked up the handblown frog. "Well, Maya has been honing her verbal skills since the day she came out of the womb, but I don't think a..." She flipped it over to read the price tag on its belly. "Sixty-five-dollar amphibian is going to change her mind. As far as she's concerned, you wear squeaky shoes."

The overhead lights were doing something odd to his complexion, she decided. His skin tone seemed warmer, almost inviting her touch. And the twinkle in his compelling green eyes did strange things to her equilibrium.

She quickly, carefully, set the frog down and started away. "So, what do you think the newlyweds would like? Do you have a price range in mind?"

Rob resisted the urge to look at his watch, even though Kate's back was to him. Waiting for a tow truck had eaten into their time. But, strangely, he'd enjoyed the challenge—from both the car seat and Maya. She was a fascinating little creature. Almost as beautiful—and prickly—as her mother.

"Something classy," he said watching her move with grace through the shop.

He remembered someone—his mother probably—telling him that Kate and her sisters used to dance together and perform at family functions. The Sisters of the Silver Dollar, he thought they were called. He wished she'd dance for him.

No. Bad idea.

"Do you like this vase?" she asked, pointing to a brightly lit cubicle with a very large, reddish-orange vessel that seemed too curvaceous to hold water.

"Nice," he said, joining her to study the piece. "But a little bright. I don't think Dad would like it."

"What colors does he favor?"

"Blond," he mumbled under his breath.

"Pardon?"

"Oh, nothing. I'm trying to picture his house, but all I can see is a big-screen TV. I think it's black."

She snickered softly. "Well, what about this one?" she asked, crossing her arms to study the cobalt-blue blown sculpture that truly defied description—and dusting, Rob guessed. He wouldn't want it in his house.

"Too blue."

"This one?"

"Too weird."

Back and forth, they hopped from one piece of art to the next like children playing leapfrog.

I'm having fun, he suddenly realized.

They paused in the doorway to another cubicle. "Maybe crystal isn't the way to go," she said. "There are other galleries, of course. But I was hoping you'd find something here. I hate to have wasted a whole morning on nothing."

Rob didn't consider the morning a waste. He'd enjoyed every minute—even arguing with Maya. He was about to say so when her phone rang.

She grabbed it from her purse. She apparently recognized the number because she said, "Excuse me a sec. It's about my car."

The news wasn't good. Rob could tell by her frown.

"I need a new starter…to start with," she said after closing the phone. "Unfortunately, given the age of my car, they have to order the part. A day or two, the mechanic said."

Kate's brain frantically darted from Plan A to Plan B to Plan C. Normally, she could get by without a car because her mother's was available. But Yetta was leaving at dawn for L.A. and would be gone four or five days.

"So, is the shop giving you a loaner?" Rob asked.

He was standing beside a six-foot sculpture that fell just this side of obscene, although Kate honestly couldn't say what it represented. "Not exactly. If I'd had the car towed to my cousin Enzo's place, I might have been able to bum a car off him, but this is a guajo…um, non-Romani repair shop."

He nodded. The overhead lights gave silvery highlights

to his tousled waves. His casual polo shirt was a cool sage, almost the same color as his eyes. Sexy. Gorgeous. But it was the concern she read in his expression that really moved her. He cared. She sensed it, and that made him dangerous. She was a sucker for kindness.

She started to walk toward the far corner of the showroom. A warm, solid hand on her arm stopped her. "Kate, wait. I have an idea. Take my truck until yours is fixed."

She shook off his hand. "Don't be silly. I couldn't."

"Why not? It just sits there baking in the hot sun every day. You're going to be driving around picking up stuff for my dad's party, right? That can't wait until your car is back on the road."

He had a point, but… "It wouldn't look right."

He closed the distance between them. "Why not? Kate, we're practically family."

"We are?"

He nodded with such boyish exuberance Kate couldn't help but smile. "Mom told me the other night at dinner that she'd adopt you in a heartbeat if Yetta would let you go. She adores you and admires you—and I'm not just talking about your cooking skills. She thinks you're an amazing person and a really fine boss."

Kate felt her cheeks start to burn. She'd never been good at handling praise. "Well, that's nice, but…"

He made an imploring gesture. "If accolades don't work, will guilt?"

"Huh?"

"Mom's been fighting a cold for a couple of weeks..If you won't borrow my truck, she'll have to do all the running around that you would normally do, right? Do you think it's fair to make an old woman—?"

Kate stopped him with a sharp squint. "Who are you calling old?"

The twinkle in his eye told her he knew he'd won. He held up the key. "Are we done arguing?"

"Two days."

"Or until you get your car back."

She reached for the keys but didn't take them. "I'll pay you…"

He let out a low groan. "You're impossible. Just take the damn truck, okay? Jeesh, try to be a nice guy and—" He stopped midsentence and pointed. "Whoa. What about that one?"

Kate frowned, thinking he was trying to change the subject, but when she glanced over her shoulder to where he was pointing, she actually forgot what they were arguing about. "Wow."

They walked closer and stood shoulder-to-shoulder staring at the unique blown-glass sculpture on a lighted dais. Not a vase or anything functional, this piece simply was. The bottom portion seemed to represent the sea—dark and mysterious, yet brimming with life. Woven into the glass were threads of metal—fish, perhaps. The "sky" embodied every sunset Kate had ever watched while sitting on the beach.

"It's gorgeous. It almost makes me cry or something."

"Me, too," Rob said, slowly moving around the pedestal.

Neither spoke as they circled the display, but Kate sensed that they were both thinking the same thing. When she looked at him, he smiled and nodded. So, did she.

She couldn't say how long they stood there, in silence, but it felt like a minute—and forever.

"I'm buying it," he said.

"I'll wait here," she said. *And guard it.* Which was silly. She was in one of the ritziest shopping areas in the world. No one was going to swoop in and steal their find.

Rob's find, she silently corrected. Rob's gift to his father and Haley. Rob. The man she had no business liking so much. None at all.

Chapter Five

"Welcome the bride and groom," someone shouted from one of the fabulously decorated tables behind where Rob was standing.

The two weeks leading up to this moment had been a couple of the most hectic in his life, but Rob was satisfied that his father—and Haley Hunt-Brighten, Adam's new bride—were more than pleased with the results.

"Lights, action, cameras," he mumbled under his breath as he stepped aside to make room for the onslaught of photographers following the wedding party into Romantique. Others were cruising the ranks, snapping shots of the beautiful people lined up to congratulate the newlyweds.

His father was tall and distinguished in his Armani suit. Haley's dress probably cost more than Rob's car, but she looked damn gorgeous in it.

Rob and his dad had golfed the day before. Snippets of wedding talk had filtered into their usual nonmeaningful conversation. Yes, she was Rob's age. No, neither of them gave a damn. They were in love.

Rob believed it. His father had never looked happier.

"She's restored my faith in humanity," Adam had told Rob while teeing off on the fourteenth hole. "She's so much more than a beautiful face. Her soul is pure, her heart adventurous."

"I'm really happy for you, Dad."

"She wants to start a family. Right away."

The last had caused Rob to send his ball into the rough, but he'd managed to keep his opinion to himself. Adam wasn't a bad father, but Rob had never gotten the impression his father was really into kids—his own or anyone else's. Why he'd want to go through parenthood a second time, Rob couldn't imagine.

Ten minutes later, his father slipped away from the crowd to join Rob near the bar, where Rob was helping to make sure the champagne flowed. "You did it, son. I'm really impressed," Adam exclaimed. "This place is fabulous, even if it is a bit out of the way."

Rob shrugged. "That's what limos and taxicabs are for. You'll never find better food. Or more privacy." He said the last tongue-in-cheek, since one corner of the parking lot had been roped off for members of the press.

"Yes, your Kate is a marvel. That lobster in endive!" He made a kissing motion with his fingers. "Thought I'd died and gone to heaven."

"Which is a distinct possibility if you eat too much of it," a woman said.

Rob and Adam turned to find Jo watching them. She stepped closer. Her tall chef's hat barely cleared the top of the men's shoulders. Rob hadn't seen her or Kate since the limos arrived. Kate's sisters, Liz and Alex, were handling the hostess duties. "Yetta is home with Maya," Alex had informed Rob when he asked.

Rob hugged his mother. "Everything is perfect so far, Mom. How are you and Kate holding up?"

"Great. She's a genius. I think your son should marry her," she told Adam.

Rob blinked in surprise. "Marry? Me?"

Adam looked equally shocked. "I didn't even know they were dating. He didn't say a word. Even though we played eighteen holes yesterday."

Rob made a time-out sign. "Nope. Stop. Off-topic. Kate and I are not dating."

"He lent her his truck," Jo confided. "You know how particular he is with his truck. It presently has a child booster seat in it."

Rob groaned when he saw his father's brows arch. He knew that look. "Mother," he said sharply. "My private life is not open for discussion. I never poked into yours or dad's. Now, if you'll excuse me, I think I'd better check on that ice sculpture. Is it just the light or does Cupid have an erection?"

His parents both turned to look at the buffet table.

"Oh, damn," Jo muttered. "That's downright naughty. I'll go find an ice pick."

Rob and his dad looked at each other and started to laugh, just as Adam's bride arrived. "What's so funny?"

As Adam explained, Kate appeared, her cheeks rosy and eyes filled with concern. "I'm so very sorry for the—"

Adam stopped her. "Please, Kate. Don't give it another thought. Haley and I are thinking about posing beside him."

Kate watched speechless as the couple pointed out the risqué sculpture to their friends. The mood suddenly seemed to rise to another level. She'd seen this happen before. Sedate and serious suddenly became tipsy and fun.

"Wow. They're really good sports," she said aloud.

Rob, who was standing beside her, said, "Yes, actually, my dad always has been. He never let small things ruffle him. Apparently Haley is the same way."

Kate looked at him. She'd done her best over the past two weeks to keep her distance. She'd made use of his truck until her car was roadworthy again, but in a moment of cowardice had persuaded Jo to return it to him so she wouldn't have to face him. Nothing could come of the attraction she felt toward him, so why court temptation?

"Well, back to—"

"Kate," he said stepping close enough to be heard over the noise. "I know you're swamped, but in case I get caught up in best man duties and we don't have another opportunity, I want you to know I'm really grateful. Everything is fabulous."

She put her finger to her lips. "Bad luck to say so before you've eaten. If everyone is full, fat and happy when this is over, then you can tell me. Okay?"

He took her hand in his and closed his own around it. He brushed his lips across her knuckles, which were rough and red from being in water. She thought she'd lost sensitivity in her fingertips, but she was wrong. She felt every little nuance of his touch. "Later then."

Kate's heart did a little sideways movement in her rib cage, and she fled back to her kitchen. To safety.

Of sorts.

AFTERWARD, no one could say how it happened. Jo had been reaching for something in the pantry. A lid? The box of salt shakers? She couldn't remember because pain blocked every other thought out of her head, or so she claimed. And Kate believed her. She'd never seen her second-in-command look so shaky and gray around the lips.

Somehow, a two-gallon can of tomato puree had fallen off the shelf and landed on its rim across the toe of Jo's sturdy black shoes. Her toes were still attached to her foot, thank God, but the swollen purple digits looked abnormally puffy and painful.

"Let me up. I have work to do," Jo demanded.

"Absolutely not. Alex, run and find Rob. He should take his mom to have her foot X-rayed."

"No," Jo said imperiously. "Not on your life."

"It'll be covered by worker's comp. Go."

"Forget it. Is your garlic burning?"

Kate sniffed the air then dashed back to the stove. She tossed the capers she had waiting in a dish into the pan. A cloud of steam billowed up. Once the cloud cleared, she added a measure of champagne, followed by sea salt, white pepper and shrimp. Her version of scampi. Once she had the concoction under control, she called for her under-chef to slowly stir in the thick white cream. Another helper was preparing the fettuccini.

Out of the corner of her eye, she saw the recent graduate of culinary school that she'd just hired reach for the shredded Parmesan cheese. "No," Kate shouted. "That's for the scampi. You're adding Asiago to that sauce. It's in the walk-in."

A hand touched her shoulder. She turned and found Rob standing beside her. His suit coat had been replaced by a white apron. "I won't be as much help as Mom, but since she refuses to leave, you might as well let me try to fill in."

Kate looked from son to mother. Same stubborn set to their jaws. "Jo, until we get the main course served, Rob can be you. Tell him what to do and don't let him get killed or maimed. My insurance can only handle so much."

After that, she didn't have time to think, let alone lust after the debonair man at her side. Occasionally they brushed against each other in passing. She could smell his fabulous cologne even over the mouthwatering aromas she was preparing. Shirtsleeves rolled up. Forearms lightly brushed with medium-brown hair. He moved with a natural grace his mother lacked, but he shared Jo's intense focus. He followed his mother's orders to the letter.

The gruff commands added to the general chaos, but somehow every plate got served. When the last server was out the door, Kate could finally take a deep breath and wipe the sweat from her brow.

"We did it," she whispered, straining to hear the general tone of the diners.

"I need a smoke," Jo said. "Help me up, son."

Kate rushed to take one arm while Rob held the other. They'd just eased her to the bench outside the back door when Jo slapped her thigh and said, "The vegan parfaits. I forgot to take them out of the walk-in freezer. If we don't get them out now, they won't be thawed in time for dessert."

Kate gulped in a breath of fresh air then pushed to her feet, arching her back slightly. "I'll get them."

"No. You deserve a break. Point me in the right direction, Mom. I can handle this."

"Absolutely not," Kate countered, blocking his return to the kitchen. "You need to get back to the party. Don't you have toasts to make or something? Besides, you're a guest. You should be eating."

"Children, stop bickering. Somebody rescue my parfaits."

They looked at each other. "She's feeling better."

"The aspirin must have helped."

Jo's low growl and threatened attempt to stand sent them both hurrying indoors. "The walk-in is over here. I think there's only one tray. The party planner wanted a vegan option for people who don't eat cake."

Rob followed her, his senses on high alert. He'd never in his life experienced such a powerful, exciting rush of emotions as he had working in Kate's kitchen. Even waiting for a verdict was low-key compared to the orchestrated flurry of food preparation. The combined energy of her assistants and various helpers along with the servers coming and going and his mother shouting orders should have spelled chaos, but he'd never felt that things were out of control. Because of Kate, who was both commander-in-chief of her kitchen and a sexy, powerful woman.

Damn, he wanted to kiss her.

And they were alone for the first time all night.

He opened the freezer door for her. The chill, so inviting after the heat of the kitchen, enticed him to step inside even though this put him in close proximity to Kate. Encircled by chrome shelves, he pivoted to take it all in.

"I'm still not completely restocked," she said, apparently noticing his interest. "We lost a lot of inventory because of the E. coli fiasco. You don't make that up overnight." Her tone was resigned. "Oh, there's the tray your mom made."

She rose up on her toes to reach for the shallow pan, which was resting on an upper shelf just beyond Rob. On impulse, he intercepted her hand and drew it between them. She tensed, but allowed him to turn it palm-up. His thumb skimmed over calloused ridges that made her skin feel different from any other woman he'd dated. Hers were not pretty fingers with long, sculpted nails.

He felt an odd pang deep in his chest. He didn't know why or what it meant.

Kate yanked her hand away and hid it behind her back. "What are you doing?"

"Something I shouldn't," he admitted before he took a step closer.

Her chin rose and her eyes narrowed—a warning, if ever he'd seen one. But he had to do what he'd wanted to all night. And while Kate might deny it later, Rob knew she felt the sizzle between them, too.

"Rob. This isn't—"

He pressed his lips to hers, stopping her protest. Not the most chivalrous thing to do, but when she melted against him a heartbeat later, he stopped thinking. His right hand moved behind her back to pull her closer. His left brushed against her neck, expecting to find the mass of curls that fascinated him, but her hair was braided and pinned—unreachable.

She made a little moan—that Rob realized a second later was the sound of regret. "No. Stop. Bad idea," she said, pushing him away.

Rob stepped back and took in a deep breath of icy air. The sharpness didn't jibe with the heat that still surged through ninety percent of his body. But as his rational mind kicked in, he admitted to himself that she was right. This was madness.

"Good call. My mother will be hopping in here on one foot if we don't show up with her parfaits," he said, striving for a normalcy he didn't feel.

He turned and picked up the tray. "Can you get the door for me?"

"Of course." Her voice was husky, the sound so sexy he almost changed direction. Almost. Fortunately, sanity was slowly returning, and with it, all the reasons why he needed to keep his distance.

Once outside, she directed him to place the tray on a counter in the kitchen. "You'd better take off that apron and rejoin the party," she said, her tone brisk. "Don't you have to make the best-man toast?"

Her reminder hit him like a glass of ice water across the face. What kind of son was he? His mom was hurt, his dad's wedding reception was only half over and Rob was playing kissy-face in the freezer.

He yanked on the tie at his waist, which only served to tighten the knot. "Damn," he said, frantically picking at the strings.

"Oh, for heaven's sake," Kate muttered.

She brushed his hands aside and took over. Her nimble fingers worked quickly, but not fast enough.

"Hmm, what's going on?" a voice asked.

Kate let out a low groan. "What does it look like?"

Rob turned his chin to see over his shoulder. Liz and Alex Radonovic were standing a few feet away with matching smirks on their faces. He quickly looked down to see if Kate had succeeded in setting him free. Not even close. In fact, she was actually leaning over, her face just inches from his groin.

"Umm…I…I'm dyslexic. I've never been able to tie anything right," he said, hoping to distract them.

"Oh, hell," Kate said sharply. "This is going to take all night. Liz, hand me that knife on the counter."

Before he could protest, the largest butcher knife he'd ever seen was resting against his belly—sharp side out, thank God. Kate looked him in the eye—and Rob could have sworn he saw her grin—before she made a slight flick of her wrist. The apron strings fell away.

"Coffee, people," she shouted, motioning toward a group gathered by the back door, where he'd left his mother. "Break's over. We aren't done yet."

Rob pulled off the apron that was hanging loosely from his neck. He handed it to Liz as he walked past.

"You're a brave man," she said, with a wink.

"You're right. I have a toast to make."

Two HOURS LATER, after supervising the cutting of the cake, Kate leaned against the back wall of the dining room and watched the man who had kissed her in the cooler step up to the microphone. A four-piece band was set up to entertain the party until the wee hours of the morning, but first, the best man had to make a toast.

"Dad...Haley...may your life together be blessed with good health, happy memories and the harmony of love, and may the road you travel together be filled with joy."

Short. Simple. Elegant.

And for no reason that made sense, tears raced to her eyes.

She blinked them away and quickly lifted her glass. It was that damn kiss, she thought, taking a chug of champagne. That and the wedding. The combination had stirred up too many emotions. She'd been down this road before. A bride. Filled with hope and wonder and fear. Wed to a man who, at face value, was all any woman could ever ask for. Tall, handsome, charming. Romani.

She and Ian had tied the knot at a tiny wedding chapel that went out of business about a month later. Then, with their attendants, Grace and Ian's friend and mentor from Reno, they'd joined a huge gathering of friends and family for a block party in the cul-de-sac in front of her parents' home. She'd danced till her feet hurt, then the limo her father had hired drove Kate and her very drunk husband home—to the little house they'd rented.

She was the first of her sisters to marry.

For love, of course.

But for another reason, too.

"Mom, I'm pregnant. Ian wants us to get married. I love him. He's fun and ambitious, but sometimes he seems so autocratic. We butt heads over the silliest things. What should I do?" Kate had asked Yetta once she'd finally admitted to herself that the *flu* she'd been experiencing wasn't the flu.

Yetta had deliberated on the question for nearly two days. Finally, she'd told Kate, "You need to marry Ian."

Any reservations Kate might have had about committing to the smooth-talking Gypsy who'd entered her life so suddenly were assuaged by the conviction she heard in her mother's firm, deliberate tone. Everyone came to Yetta for advice. Only a fool would ignore the word of a Romani fortune-teller, right?

Kate took another gulp of champagne. The bubbles burned going down her throat.

Tempting as it was to blame her mother for what had followed, Kate was a realist. No one had forced her to say "I do" in front of the Elvis-impersonator justice of the peace. She could have listened to the little voice inside her head that said, "You don't need a man to help you raise this child. Not if he's the wrong man."

But she hadn't trusted her instincts. And she'd paid dearly. As had her family and her daughter.

Now, her instincts were harping again. The voice in her head said, "Run." From Rob? Or Ian? *Both,* she decided.

There would be no repeat of that kiss. No matter how wonderful it felt.

"Kate."

Rob had spotted her standing alone at the back of the room when he'd made his toast. She was sipping from a champagne flute. He'd never seen her drink anything but cola. Was she celebrating? She certainly had a right to. The reception had been an unqualified success, but he had one more thing to do before he could call it a night.

"Here's the woman of the hour," he told the three reporters—two men and a woman—he'd asked to follow him. "Gentlemen. Ms. Chamberlain. It's my privilege to introduce Katherine Radonovic Grant. She and her sister, Grace, own Romantique."

"Hi," the senior of the two men said. "Nice to meet you. Thanks for all the samples you sent out to us. Delicious."

"Yeah. What were those rolled-up thingies?" the heavyset man asked. "I'd like to get my wife to make them. Where do I get the recipe?"

"Do you mean the dolmas? They're stuffed grape leaves. I add my own twist. I'm so glad you liked them."

"Kate and her staff put in hours designing a personalized menu for the bride and groom," Rob said. "And I just happen to have copies of it for you."

Kate appeared surprised but her smile didn't change. Something was up. Was she mad at him about the kiss in the freezer? He didn't blame her. It was a stupid impulse. He planned to make sure it didn't happen again. Once this party was over, there was really no reason for them to see each other.

"I understand this restaurant was closed recently because of an E. coli scare. What's that about?" one of the journalists asked.

Kate's shoulders stiffened.

"The unsubstantiated charge came from a man who is looking at serious jail time," Rob said without giving her a chance to answer. "A thorough investigation failed to turn up any trace of contaminants. Isn't it a shame how the innocent wind up paying for one man's malicious accusations? Thank God Kate stood up and fought for the truth."

The reporters asked a few more questions before they wandered off to sample his mother's fabulous cake.

Rob let out the breath he'd been holding, then turned to Kate, who appeared slightly shell-shocked. "Sorry for jumping in that way. I was afraid that question might come up and I didn't get a chance to warn you. I know you're completely capable of handling reporters, but I figured there was a reason you normally put this kind of thing in Grace's hands."

She set her empty champagne flute on a table then looked at him. "You're right. I'm happiest behind the grill, not being grilled by reporters. And I appreciate everything you did for me…for Romantique, but Rob…" She frowned and took a breath.

Rob had a feeling he knew what she was going to say— that the kiss they shared was a mistake and they shouldn't see each other again. And even though he agreed with her in theory, he wasn't ready to hear the words.

"Oh, look, Dad and Haley are getting ready to smash cake in each other's faces. Don't want to miss that. I'll call you later. Maybe we can settle up the final bill over a drink."

She didn't argue. How could she? He'd tied their future meeting to money. A trick he'd learned years ago. People were usually willing to talk if you offered a strong incentive.

Chapter Six

"Ethically, I can't discuss your daughter's case with you, Yetta," Rob said as gently as possible. A week and a half had passed since the wedding and he'd only seen Kate once—not for that drink he'd suggested. When he'd called to set up the date, she'd explained that his PR efforts on behalf of Romantique had been such an unqualified success she was too busy to spare a minute.

"Grace will fax you the final bill," she'd told him.

Not what he'd hoped to hear, but then she'd added, "You're our hero, Rob. Any time you're hungry, you know you're welcome here."

He didn't want food. He wanted…he wasn't sure what he wanted, but Kate was an increasingly familiar face—and sexual fantasy—in his dreams.

When Yetta had called the night before and asked him to stop by her house on his way to work, he'd been happy to comply—on the off-chance he'd get to see Kate. Plus, he had a gift for Maya. Okay, a bribe.

Eric, one of the lawyers in his office, had taken Rob to dinner last night. He'd been married in college but had divorced wife number one to marry wife number two after he'd handled her divorce. She'd brought two children—a boy and a girl—to the union, and they'd since had one more of their own.

Responsibility for the three youngsters had fallen entirely on Eric's shoulders after his wife took off with another man, and when Rob first arrived in Las Vegas, Eric had been in the habit of bringing the children to work with him. As a result, his job performance had suffered.

"If you want to date a single mother, you start by courting the child," Eric had counseled after Rob had accidentally mentioned Maya. He'd quickly tried to disabuse his colleague of the notion that he had designs on Kate, but the idea of making friends with Maya had stuck. Which explained the present in his pocket.

"I've had the most disturbing dreams this past week," Yetta said, interrupting his thoughts. "I'm very worried about my daughter and my granddaughter."

"I can appreciate that, but Kate was my client, and anything we discussed is privileged. Since she's working with someone else now, I don't really know what's going on in her custody battle. Why don't you ask her?"

"I did. She said everything is fine. But Katherine is a lot like her father. Plays her cards close to the chest, as they say."

Rob took a drink of butterscotch-flavored coffee and looked out the window to his right. He could see the house next door, which belonged to Rob's former client Claude Radonovic, Yetta's brother-in-law. Claude, Rob knew, was now living with his eldest son and had rented the home to Jurek Sarna. Jurek, who was Yetta's shirttail cousin, was also the birth father of Grace's fiancé. Rob spotted Jurek standing in front of the house with a hose. According to Jo, Jurek was recovering from a bout of cancer.

"How's Nick's dad doing?"

Yetta, who was sitting across from him at the round table, took a sip from her cup then said, "Much better. He's planning on visiting Grace and Nikolai in Detroit as soon as he's up to it."

"Mom told me the story about Nick meeting his dad after all those years. Must have been pretty emotional."

"Yes. The possibility of establishing a relationship with his son has really lifted his spirits. Jurek may have signed away his rights to raise Nikolai, but he never stopped being Nikolai's father. Not deep inside."

Rob nodded as though he understood, but he didn't. His father had lived in the same house with Rob and his mother until Rob was seventeen, but Adam had never been overly involved in Rob's activities. He'd provided for his family, but his life revolved around his classes, his writing and golf.

"Are you telling me this because you think Maya's father feels the same way?"

Yetta smiled. "No. I'm not sure why Ian appears so determined to reestablish a relationship with his daughter. At one time, I was willing to give him the benefit of the doubt, but he proved unworthy. Unlike you."

Rob blinked. "I beg your pardon?"

Yetta chuckled warmly. "You have been nothing but a boon to this family."

"Well, that's nice to know. I'm a lawyer, I don't hear that a lot."

"You breathed life into Katherine's restaurant."

"No. Not me. Kate did all the work. I...was mostly in the way."

Yetta looked at him shrewdly. "You're quite modest for a young man. But you can't deny what you did for

MaryAnn." MaryAnn Radonovic was another of Rob's clients who had been caught in the same net as Charles Harmon. She was married to Claude's youngest son, Gregor. "Claude was at the hearing. He said your eloquence alone got the poor girl into one of the best psychological facilities in the area instead of going straight to jail."

"MaryAnn needed help. The judge saw that. And Grace's letter went a long way on MaryAnn's behalf. I just did my job." He pushed his cup away. "Not to change the subject, but is Liz around? I wanted to talk to her about my mom. She can't seem to shake this cough. The doctor who X-rayed her foot wanted to run tests, but Mom refused. Maybe some herbal tea would help."

His mother's cough was only one more problem he'd had to deal with this past week. Two people in his office had the flu—he hoped. If they'd called in sick just to avoid hearing their performance reviews, he would soon be even more shorthanded than he was now. Plus, he'd offered to oversee the shipment of his father's wedding presents. Who knew there'd be a zillion?

"Elizabeth and Katherine are out back by the pool. They're trying to talk Maya into taking swimming lessons."

"Maya's going on five and she doesn't know how to swim?"

"Oh, she thinks she does. She gets around with the floaty things on her arms, but she won't get her face wet. For a smart child, she can be downright muleheaded over certain things. And swimming is one of them."

Rob didn't like hearing that. "I was a lifeguard at our community pool for six summers. And I taught Red Cross swim lessons. I'm from the earlier-the-better school of swimming."

The look in Yetta's eyes told him she agreed. "Well,

maybe a male teacher would have better luck with Maya. She pretty much gets around her aunts and her mother."

She motioned for Rob to follow her through the house to the sliding glass door that connected to the backyard. He glanced at the decor in passing. The home was slightly shabby, slightly cluttered, but he felt an immediate connection to the underlying essence of the place. This was a home filled with love.

He dashed around Yetta to open the door for her. She smiled, as if surprised by his gesture. "My mother's influence," he said sheepishly.

"A good woman," Yetta replied with a wry look.

"Hello, everyone," she called out a second later. "Look who's here."

Rob followed her out. A covered patio ran the length of the house and was home to a lush flower garden at one end as well as a hodgepodge of padded chairs and small tables. Just beyond the line of shade lay an oval oasis of blue surrounded by concrete. In close proximity, a large green umbrella fluttered in the wind above a glass and metal table and six chairs.

Kate, Liz and Maya stood together near the shallow end of the pool. Liz, in a navy-blue one-piece suit, stood on the top step in water up to her ankles. Maya—also in a swimsuit, a bright orange two-piece with a little skirt that was gathered at one hip—stood between the two sisters.

Kate lifted her hand to shield her eyes as she looked at him. "Rob? What are you doing here? Is Jo okay?"

"Fine." *I hope.*

"I asked him to stop by," Yetta said. "I wanted to know where we stood regarding you-know-who." She lowered her voice with the last word.

Maya looked up with interest.

Kate, who was dressed in her checkered chef's pants and sleeveless white tank top, gave her mother a severe look. "Maya knows what's going on, Mom. I read her the letter from my new lawyer. She said he sounds like a very nice man."

Unlike me. The icky one with squeaky shoes.

"I'm glad to hear that," Rob said. "I talked to several people who said he's experienced and compassionate. He'll make sure your rights aren't trampled in any way."

He patted his pocket for his sunglasses, but he'd left them on the table with his keys. Damn. It was really tough to look at Kate without remembering how it felt to hold her in his arms and kiss her.

He pushed the memory away and said to Liz, "I was wondering if you could recommend some herbal tea for my mom. To help ease her cough. She says she's having trouble sleeping because the cough wakes her up."

Before Liz could reply, Yetta made a chopping motion with her hand. "You can e-mail him some literature, Elizabeth. What's important now is the fact that Rob is a licensed swimming instructor."

He demurred, trying to downplay Yetta's overstatement of his credentials. "Was. In high school and my first year of college. It's been a while."

"What? Like two or three years?" Liz quipped with a wink.

"Slightly longer."

"I don't want to go to swimming school," Maya said, crossing her arms belligerently. "I already know how to swim."

Kate went down on one knee. "Maya, you're a wonderful kicker and very bold when you're wearing your floaties, but you also have to know how to swim when you don't have them on your arms."

"Yeah, kiddo, being able to dog-paddle is important," her aunt said. "Let me show—"

"No," Maya snapped rudely, brushing Liz's hands away. *Brat.*

She pivoted to stare at him as if she'd heard his silent comment. Rob fought to keep from blushing. Distracted by the little girl's unspoken antipathy—and possibly because he rarely turned down a challenge—he heard himself say, "I have a suit in my gym bag in the car. I could come back after work. I bet I could have Maya swimming like a fish inside a week."

Kate stood up. "But...you're a lawyer. Isn't giving lessons to four-year-olds a bit beneath you?"

"How often do I get to save a life? And that's what learning how to swim can do." He looked at Maya and said, "Unless someone's...chicken."

Her chin came up just the way her mother's did when challenged. "I don't like you."

"I know. And I wish you did. But you can still learn from me. If you're brave enough to try."

She looked at him a few seconds, then turned and ran to her mother. "Mommy..."

Kate picked her up and walked under the shade of the umbrella. He couldn't hear what they were saying because they spoke in whispers. Liz apparently got tired of waiting because she dove into the water and started swimming laps. Yetta motioned for him to follow her back under the overhang where it was significantly cooler.

"This is a turbulent time for my granddaughter. She's

particularly sensitive to her mother's feelings, and Katherine is a ball of nerves. Too much on her plate, as they say."

"I'm sure it can't be easy running the restaurant alone."

"Oh, that's a small thing compared to Ian's return. My daughter is an all-or-nothing kind of woman," she said, looking to where Kate was standing. "If she gives her heart, she gives every ounce of her spirit, trust and loyalty, as well. When Ian betrayed her, he broke her faith in love."

He looked at her, wondering if she was telling him this for a reason.

"Wounds that fester never heal properly. I'm afraid that Katherine will never allow herself to trust again if she doesn't resolve things with Ian," she said.

"You don't think she should fight to retain sole custody."

"Rom men will defend to the death what they believe is theirs. Ian's honor—what's left of it—is at stake." She made a dismissive motion with her hand. "But if he were to win Kate back, the challenge would be gone and sooner or later he'd revert to his old ways."

Grant planned to win Kate back? Was that possible? They shared a child. Wouldn't any mother want to give her daughter a happy, two-parent home if the possibility presented itself?

Yetta startled him when she laid her slim white hand on his shoulder. "Breathe, my dear boy. I said that's what Ian wants. Not what Katherine has in mind."

He blinked in surprise at her cheerful tone. Her silver hair made her regal, not old. Smooth skin and uncanny brown eyes so dark they almost seemed black. Bewitching.

Before he could speak, Kate joined them. Maya had disappeared. "Thank you for offering to help, Rob, but we're going to have to take a rain check. Maya's convinced herself she's sick."

"I'm sure we'll see a remarkable improvement once Rob leaves," Yetta said. Her tone seemed nonjudgmental to Rob, but he could tell by the way Kate's shoulders stiffened that she took her mother's observation as criticism.

"Hey," he said before she could reply, "I don't blame her. I'm a stranger. And a man. Maybe if you had a couple of other kids around at the same time—made it a real class, she'd feel less like she was on the spot."

Kate blinked, obviously surprised by his suggestion.

"That's a really good idea," Yetta said. "Maybe Gregor could bring Luca and Gemilla over. I remember MaryAnn taking Luca to lessons when he was little, but I don't think Gemilla knows more than what she's picked up from her brother."

"Mom, Rob is a busy lawyer. He gets paid big bucks—"

He cut her off with a laugh. "Not to swim. Consider it payback for all the work your family's sent my way. I know things have been tough for your cousin and the kids with MaryAnn away. This might be nice for them. How 'bout Saturday morning?"

Kate still didn't appear convinced. "Not early. Fridays are our busiest night."

"Say midmorning. Ten-thirty?"

"O…okay."

Rob could tell she wasn't enthused but, oddly, he was. In fact, he could hardly wait.

He was about ten steps away when he remembered the gift in his pocket. He decided to leave it there. Maybe it would look less like a bribe if he gave it to her after she learned to swim.

"KATIE. God, you look great. It's so good to see you. Did you bring Maya?"

Kate's temper spiked. *Typical Ian. Everything was always about his agenda.*

Today was Friday. Last day of the week and what was surely going to be the longest day of her life. Her attorney had called shortly after Rob's visit two days earlier. He had news. She and Ian were scheduled to meet face-to-face. "Just to feel each other out," her lawyer had said.

Kate shook her head, managing to keep inside all the things she'd waited so long to say. She'd promised her mother and Liz that she wouldn't lose her temper.

"Don't call me Katie. And, no, Maya isn't with me. She won't be allowed anywhere near you until the court orders it."

His chin dropped to his chest, as if she'd struck him. "Why? Do you think I'd harm her? I'm an embezzler, not a pedophile."

Before Kate's attorney could pull her back, Kate leaned across the table and said, "You're a two-bit thief and a worthless excuse for a husband. You're a lot of things, Ian, but the main thing you are is a flight risk." Although looking at him, she wondered if that was true. He was pale. Too thin. And weak-looking.

He gave a feeble laugh. "Do I really look that dangerous?"

"I know you, Ian. You could be on life support, and still find a way to screw up my life. I'm demanding that you not be allowed to spend any time with our daughter unsupervised."

His skin had the cast of day-old mashed potatoes. He made a "whatever" motion with his hand, which ended up flopping uselessly to the table. "I'm not going anywhere,

Katie. I can't even get up to pee without help. You don't have to worry about me stealing our daughter."

She lowered her voice. "But I do, Ian. I used to have nightmares about you talking your way out of jail then walking off with Maya. I'd spend night after night in a futile chase. You know how we Romani feel about dreams—that they forecast the future."

He acknowledged her assertion with a grimace.

"Eventually, those dreams faded because you were safely behind bars, but now…here you are. You look sick, but maybe you're faking this just to get close to Maya. I don't know and I'm not taking any chances."

"You really hate me, don't you?"

"The absence of love isn't necessarily hate. But I do hate what you did." She couldn't allow sympathy—or the memories of the good times they'd shared—to cloud her judgment. "I loved you once, but now I really don't give a damn what happens to you, except for how it might affect Maya. I don't wish you dead—just not living in the same town."

"God has forgiven me, so how come you can't?"

God? Was Rob right? Had Ian found religion in prison? "To forgive you would be to excuse what you did. I want my daughter to know that lying, cheating and stealing result in losing things that matter to you."

He didn't say anything for so long Kate wasn't sure he was still breathing. "You didn't used to be so hard."

She picked up her purse. In a low, harsh growl, she said, "You're right. I used to trust people. I used to trust you. But then you stole the money left to my mother by my recently deceased father. While I was grieving, you ran off with another woman, leaving me—and your daughter—

homeless and broke. Yes, I'm a bitter, dried-up old woman, and you can thank yourself for that."

He lifted his eyes to look into hers. "You're still young and beautiful, Katie."

"Don't call me that. I'm not your wife, Ian. I'm the mother of your daughter and always will be, but other than Maya, we have nothing in common. Nothing. The only reason I'm here is because the state of Nevada and this poor misguided young woman seem to think you have some redeeming value. I stopped believing in you the day the cops hauled you back from the border with a blond bimbo in handcuffs beside you."

He started to speak, but before he could get a word out, she added, "I'll get through this because I don't have any choice. I have to be strong for our little girl, who sees her best friend's daddy and doesn't understand why she doesn't have one."

She ignored the spark of hope she saw in his eyes. "The state says I have to let you back in Maya's life, but that doesn't mean you'll ever be a part of mine."

The young public defender or whatever she was—a willowy blonde—started to speak, but Kate cut her off. "I'm done here. I said what I came to say. But I want your client to know that I plan to watch his every move where our daughter is concerned. If he hurts Maya or tries to turn her against me, he's going to wish he was back in prison with guards to protect him from a mother's wrath."

She left without looking back. For reasons that had been explained to her, but in her anxiety she'd forgotten, the meeting had been held in the conference room at Rob's law offices. She'd been to the first-floor suite in the well-appointed professional complex once before, but never to this part of the building and she was turned around. Lost.

She started toward what she thought was the front entrance, but stopped when she heard a familiar voice.

"Integrity, man. Either you get the concept or you don't. And I won't have people working for me who think it's okay to bill a wealthy client for time spent on the golf course. Or at your kid's soccer game. Or whatever."

She froze. That was Rob's voice, although she'd never heard him that vociferous.

She glanced around. She recognized where she was. Rob's office was just ahead. That wasn't the direction the loud voices were coming from, but she wasn't taking any chances. She turned to leave and bumped into the man she'd hoped to avoid.

"Kate."

His face was slightly flushed, and there was a tension in his brow that she'd never seen. He seemed puzzled to see her.

"Hi. Meeting here today. Sorry. I got turned around. I'm looking for the door."

His eyes opened as if realizing why she was there. He leaned toward her and in a gruff whisper asked, "Do I need a gun?"

"What?"

"You had this look—as if you'd been wrestling with the devil. Is he still here? Do I need a gun?"

His small attempt at humor was oddly calming. She felt her shoulders relax. "Do you have one?"

"Naw. They scare the crap out me, but for you, I'll buy one."

She snickered softly. "Well, I'm not a big fan of guns, either. Not since Grace got shot."

"Understandable. How do you feel about iced mochas?"

"Much less lethal, although they are a danger to my thighs."

"Are you willing to risk the calories?"

"Possibly. Why?"

He glanced over his shoulder at the office he'd just stepped out of. "I think we both need a drink—and it's too early for booze."

The offer was tempting. "I…I don't know."

He put his hands together. "Please. I could really use someone to talk to who isn't associated with this place."

Since Maya was at the Hippo with Alex, she gave in and followed him to his car. She sank against the soft, sun-warmed leather. The car still smelled new and the luxury was infectious.

The day was relatively cool and when Rob asked if she'd like the top down, she nodded yes. The wind played havoc with her hair, and she didn't care. "There's a Star-bucks about half a mile down—"

He shook his head. "I found a drive-through right up here. And since I've got you, I'd like to make the most of the opportunity."

"To do what?"

"Pick your brain."

"Concerning?"

"Whether or not I should buy a house. You know Vegas, right? Everyone tells me the housing market is insane. If I don't buy, I'll regret it, but a part of me says only an insane person would live in a desert."

She laughed. "I went to school in upstate New York and I spent a couple of years in Colorado and New Mexico working at resorts, but I've always called Vegas home. To me, nothing compares to the pure beauty of Red Rocks or the Valley of Fire. The desert is constantly changing—and you never take it for granted. Like life."

Rob hadn't expected to hear such passion about a place that felt so alien to him. He missed the cool breezes that raced in ahead of a fog bank that could swallow the Golden Gate Bridge in a matter of minutes. He missed the green. But Las Vegas did hold a certain appeal.

They pulled into the express lane at the coffee shop and placed their order. Two iced mochas. Blended for him. On the rocks for her.

"So, where is this house you're looking at?" she asked as he pulled into traffic.

"The other side of town. I doubt if you have time—"

"Actually. I'm free until three when I have to start prepping for tonight. Fridays are always crazy, but we hired two new cooks and your mother is having fun whipping them into shape."

"Not literally, I hope."

"No. She's actually very kind and a much better teacher than I am, which is why she asked me not to come in until I absolutely had to."

Rob had never seen this side of her—relaxed and playful. Was this a reaction to the stress of her meeting with her ex? Did he care? Maybe they both just needed a break.

He handed her his phone and said, "Hit number sixty, would you? I was supposed to meet my Realtor at the house after work. Maybe she can meet us there early."

She could. And would. Apparently the woman thought she had the sale wrapped up. Too bad Rob was so ambivalent about relocating to Vegas. His mother argued that he should at least rent a house, if he didn't want to buy. But even the idea of signing a lease was enough make him queasy.

He didn't know why he wasting his time looking at a place he probably wouldn't buy, but at the moment he was content to have Kate at his side as he headed toward the posh new development east of Henderson.

"Liz's house is only a mile or so from here," she volunteered as they turned off Boulder Highway. "And my cousin Enzo's auto repair shop is over that way."

"Speaking of cars. How's yours running?"

"Great." She took a noisy slurp of her drink. "Have you talked to your dad lately? Are they back from their honeymoon?"

He smiled at her quick diversion. She never let the focus stay on her for long. "E-mail. They had a great time in Tahiti. Photos to follow. Oh, and they absolutely loved the glass sculpture you helped me pick out. Dad said Haley cried when she saw it."

"Haley is nicer than you expected, isn't she?"

"Yes, although I shouldn't have been surprised. Dad always had good taste in women—even when he was married to my mom."

Kate heard something unexpected in his voice. Bitterness. She shifted to look at him. "From what I could see, your parents get along well. Jo actually seems to adore your dad. Did I miss something?"

He shrugged. "Not really."

But she sensed there was more to the story. Come to think of it, Rob had seemed stiffer around his father than he was with her and Jo. "You aren't close. Is that it?"

"Let's just say I love him, but I don't necessarily respect some of the choices he's made in the past."

Kate had only recently learned about some of the mistakes her own father had made when he was alive. Poor Grace had taken the revelations pretty hard, but then, as the baby of the family, she'd been closest to Ernst.

"My dad was no saint," Kate said. "What's that saying? Something about being able to pick your friends, but you can't escape your family?"

He chuckled but didn't reply. Kate watched the cityscape fade away as they neared the new housing development that included several lakes, an upscale casino and a very high-end shopping area. She'd heard that one of his neighbors was a popular Canadian singer/pop star who had a show on the Strip.

She and Ian had lived in a wealthy housing development, too. For a short time.

Half an hour later, she was seated at a breakfast nook in a gloriously sunny kitchen. While Rob talked to Ginny Lewis, a fiftysomething woman with curly blond hair and lots of jewelry, Kate looked around, picturing the kinds of decorator touches she'd add if she lived there. Window treatments. Something tailored and classy that didn't take away from the view.

Rob joined her, making her scoot over to give him room to sit down.

"What do you think?" he asked.

"It's gorgeous."

"But…" he said, as if hearing her unspoken qualification.

"It's so big. Smart from a resale point of view, but one could go broke trying to furnish it."

Rob let out a soft hoot. "The woman makes a joke. That's encouraging. I was afraid that meeting today might have done you in."

She tossed up her hands casually. "Me? I'm fine. My main concern at the moment is Maya."

Me, too, Rob thought. Because tomorrow he was expected to show up at Yetta's and teach a little girl who hated him how to swim.

"Are we still on for swim lessons? If you'd rather postpone…" He'd wrestled with this dilemma for days. And nights. One minute, he pictured himself coaching Maya to a trophy at some future swim meet; the next, he'd see himself taking Kate in his arms and making soul-filling love with her. Last night, he'd imagined Maya standing between her parents while they renewed their marriage vows. He was afraid he might be cracking up.

"Are you kidding? Mom jumped on that idea you had about inviting some other kids. She's a sucker for men in need."

Rob wasn't sure what that meant, but he was distracted by the saucy twinkle in her eyes. Flirtatious, even. Which brought up the memory of their kiss in the freezer. What would that have been like if she'd initiated it?

Ginny, who'd dashed out to her Hummer for some information on the home, returned, walking briskly. "Did I hear you say something about swimming? This place has a pool, you know. How many children do you have?"

"One. She's four and a half going on twelve," Rob answered, standing up. He offered his hand to Kate to help her rise, but she ignored it, standing up on her own.

"We're not married," she said bluntly.

Ginny, who was consulting her paperwork as she walked away, called back, "No problem. I've made tons of sales to unmarried couples."

"But—"

Rob cut her off with a boyish wink so playful Kate's insides went a little haywire. She almost had to sit down again because her knees suddenly felt disconnected from her body.

"Technically, it's a lap pool, but there's plenty of room to put in something more child-friendly," the Realtor said, urging them to move along. "You can check it out from the window in the formal dining room before we go upstairs, then we'll take the exterior staircase to the patio."

Rob grabbed Kate's hand and tugged her after him. Normally, she'd have pulled back, but Rob's hand felt solid and friendly, not domineering. She liked the feeling. She liked Rob. Too much for her own good? Probably.

Forty-five minutes later, they bid Ginny goodbye and got into Rob's car. Neither spoke right away. Kate was still mulling over the fact that she'd toured a gorgeous house—one she'd have bought in a heartbeat if she'd had the money—and had more or less pretended to be Rob's significant other. She didn't play games, so why the ruse? Because it felt good to be part of a couple again? Or because it felt good to be with Rob?

"You didn't like the place, right?"

Startled out of her ponderings, she glanced sideways. "I think it's fabulous. Too big for one person, in my opinion, but it would make a lovely home for the right family."

He had his sunglasses on, so although he looked at her while they waited for the light to change, she couldn't tell anything from his expression.

"Can I ask you something and count on an honest answer?"

His serious, lawyerly tone made her heart speed up. "You don't think I'm honest?"

"I think you're brutally honest when it comes to business, but in your personal life…well, is it true you haven't been on a date since your divorce? I don't mean that to sound judgmental. I haven't exactly jumped right back into the dating pool myself."

"Because your girlfriend broke your heart?"

He shook his head. "No. I'm the one who called off the engagement when I realized we were getting married for the wrong reason—to make her dad, my boss, happy. There came a point when I realized we had two completely different agendas. She was into the social aspects of a wedding and wanted to explore the concept of being married. I…I wanted something else. I'm not sure what exactly."

"Your mother's been concerned because you're still living in a residential hotel and you don't have any friends. She thinks Vegas is just a layover in your life."

He pulled into traffic and didn't respond right away. When he answered, his tone held a note of dry humor. "Mom's almost as intuitive as your mother—and Jo's not even Romani."

Kate waited for him to elaborate.

"I didn't want this job. The Vegas office has had a lousy reputation almost since the day it opened, so being sent here was definitely a step down the ladder of success. I'm sure the senior partners expected me to quit rather than suffer the humiliation, but I'm a little too bullheaded for that."

She smiled. She'd been called that, too.

"My plan was to whip the place into shape then get out. The fact that Mom lived here was a nice bonus, but not a huge motivating factor. We're both pretty independent people. And I really haven't had the time or inclination to date—until now."

"Do you mean me? No. We can't date. I'm all wrong for you."

He could tell she believed that. But he also sensed a connection between them that deserved a chance—even if it went against every rule in his book.

He looked around to get his bearings. They were midway between his place and the office. Two quick turns and they pulled into the parking lot of his temporary home. One well-placed tree offered enough shade that they could sit in the car without roasting.

Kate pushed her sunglasses to the top of her head and squinted at him. "Are you trying to corrupt me?"

"Can you be corrupted?"

"No. But thank you for asking." The hint of humor in her tone gave him hope. He leaned over and kissed her. Quick, friendly, unthreatening. An invitation to play.

She didn't pull back. Or slap him. In fact, she smiled. "If I were at a different place in my life, I'd probably take you up on your offer, but…"

"A little corruption might be just what you need. Lord knows I could use some." Then, he kissed her again—the way he had in his dreams.

The small car didn't afford much room to maneuver, but he pulled her to him. She felt even better than he'd imagined. Warm, womanly. Her arms settled around his neck. He caressed her back. Lean but muscled from her work.

Her scent was sweet and it touched a chord deep in his memory. "What kind of perfume are you wearing?"

She startled, as if suddenly remembering where she was. She pushed back. "That would be eau de Play-Doh. I was helping Maya make a castle for her Little People this morning."

"That's it," he exclaimed. "I don't think that smell has changed since I was a kid."

She cocked her head and ran her finger along the edge of his jaw. "You're still a kid compared to me."

He nipped at her finger when it got close to his chin. "True. You're practically ancient."

She frowned and poked him on the nose. "I'm four years older than you."

"I know. Which is why we're going to bury—no, cremate—this nonissue here and now. Okay?"

She didn't look convinced, so he added, "Hey, my dad just married a woman nearly thirty years his junior. Didn't seem to bother either of them."

"But—"

He cut her off. "You're not going to say something sexist about older men and trophy wives, are you?"

The corners of her mouth curled up impishly. "Maybe."

"Well, forget it. According to Haley, she stalked Dad. She hunted him down and twisted his arm to go out with her."

"Why?" she croaked. "I mean, he's an attractive man, but…"

"LAFS."

"Laughs?"

"L.A.F.S.," he spelled. "Love At First Sight."

Kate's chuckle turned to a belly laugh. The magical sound made his heart do crazy, almost painful, maneuvers. Since when had humor become such a turn-on? he wondered.

"Well, I'm glad your dad and Haley got their storybook ending," she said, sitting back, "but, I'm a single mom with a daughter who is scheduled to meet her parolee father in the very near future. The only happily-ever-after I can expect to see anytime soon will come at the end of the fairy tales I read to her at night."

She consulted her watch and told him, "It's getting late. I enjoyed the house tour, but I'd better go home and change for work."

Rob didn't argue, but a guy could dream. And tonight he probably would. X-rated, no doubt.

Chapter Seven

The next morning came a little too soon for Rob. He'd spent a restless night tossing and turning. A combination of guilt and regret stemming from his fizzled attempt at seduction and his ongoing frustration at work. Kate had been right to shoot down his suggestion. She needed to stay focused on Maya. He needed to keep his mind on his job.

Simple.

So when—if—he saw her this morning at swim lessons, he'd apologize for being an idiot.

As he looked around Yetta's backyard, he could see only men—and little kids, from toddlers in their fathers' arms to a pensive-looking youngster Rob recognized from court. MaryAnn's son. *Luke? Lucas? Luca.*

Yetta joined him. "I hope I didn't invite too many. Once I put the word out, men seemed to come out of the woodwork. I had no idea there were so many fathers who wanted to spend quality time with their children."

Rob had a feeling that was a lie. Yetta *knew* things. "The more the merrier, but since the pool is rather small, maybe we should break into groups by age and experience."

This proved to be no easy task, so he enlisted the help

of Kate's cousin, Gregor. The man had lost weight since Rob last saw him. He seemed to have grown up, too. Visiting your wife in a mental institute might do that to a person, Rob thought.

"Do you know any of these people?" Rob asked.

"Yeah, almost everybody. Most are shirttail relatives. That tall guy over there is my brother Enzo. He and his wife have three older kids, then out of the blue, Bubba, showed up."

"Bubba?" Rob repeated, squinting at the lad in his dad's burly arms. The kid looked like a black-haired Pillsbury Doughboy.

"His real name is Burdick Anders Radonovic. Don't ask."

"Gotcha."

One by one, Greg identified the six fathers and seven children. Greg's distant cousin Nathan, a mousy-looking fellow with a pronounced overbite, brought twins Gretel and Lucinda.

Maya, Rob noticed, was MIA.

"Gentlemen, front and center," he hollered over a cacophony of high-pitched squeals. "Here's the game plan."

Rob had rehearsed his speech in front of the mirror that morning. He'd even gone online last night to make sure the technique for teaching children hadn't changed dramatically since his Red Cross training. One Web site he'd run across had intrigued him so much he'd ordered four copies of its book, *Stewie the Duck Learns to Swim*.

I'm going to need more copies.

He felt capable of teaching these dads and their kids, but the minute Kate and Maya walked out of the house to join the group, Rob's confidence evaporated. The look Maya gave him made him want to flee to the nearest bar for a shot of liquid courage.

You're not a wimp. She's a kid. Suck it up, man.

The silent pep talk worked—or maybe it was the air of desperation he sensed in the fathers. They'd either volunteered for this task or—like him—could find no graceful out. They had kids who didn't want to be here and they looked about ready to dunk said kids in the water.

He yanked off his Old Navy T-shirt and marched to where Maya was standing, her fingers white-knuckled from her grip on her mother's hand. He passed his sunglasses to Kate, even though the glare was almost enough to blind a person.

"Maya," he said, going down on one knee, "you're going to turn five on your next birthday. That's old enough to understand that being able to swim is very, very important. If you accidentally fell in the water and no adults were around to help you, you might drown."

She frowned and looked over the group of kids. "Bubba's a baby. He doesn't even walk."

"But he could still fall into the water." Rob glanced at Kate. She had a rumpled, just woken up look that made him want to race back to bed with her.

Maya kicked him squarely in the shin. Her bare foot didn't hurt but it got his attention. "If you can kick that well in the water, you're going to be swimming in no time."

"I already know how to swim," she declared.

"Prove it." He put out his hand. "Come on. I dare you."

Kate watched the power struggle between Rob and her daughter with mixed emotions. She wanted Maya to learn how to swim and had been utterly stymied and frustrated by Maya's fierce determination not to take lessons. She hoped Rob would be able to accomplish the task. At the same time, she knew this exercise wasn't entirely about swimming. It was about trust. Or more specifically, about trusting a man.

She stayed in the background as Rob organized the men and their children. Her mother came to stand beside her.

"Relax, dear. He seems very capable."

Kate nodded but didn't comment. To ease her tension, she looked around at the men. "Who's that?" she asked, seeing one she didn't recognize.

"Mac. He's Zeke's new protégé," Yetta said. Blond and buff, he appeared to be quite young. His early twenties, Kate guessed. His swim trunks reached his kneecaps. He was carrying an infant, probably only two or three months old.

"That's a pretty tiny baby," Kate said. "Does his wife know he's here?"

A low rumble of laughter sounded behind them. Kate turned to see Zeke Martini, the gray-haired policeman who had organized the undercover roust that had cost her family so much. Kate didn't ask why he was here. She knew his children were grown and lived in California with his ex-wife. She knew that Yetta had gone to lunch with him a few times. The two had become friends.

Personally, Kate was still a little wary of the man, whom it could be argued had used her Romani family to catch a master criminal, but her sisters seemed more inclined to forgive and forget. "Not much escapes Mac's wife's attention," he said. "She's a newspaper reporter. She told Mac this would be a bonding experience."

Kate looked at the young cop, who seemed very much out of his element. Scared even.

Rob addressed his group. "It's important to get your initial introduction to the water out of the way fast. The longer you have to fret about something, the more nervous everyone gets. Just pick your child up." He demonstrated with Maya, who stiffened like a piece of wood. "And get wet."

He walked briskly down the steps, keeping his grip firmly on her daughter, even though Maya let out a howl and tried to climb up his neck. He bounced around and chattered to her, making goofy faces that distracted her enough to end the noisy tantrum.

"Girl's got a set of pipes on her," Zeke said.

"She knows how to say what she wants even if it's not what she really wants," Yetta replied.

Kate looked at her mother, wondering if there was a message in that cryptic remark for her, but her attention was pulled back to the action as the other fathers entered the pool. Nathan was having a hard time of it trying to get the twins to stay separated. He wanted one of the little girls to sit in a chair while he worked with the other, but neither would have anything to do with that plan.

"Maybe I should—" she started, but Zeke shouldered past her.

"I guess I look enough like a grandpa to gain her trust."

Kate's mouth dropped open as he emptied his pockets and removed his shirt and belt. His khaki shorts rested on lean hips. He was thin but not skinny and still very muscular. He didn't look bad for his age. She glanced at her mother, who had a funny look on her face.

Once Zeke had made friends with the spare twin, he carried her into the water, making sure to stand right next to her sister and father.

"Okay," Rob called out. "That was simple. Now, we all know what comes next, right? You can't swim if you don't get your head and face in the water. People drown because they panic. As the law enforcement officers in our midst can tell you, the best way to diffuse panic is through experience and practice."

The pool was a bit crowded in the shallow end, so Rob stepped close to the invisible line where the deep end started. Kate's heart rate sped up. She hoped he knew what he was doing.

"Like I showed Maya a few minutes ago, we need to start by blowing bubbles."

The hilarity that ensued eased some of Kate's anxiety. *He's actually doing this.*

After about five minutes, Rob whistled and said, "Next, we do this underwater. I'm from the blow-in-the-face school of thought, but you'll figure out what works best for you. I do suggest you make eye contact with your youngster, then count and bounce. Like this. One…two…three."

Rob's heart was pounding in his chest as he tightened his grip on Maya's shoulders and sank under the water. He kept his eyes open and watched the surprise and abject horror in her eyes as he dunked her. But she didn't gulp in air.

He rocketed them out of the water.

She sputtered and sucked in a breath that seemed primed to turn into an ear-splitting cry, but Rob spun her around and held her overhead, praising her nonstop. "Good job, Maya. You did it. You didn't take in any water at all, did you? That was amazing. And brave. You showed all the kids exactly how to do it."

She closed her mouth and looked around.

As it dawned on her that she was, indeed, the center of attention, she relaxed and tucked her head into his shoulder, shyly.

The gesture, so small and yet so trusting, melted Rob's heart. "Give it a try, everyone. One…two…" He felt Maya tense, but this time her fingers didn't nearly pierce his skin. When they came up, she was laughing.

Some kids weren't. The baby was choking. Rob trotted over to help. Maya laid a hand on the child's chest and the baby stopped sputtering. "She's okay."

Rob felt a shiver travel up his spine. He looked toward the house where Kate had been standing. She wasn't there. He'd ask her later. Does your kid have special powers? Oh, yeah, that would go over well.

KATE HID OUT in the kitchen until the noise out back subsided. In theory, handing your child over to someone else for swimming lessons was a good thing. But actually watching Maya being dunked by a man she barely knew and who made her want things she really had no business wanting was too much. She did what she always did in times of crisis. She cooked.

"What are you doing in here?" her mother asked as Kate pulled a tray of cookies out of the oven.

"Treats. I think the kids and the dads are going to need nourishment, don't you?"

Yetta didn't answer, but she took a plastic plate from the cupboard and arranged a heaping mound on top of it.

"There's fresh lemonade in the fridge," Kate said.

"I can only carry one thing at a time. If you don't bring the drinks out, I'll send Rob in."

Kate stifled a groan. Her mother was playing matchmaker. And none too subtly. But, despite the tingle she got behind her knees every time Rob kissed her, Kate wasn't going to follow through on the attraction. She couldn't. Maya was her predominant concern at the moment and Maya didn't like Rob. After this morning, she probably wanted him dead.

Or not, she thought a couple of minutes later when she went outside carrying a tray laden with ice bucket, plastic glasses and a pitcher. Maya was sitting on Rob's lap at the table under the umbrella. The other fathers were gathered around, too. Half the children—the boys mainly, were playing in the covered sandbox with MaryAnn's son, Luca. The girls were either with their dads or in Maya's playhouse.

Luca's little sister, Gemilla, was perched on Gregor's lap. That's why she's still with Rob, Kate decided. Maya was very sensitive to other children's needs and poor Gemilla had had a difficult time adjusting to her mother's absence.

"Anybody thirsty?"

Kids surged around her. Rob stood up, setting Maya in the chair, before he reached out to help. The courtly gesture touched her.

"Everyone survived, I take it?"

His expression went from happy to wounded so fast she almost laughed. "Of course. Did you doubt me?"

As she poured lemonade into wobbly cups, she said, "Don't take that the wrong way. Each of my sisters tried to get Maya to dunk her face and failed miserably."

"Ah, well, Maya wasn't four and a half then. She's grown and matured, right, Maya?"

The little girl nodded. "But I don't want to do it again today."

Rob laughed. "Not a problem. But after a few more lessons, your mother won't be able to keep you out of the pool. But always remember that you can only go in the water if an adult is watching you, right?" he added his tone stern.

Kate stepped back to observe Rob interact with the fathers. For a guy, who—according to Maya—didn't like kids, he seemed like a natural. Relaxed and gregarious. She found it hard to believe that he didn't have a family of his own.

An hour later, when she walked him to his car, she asked him about the odd dichotomy. "How come you're not married with two or three kids?"

He shrugged, which made the gray T-shirt he was wearing emphasize his great chest. "Law school. It's a commitment even more demanding than a wife." He winced. "Not that all wives are demanding," he quickly qualified, "but most relationships require time and energy, and when you're studying and writing papers and taking tests, you don't have the oomph to do much else."

She smiled at his gaffe. She understood what he meant. He wasn't a chauvinist. Not like Ian. "Was your last girlfriend the closest you've come to marriage?"

He nodded. "I didn't date much in college. How 'bout you?"

"I apprenticed in a male-dominated profession. If you're a woman, fairly attractive and single, you get asked out a lot."

"And since you're gorgeous, you must have had to fend off advances left and right."

Embarrassed by the compliment, she said, "I always made sure the person I was flirting with understood the ground rules. I didn't sleep around. I had one disastrous experience early on and that taught me a valuable lesson."

"What was that?"

"That a great chef isn't necessarily a great person. I thought I was in love. He was older. Italian. Very passionate. I found out a couple of months into the affair that he had a wife, and ten kids in Italy."

"What did you do?"

"Quit. Well, first I walked around with the biggest,

sharpest knife I could find, plotting revenge. But he was smart enough to stay away until I cooled down. Then, I loaded up my car and headed home."

The irony never ceased to amaze her. If not for that treacherous ex-lover, she never would have met Ian.

"I tried to drive straight through and couldn't make it. I stopped at a convenience store in Kingman for a soda and while I was there, I struck up a conversation with a complete stranger, whom I later married," she added under her breath.

"Ian?" He sounded shocked.

"He didn't ask for a ride or anything. Just my number, in case he ever made it to Vegas."

And I gave it to him.

"When he called a few weeks later, it felt like fate."

He didn't say anything for a minute. "I heard some talk about your mother's prophecies. Did you think Ian was your destiny?"

"Maybe. Or maybe he's the past I can't avoid," she muttered.

"Is there a chance you two might get back together?"

"No." He didn't look convinced so she added, "Ian is a liar and a thief. He stole money from people I love, then ran away with another woman when my uncle started asking questions about his retirement fund. As far as I'm concerned, he's poison. The first taste nearly killed me. There won't be a second."

Because he looked so sympathetic, she felt compelled to add, "But that doesn't mean I don't still feel guilty about giving up on my marriage vows. I hate to lose. Just ask my sisters."

"For better or worse does have some limits. Just ask my mother."

That bitterness again. She wanted to ask why, but she didn't get the chance. Gregor and his two kids walked out of Yetta's house and headed their way. "Hey, man, nice ride."

As the two men talked, Kate's thoughts returned to her failed marriage. She'd been completely oblivious to Ian's cheating. She could excuse herself to some degree for not realizing he was stealing from his clients, but to miss the clues to his philandering was ridiculous.

She'd known something was wrong in their marriage, but she'd blamed his inattentiveness on business. The economy. Stress. Looking back at those months before Ian disappeared, only to be caught with a suitcase full of money and another woman at his side trying to cross into Mexico, Kate couldn't believe how naïve she'd been.

But she'd promised herself she wouldn't make the same mistake again. And while Rob wasn't the *same* mistake, getting involved with him at this time in her life wouldn't be a good idea—no matter how handsome and beguiling he was.

"Oh," he exclaimed suddenly, turning back to Kate. "I almost forgot. I have something for Maya."

He lifted a small, green velvet bag off the passenger seat of his car and handed it to Kate. "Would you give this to her for me? She did a really good job today. Tell her I said thanks for not giving me too hard a time. I gotta take off. I'm meeting with one of my colleagues this afternoon. The one who mishandled Ian's parole hearing." He shook his head. "She's a great gal and a terrific lawyer—when her mind in on task, but her mom's sick and she's juggling a lot. I'm going to try to help her work on time-management issues."

He gave her a jaunty wave as he drove off. Kate gingerly

opened the drawstring on the bag and peeked inside to find a frog made of bright green glass.

Damn, she thought. Kind, caring and thoughtful. The man was way past dangerous. He was very close to perfect.

Chapter Eight

Kate rolled over onto her stomach and pulled the light cotton blanket over her head. She wasn't ready to face the world—especially not a world where Maya and Ian were reunited.

At least, their first meeting hadn't gone very well, she thought sourly, recalling the brief encounter that had taken place yesterday at the Hippo.

Alex had offered her house as neutral ground—after school and out of the public eye—but safely within the compound. Unfortunately, one of Kate's assistant chefs had called in sick at the last minute, so Kate had had to drive back across town at rush hour, which set her nerves on edge—more on edge than they'd already been.

She and Maya had arrived only minutes before Ian and his attorney. She'd tried to distract Maya with a book, but her ever-intuitive daughter hadn't been able to sit still. She was darting from play area to play area when the door opened and Ian walked in.

Like a bunny caught within paw's reach of a hungry lion, Maya had frozen and stared, unmoving, as he walked toward her. When he leaned down and called her name, "Maya…" in a slightly out-of-breath, raspy voice, the little girl had let out a yelp and dashed to Kate's side, burying her face against her mother's leg.

Except for a couple of furtive glances, Maya had stubbornly refused to look at Ian again. Even when he offered her an extra-large candy bar.

The gift had irked Kate to no end.

"Bribes? Aren't you the man who said your children would never be poisoned by processed sugar?" Ian had been full of idealistic theories about parenting when she'd been pregnant, but almost as soon as Maya was born, his attentions had turned elsewhere. To work, to making—and stealing—money.

Ian had given up trying to break through Maya's atypical shyness a short while later. Once he was gone, Kate and Maya had walked home.

"So what was that about? I thought you were anxious to meet your dad."

Maya had shrugged her shoulders. "Will he come back?"

"Do you want him to?"

"Uh-huh."

Then he probably would. Unfortunately.

ROB WAS STARTING his third week in his new role as lawyer-slash-swimming instructor. Contrary to his hope, he'd seen very little of Kate. Maya had missed the second Saturday class because of a bout with the flu, which Kate then caught. According to his mother, Kate had even missed a couple of days of work, which was practically unheard-of.

He'd sent her flowers but hadn't heard if she liked them or found the gesture too pushy.

He'd been back to the Romani compound twice outside of class. Once to have coffee and cake with Yetta—her way of thanking him for the swim lessons, she'd claimed. And another time for a barbeque at Gregor's. To Rob's surprise, he'd found both experiences most revealing.

Kate's mother had been very generous with details about Romani life, including some tantalizing glimpses into Kate's childhood and teen years. Gregor's hamburger patties were a bit like the charcoal he cooked them over, but Rob had enjoyed his ex-client's company. Plus, Luca and Gemilla, while not quite as fascinating as Maya, were sweet kids and very eager to please.

Later, Gregor's brother, Enzo, and another guy from the dads' group had dropped by. The ensuing conversation had covered a wide range of topics, from sports to potty training. Rob had enjoyed himself more than he could have predicted.

He was actually looking forward to class this morning, to see his new friends. He was especially curious how Greg's job interview had gone. One of Rob's other clients had mentioned the need for a part-time handyman, and Rob had recommended Gregor.

He knocked on Yetta's door.

"Yes? Oh, it's you." Kate's sister, Liz, opened the door for him. "Come in. Cup of coffee?"

"Sure. Thanks. I'm a little early. Is Yetta around?"

Rob hadn't spent much time with Liz, but they'd bumped into each other coming and going a couple of times.

"She's next door helping Jurek pack. He's flying to Detroit tomorrow to visit Nick and Grace."

"Oh, that's good. He must be feeling stronger."

She handed him a large mug. "You can wait here or go out back. Your call. Maya's playing in Mom's flower garden. But I should warn you, she's been a real brat this morning."

"Really?"

She nodded. "She had her first meeting with her father. He came to the Hippo after the other kids had gone home. She said she remembered him, but she didn't. Not really."

"That must have been hard on her and Kate."

"Well, Kate didn't help matters because she's still so mad at him she can barely look at him without snarling. Maya picks up on that kind of thing. She's confused and upset. And Kate's so prickly you have to tiptoe around her."

"Oh."

"She's out back. Pouting."

"Kate?"

That made Liz smile. "Maya. Kate's sleeping in. She had a long night. Her dishwasher broke down." She might have said more but the phone rang.

Rob sipped the cup of coffee Liz had handed him, wondering if he should try to call off swim class.

"I'll be right there," she said to the person on the other end of the line. She hung up the receiver and turned to look at him. "Will you do me a huge favor? Keep an eye on Maya while I run next door. Mom needs help organizing Jurek's meds. Thanks."

She dashed away before he could answer. He glanced at his watch. The Dads Group, as they were calling themselves, wasn't scheduled to arrive for another twenty minutes. He always came early in hopes of bumping into Kate. This was the first time he'd been asked to babysit.

Curious, he stood up and walked to the sliding glass door that led to the covered patio. He could see Maya sitting on the ground in front of a flower bed. She appeared to be making something out of the petunias.

As if sensing his attention, Maya turned her head to look at him. Rob's heart did a little jump.

She suddenly scrambled to her feet and raced to where he was standing. Rob opened the door in anticipation of her coming in the house. She didn't. She stopped just opposite him and said, "I already have a daddy."

Whoa. "Um...I know. What are you doing with the flowers?"

She gave him a serious look. He wasn't sure she was going to answer him. "Playing dress-up."

"Really? How do you do that?"

She let out a put-upon sigh. "Oh, come on. I'll show you."

Rob followed her to the shaded nook where Yetta's green thumb was most evident. She pointed to the ground. "Sit down. You can be Holly. I'm P'tunia."

He was glad he'd pulled on sweats so he didn't have to sit on the cement in his swim trunks. Once settled, he accepted the flower Maya held out to him. A pale pink bell-shaped flower with furry yellow stamens. *Oh.* "Holly. As in Hollyhock."

Maya nodded. "Hock is her last name. My last name is Grant. That's my daddy's name."

"I know."

She looked at him but didn't say anything for a minute. "Holly and P'tunia are friends. They go to flower school together. Tomorrow there's going to be a party and they want to look nice."

"I see. So they need new outfits?" he guessed.

He watched her tiny fingers gently invert her royal purple petunia and impale it on a twig. She indicated Rob should do the same with his flower, but his hands felt too big and clumsy. What if he ripped her poor flower in half?

"Um, could you help me with this?"

With exaggerated patience, she walked him through the process. "They can't dance if they don't have legs."

"Got it. Do they need shoes?"

"No. They're Romani. Roms dance with naked feet. Like my mommy taught me."

Naked feet. He tried his best not to smile, not wanting to offend her. Once she had both flowers to her liking, she handed his back to him.

"Now, we have to do their hair."

Rob was afraid to ask. He leaned forward to watch as Maya plucked a few strands of grass. To avoid copying her, he reached overhead to snap off a bit of asparagus fern. He wrapped the prickly greenery around the top of his stick as Maya had done then showed it to her.

She studied it a moment. He couldn't tell if it met with her approval or not. Before he could ask, a voice said from behind them, "What's going on?"

Maya looked up, then tossed her flower away and launched herself into her mother's arms. "Mommy. You're awake. Auntie Liz said you needed to sleep 'cause the washer broke."

Rob scrambled to his feet, too, letting Holly tumble to the sidewalk. "We didn't wake you, did we?"

Kate, who looked sleepy and all soft around the edges— and totally desirable—shook her head. "The phone rang. Mom said to tell you Nathan Barnes and the twins won't be here today. One of the girls has an ear infection."

"Gretel," Maya said with conviction. "Lucinda's fine."

He looked at mother and daughter and his heart did a funny little dance on naked feet. He wanted to be inside the circle, instead of outside.

Maya suddenly turned her head and looked at him. He

felt as if she were peering into the very heart of him and seeing his dreams displayed like dancing flowers. He suppressed a shiver. "I'd better go get ready for class. Thanks for showing me your flowers, Maya."

He started away but had only taken two steps when Maya let out a wailing cry. "You stepped on Holly. Mommy, he killed her."

Rob turned. Sure enough. Squished flat on the pavement was a red-and-green blob. *Oh, God.*

"I hate him, Mommy. He has mean shoes."

Rob looked down at the flip-flops he'd picked up at Target. His four-hundred-dollar Bruno Maglis—the much-maligned, *squeaky* shoes—were safely stowed in his closet. Who could have guessed cheap shoes were just as evil?

"Maya, I'm sorry. I—"

She sobbed noisily against her mother's shoulder. Kate looked a little baffled and still not quite awake. He'd blown it. Again. So much for making headway with mother and daughter.

"I…I'll be over by the pool. If Maya doesn't feel like participating today, I understand."

Kate watched Rob leave. He was upset, but she really didn't know what to say. Maya had been unusually emotional lately. Ever since her bout of flu, actually. First, she'd been lethargic and grumpy. Then, increasingly crabby and reluctant to leave the house. Kate attributed some of the changes in her daughter's behavior to that first meeting with Ian.

She stood still and let Maya cry. Once the tears had abated, she pulled back to look at her daughter. "Wow, that was a flood. All over a flower that got accidentally got stepped on?"

"It was Holly. She was *his* flower."

The emphasis on the word *his* made her wonder what was really going on. "What's wrong, honey?"

"I want my daddy."

Ahh. "You saw him and wouldn't even talk to him."

The child didn't reply.

"Maya, remember when you were sick? You slept a lot and didn't feel like playing, did you?"

Maya frowned. "No."

"Well, your father has been sick, too. He needs to rest. To start out with, you'll only see him once a week, but maybe you can spend more time with him after he gets better. We talked about this, remember?"

"Does the lady who was with him see Daddy every day?"

Maya was jealous. "I don't know," she answered truthfully. "She's his lawyer. That's the same job Rob has… when he's not teaching swimming."

She watched her daughter turn her head to look at Rob. Kate did, too. And her heart made a funny jump. She focused on her daughter again. "Are you going to swim this morning? I have a meeting, so if you won't want to do this, I'll have to see if Grandma can watch you."

Maya hopped to her feet. "I'll stay here."

"And you're going to be a super nice, sweet and agreeable person, right? Because even if we don't feel well or we're worried about something that is happening in our life, we don't take that out on our friends. Right?"

She waited until Maya looked at her. "Uh-huh."

"Good."

Chapter Nine

Kate wasn't certain her daughter would cooperate with Rob this morning, but she couldn't stay and help. She'd agreed to meet with Ian—sans lawyers. An informal chat, he'd said. A chance to apologize.

She knew this was a bad idea, but a part of her really wanted to hear him say, "I'm sorry."

She drove to the house where Ian was renting a room. Knowing he was less than ten miles from the compound did little for her peace of mind.

Ian's lawyer met her at the door. "I thought we were lawyer-free today," Kate said, hesitating. Was this a trick of some sort to get Kate to give up her rights?

"I check on him every morning to make sure he has his meds for the day," the woman said. "I was just leaving, but I'd be happy to show you to his room."

Kate sensed the woman's antipathy, well hidden beneath her diplomatic greeting. She led the way without speaking and knocked softly on a partially open olive-green door.

"Is my wife here?" a familiar voice called out.

Kate's temper spiked. "I...am...not...your wife," she said, marching into the room.

Ian was sitting in a recliner that had been positioned near the room's only window. He smiled as if she'd just breezed in with a kiss and hug. "Good morning, Katie. Thank you, Andrea."

Kate heard the door close behind her, but she couldn't pull her gaze from her ex-husband. Sympathy warred with ire. Ian looked like hell. The previous times she'd seen him, he'd been neatly groomed. Although painfully thin, he'd still looked…like Ian. This morning, dressed in a white T-shirt and boxers covered by a light cotton robe, he looked ancient. And ill.

"You look awful."

He snickered softly. "Well, you don't look so hot yourself. Were you out late on a hot date with your gaucho lawyer?"

Only in my dreams. Kate felt her face flush. "I was beating a cranky dishwasher into submission," she snapped.

"The mechanical kind, I hope." Ian chuckled at his joke. "You never were much of a people person. An empty kitchen and a restaurant filled with invisible customers— your idea of heaven, right?"

Kate swallowed her anger. She wouldn't let him provoke her. This wasn't about her. Or him. This was about Maya. "Actually, I have several employees who claim I'm the best boss they've ever had. I guess that proves people can change. But the real question is have you?"

"I still love you, if that's what you mean."

Kate closed her eyes. Typical Ian. "That's a lie, of course. You never loved me. You loved the connections I brought you. The patsies."

"Katie, honey, you don't—"

She stopped him. "I do mean that, Ian." She could play

the mind-reader card, too. "I'm here because you said you wanted to talk about Maya. So talk."

"She hates me, doesn't she?"

"You're a stranger, Ian. You can't expect her to welcome you with open arms just because you show up with candy."

"Well, what am I supposed to do?"

Go away and leave us alone. "Be patient," she said instead. "She's a kind and loving child. She'll warm up to you in time."

He sat up a little straighter. His hair had been buzz-cut in jail and was slowly coming back in—she could see silver where before there had only been black. But his black eyes still flashed with well-remembered arrogance. "I heard you're seeing that guy who used to be your lawyer. The young one. He's just moved here, right? Probably thinking about settling down, having a family."

Rob? He asked her here to talk about Rob?

"That would be Rob's business. Not yours."

"But, Katie, a man has a right to know who his competition is, doesn't he?"

She walked to where he was sitting and leaned over just close enough to make sure he could see her eyes. "Rob Brighten has no competition."

Then she left.

"'ROB HAS NO COMPETITION'? You just said that to make a point, right?" Liz asked.

The two sisters were sitting in their mother's backyard. Maya was playing at Gemilla's. Kate had no idea where Yetta was. Instead of rushing home from Ian's, she'd dawdled at the market to avoid bumping into Rob again. Liz had shown up a few minutes later. And while she and

Kate weren't particularly close, Kate had needed to talk to someone.

"Of course," Kate said, fighting the urge to pace from one end of the yard to the other. She wished Grace was here. "I wanted to punish him. I wanted him to think I had this fabulous life with a handsome young lover. When did I turn into such a shrew?"

Her sister chuckled dryly. "I'm sure we could pinpoint the exact moment if we tried."

Kate stuck out her tongue, but she knew her sister was trying for humor—the way Grace would have. "But since that would probably just add to your depression," Liz quickly added, "Let's move forward instead."

"What if I can't?"

"What do you mean?"

"Maya's a mess, too. She's very sensitive to what's happening around her, especially when it involves me. I know that her bad attitude lately is partly my fault. I'm angry at Ian and frustrated at work. Even with Jo helping, I still have too much to do."

"Because Grace is gone."

Liz poured them each some iced tea from a pitcher. The bowl of browning apple slices was left over from swim class, Kate assumed. She wished now that she'd stayed. She loved watching Rob interact with the fathers and the other children. He was even making progress where Maya was concerned, although he probably didn't think so.

Maya had placed the green glass frog on her bedside table and always told it good-night, right after her fish.

"You and Grace are partners, right? When one partner leaves the business, isn't it common for that partner to sell her share?" Liz asked.

Kate took a drink. Honey and mint tea. "Ummm. This

is good. Where'd you get it? I wouldn't mind serving it at Romantique."

"I made it. Three mints and a couple of other herbs. Don't change the subject."

Kate leaned forward and plopped her chin on her palm. "I can't afford to buy Grace's share. She's invested way more tha—"

"I meant to another buyer. Someone who loves the business as much as you do. Someone like…Jo."

"Jo?" She sat up straight. "Do you really think she'd be interested? Grace put a lot of seed money into the place. What makes you think Jo could afford to buy Grace's half?"

Liz had that cat-ate-the-mouse look on her face. Of all Kate's sisters, Liz was the most observant. She watched and listened when everyone else was shouting. She saw things others missed. "Jo and Mom got together for lunch last Monday. I happened to pass by here. They were discussing the idea. Jo said she was afraid to suggest it because you might think she was trying to horn in on your success. And she knows how close you are to Grace."

Kate was touched, deeply. "I love that woman. Do you think Grace would go for it? Romantique is as much her baby as mine."

"I know that. But Mom thinks our little sister is going to be thinking about living, breathing babies pretty soon." She paused a second then added, "I've heard Grace say how guilty she feels about not being here to help more. Why not ask her?"

Kate thought a moment. The idea not only sounded good, it felt right. She stood up. "I think I will. Right this minute." She started to walk away, but paused and added, "Thanks, sis."

"KATE. MOM. What are you two doing here?"

Rob had been at his desk all morning going over employee evaluations that the personnel manager had forwarded from home office. One of his two lowest-producing attorneys needed to be let go. April, the woman who'd mishandled Kate's case, and Kwen, who had finally stopped bringing his children to work, had been singled out because of low numbers. According to the memo Rob had received, both lacked the drive the senior partners felt was a requirement.

Rob disagreed. He felt the two were excellent litigators whose work had suffered lately from outside stresses in their lives. Kwen's shaky marriage and concern for his children and April's mother's situation were human, real-life problems. Firing either of these people wasn't going to be easy.

He stood up as the two women walked in. "You're both smiling. That's good. Isn't it?"

"I'm buying Grace's half of the business," his mother said. She sat down in one of the two chairs opposite his desk. She seemed a bit breathless—from excitement?

He looked at Kate as she explained. "I talked to Grace last Saturday. I gave her the weekend to think about it and come up with a price if she wanted to go through with it. She and Jo discussed numbers this morning. We're ready to make it legal."

"Really? Grace agreed to sell her share of Romantique?" From the little he knew of Kate's younger sister, this idea seemed rather unexpected.

"Her life is in Detroit now, not Las Vegas."

"And she also agreed that Kate had a right to ask for a totally committed working partner," his mother added.

"Nikolai said it was Grace's call, but given the fact she

has a wedding to plan and a house to decorate, she decided she could use the time and money to settle into her new life."

Kate had heard the news that morning with a mixture of relief and regret. She missed her sister desperately and wasn't sure she could make a go of this on her own—even with Jo's full support. But both sisters knew the present situation wasn't fair to either of them.

She watched as Rob and his mother discussed the details of the sale. On one hand, Kate felt a giddy kind of lightness—as if the thumb that had been pressing down on her was suddenly removed. On the other, her emotions hovered on the verge of tears. So many changes...

As if sensing her turmoil, Rob looked up and smiled. "I think this is going to be a fabulous move for both of you. Do you know what you should do now?"

She shook her head.

"Celebrate. How 'bout I take you two lovely ladies to lunch? Romantique is closed on Mondays, so you don't have any excuse not to go."

Jo coughed into her hand. She seemed to struggle to catch her breath. Kate had seen this happen all too often lately, but Jo insisted it was just a touch of bronchitis.

"I'd love to, son, but you've been such a nag about seeing the doctor for this stupid cough, I set up an appointment for today."

Rob sat back in surprise. "You're kidding. I thought I was going to have to hog-tie you to get you into the clinic."

Jo crinkled her nose. "So I hate doctors. I'm not alone, you know. But Yetta gave me the name of the lady doctor she sees. So I agreed to give her a try."

"That's great, Mom. I'm really glad," he said. Then he looked at Kate. "So, are you free for lunch?"

Surprisingly, she was free for the rest of the day. The three- and four-year-old students at the Dancing Hippo were on a field trip, and Yetta had offered to take Maya, Gemilla and another friend out to dinner for Gemilla's birthday. Afterward, the girls would enjoy a marathon movie night and sleep in Maya's room. Kate hadn't been invited, but that was okay. Maya had been particularly clingy lately and this seemed like a positive change.

"I have a better idea," Jo said. She produced her saddle-bag-shaped purse and started digging in it. "I've got just the thing. And it's free."

Rob grinned. His mother loved a bargain. And she looked better than she had in days. Weeks. Maybe she had been suffering from a lingering cold. Or maybe being part owner of a restaurant was just the shot in the arm she needed to feel good about her life.

As they waited for Jo to find whatever it was she was looking for, Rob glanced at Kate. Gorgeous. And surprisingly relaxed.

"Here it is. An overnight spa escape for two. To Mesquite."

He shook his head. "Mesquite? Where's that?"

"About an hour east of here," Kate said. Her smile looked indulgent, not put off.

Jo handed her the trifold flyer. "I bid on this at some fund-raiser they were having at my apartment complex. It has to be used this month. You could both benefit from a massage and a nice dinner, right? You take it."

Kate passed him the brochure without comment. Rob studied the glossy photos. Green golf courses. Purplish moun-

tains in the background. Aqua blue swimming pools surrounded by palms. The spa package included two massages,
and the choice of either a mud bath or a pedicure. Plus, dinner
at the hotel's restaurant and a night in one of the luxurious
suites. "It looks great, Mom, but you should use it."

"He's right, Jo. You could head over there after your appointment. I'd be happy to cover lunch tomorrow."

Jo shook her head and stood up. "I'm a partner now. I
don't plan on starting out by going on vacation. Nope. If
you don't use it, that means I wasted my hard-earned
money on nothing. Shame. Shame. Now, I have to run to
make my appointment. Call me from Mesquite and tell me
how the food is." And she left.

Kate sat back in her chair looking slightly stunned.
"Wow. I had no idea. She's even pushier than my mother
when it comes to matchmaking."

She sounded amused, which gave Rob hope. Now was
a horrible time to leave the office. But he would. For a
chance to be with Kate. Plus, it would give him time to mull
over his personnel dilemma.

"You aren't by any chance interested in taking her up
on the offer, are you?" he asked.

"I don't know. Are you?"

He straightened the papers in the file and locked them
in his desk, then stood up. "Yes."

She looked around. "Can you do that? Just walk away?"

No. There would be all kinds of hell to pay, but… "I'm
pretty sure I feel a cold coming on." He pretended to cough.
"Mom gave it to me." He faked a sneeze. "Wouldn't want
to give it to my colleagues or clients, right?"

He walked around the desk and held out his hand. "They
say prevention is the best medicine, so let's go get healthy."

Kate hesitated just a second, then she laughed and stood up. "A massage sounds like heaven. But the mud bath? I don't know about that."

"And I'm sure the restaurant won't be as good as Romantique," he said, his heart starting to race.

She pulled back on his hand before they reached the door. "What about the room? I'm not sure…"

He shrugged, keeping his tone casual. "If we decide to stay over—for whatever reason, we can get another room. Okay?"

Her grin returned. "Okay."

Chapter Ten

Kate took her time strolling through the lush landscaping of the Casablanca's pool area. The massive cascading waterfall looked inviting. Maybe she'd go for a swim after her massage.

No. Wait. After my pedicure.

She and Rob had argued the pros and cons of mud bath versus pedicure and he'd almost convinced her to try the former. But when they arrived at the hotel and tried to book their appointments, they were told that only one slot at the mud bath was open. Kate generously took the pedicure option and sent him off with an attendant.

The thought made her smile. She'd already had one of the best days of recent memory. The drive to Mesquite had flown by. She'd learned a lot about Rob—his compassion for the people he was being told to fire, his love of the law and the reason he felt so strongly about teaching kids to swim.

"My best friend in junior high lost a sibling to an accidental drowning. It was one of those moments in your life when you suddenly realize what death means. It was senseless. Excruciating. I signed up for the Red Cross classes and eventually started teaching water safety courses. For Kyle. And his family."

Kate had been touched. And while she wasn't ready to admit it to him, that story had been the little nudge that put her over the edge. She was well past *like* and very close to *love*.

But she still wasn't ready to act on her feelings. She'd agreed to check into the single room that went with Jo's gift certificate because it gave them a place to change clothes and freshen up before dinner. Did that mean she wanted to spend the night with him? No. Well, maybe.

She looked at her watch. Ten minutes until her appointment. Impulsively, she plopped down in a chaise longue and pulled out her phone to call Grace.

"A mud bath?" her sister exclaimed after being told about Kate and Rob's spur-of-the-moment trip. "Doesn't that require a person to sit still? In a tub of mud? That doesn't sound like Rob. And you! A massage *and* a pedicure? Are you on drugs?"

"Maybe I'm turning over a new leaf. From now on, I'm going to be a calmer, more relaxed Kate."

After Grace stopped giggling, she said, "Okay. 'Fess up. This radical change of attitude can only mean one thing—you're in love."

Kate knew that lying to Grace was usually futile.

"Am I crazy? The timing couldn't be worse. Ian is making noise about us getting back—"

Grace let out a howl. "No way. Katherine Ann Grant, if you even hint about hooking up with Ian again, I'm getting on the next plane to Vegas to knock some sense into you."

"Don't worry," Kate said firmly. "I only mentioned that because Ian has made it clear he isn't going away anytime soon. Who wants to start a relationship with that kind of craziness hanging over your head?"

"Remember how Dad used to take us hiking in Red Rocks when we had something big on our minds?" Grace asked.

"The only time Dad and I spent together was at a craps table."

"Oh. Well, then that's where you should go. Shoot a little craps tonight and see if Dad shows up. He always had Ian's number. Maybe he'll help you get some perspective on what you should do. But if you want my advice, go for it. Rob seems like a great guy."

"So did Ian when I first married him."

Grace let out a little gasp. "You realize, don't you, that this plays right into Mom's prediction for you?"

Kate stood up. "No. Stop right there. Mom endorsed Ian, remember? She urged me to marry him. That just proves that Mom and I have never been on the same wavelength."

Kate and Grace had had this conversation before. "If a person can predict the future, shouldn't that person do everything in her power to help the people she loves avoid heartbreak?"

"Oh, sis, that's not how this fortune-telling thing works. I used to feel the same way. I resented Mom for not giving us any warning about Dad's stroke, but now that I've experienced a bit of…well, second sight, I can understand how Mom might have got it wrong. You should talk to her, Kate. Tell her how you feel."

Kate quickly ended the conversation, citing her need to make her massage appointment. Her sister was a natural-born peacemaker, and Grace was passionate about their Romani heritage. Kate wasn't.

Maybe I'm a natural-born skeptic.

As she walked past the inground jetted spa with its very own miniature waterfall, Kate thought about the talk she and her mother had had just before Kate left home for the Culinary Institute of America.

"This is the right choice for me, isn't it, Mom?" Kate had asked. Her sisters had chosen conventional colleges to attend. Kate had always gotten passing grades in school, but she didn't love it. What she loved was cooking.

"I've already told you your prophecy, dear, but that involves what I guess you'd call the big picture. You're asking about this specific path you're taking, right?"

Kate had nodded, a little embarrassed to admit her qualms—especially since she felt ambivalent about her mother's predictions. One part of her believed that chance and circumstance played a huge part in what choices were available to a person. Another part wanted to believe there was a master plan that mapped out her future. But she'd always been disappointed in her prophecy. It was so…bland.

"You can't escape your destiny—nor avoid the past, when the two intersect," her mother had told her. What did that mean to a young woman poised to conquer the culinary world? Destiny and the past? The words were just rhetoric to a girl starting out on her own path.

"I wish I could tell you that going to cooking school will bring you fame, fortune and the man of your dreams, but I can't," her mother had said bluntly.

"Why not? Dad says you can see the future. You have the gift. He doesn't do anything without talking to you first."

Her mother had frowned then. "I wish that were true," she'd murmured in a tone that had made Kate realize there was much about her parents' relationship that she didn't know.

"What I see are glimmers. Possibilities, for sure. Probabilities? Maybe. But I don't need a crystal ball to know that you will make a wonderful life for yourself, Katherine. You're strong, ambitious and you've always achieved any goal you set for yourself. This road you've chosen won't be easy, but it's the right path for you. I'm sure of that."

The right path.

She paused at the intersection of sidewalks. To her right was a shortcut to her room. Rob was probably done with his mud bath by now. She could go up to their suite and start something her libido would vote for, hands down. Or she could get a massage.

She tossed up her hands and gave a low chuckle. Maybe an hour of pure relaxation would add clarity to her jumbled emotions. She dashed the last few steps to the building that housed the spa. "I'm here for my massage," she said, opening the door.

ROB WALKED to his room—the room he and Kate had checked into two hours earlier. He felt slightly woozy. His senses tingled—as if he'd sloughed off a layer of body armor in the gooey heated mud. The massage that had followed was both soothing and revitalizing. He felt alive, ready to embrace life—if he could find his footing.

And Kate.

"Kate?" he called, opening the door.

They'd left their quickly packed overnight bags open on the bed after hanging up the things they planned to wear to dinner. Kate's cosmetic bag was sitting on the dresser. He could smell her presence, even though his mind said that wasn't possible.

He glanced at the clock and realized she was still getting her massage. Restless, he strolled to the window to see if he could spot the golf course he'd overheard the concierge talking about. The window faced southwest. The highway was visible, as were the mountains and a green swath that marked the course of some river.

Kate had pointed out several spots of interest on their drive, including Valley of Fire State Park. Seen through her eyes, Rob was beginning to appreciate the stark, haunting beauty of the desert.

But it's not the ocean. It wasn't home. And even if he bought a house—like the one he and Kate had toured—that didn't mean he was ever going to feel settled here. Right?

Pacing to the bed, he sat down and picked up the remote. His fingers itched. The list-making part of his brain was already starting to click and fidget. If he had a legal pad in front of him, Rob knew he'd have two columns started: *Vegas* and *SF.*

He could picture the lopsided nature of the list. There was no comparison between the two cities. But Vegas had something San Francisco didn't—Kate.

Kate.

How had she managed to insinuate herself so completely into his conscious and unconscious thought? He'd catch himself thinking about her a dozen or more times a day. He'd wonder how Maya was doing in preschool. If she'd met with her father again. If she was confused and anxious. If her mother got home safely after work. What if the car broke down again? This time on a dark street at two o'clock in the morning?

He sprang out of bed and started to pace. "What is wrong with me?" he muttered.

The answer was there. A shimmering, undeniable revelation that had crystallized in his mind while he was flat on his face on the massage table. He was in love with Kate. And Maya, too. But what to do about the fact wasn't simple.

He paused at the closet. A dress, a robe and a short-sleeve blouse hung at eye level. Two pair of shoes—slip-on deck shoes and sling-back pumps—rested neatly on the floor.

The shoulder of the dress had slipped partway off the hanger so he straightened it. The fabric was silky. In the dark closet it looked black but he'd seen Kate take it out of her suitcase and knew it was a rich, deep plum color. He couldn't wait to see her in it. He wanted more than anything to be able to help take it off her. To spend the night wrapped in each others' arms making hot, passionate love.

He'd barely managed to push the thought from his mind when he heard a sound at the outer door. The instant he saw her he recognized the bemused, slightly foggy look on her face. Pure and utter relaxation.

He backed up to give her space. "You enjoyed your massage. I can tell."

She smiled and nodded. "It was heavenly. I think I had an out-of-body experience and when I came back, I was in somebody else's body. Someone with pink toenails. Look." She sat down on the end of the bed and lifted one leg so Rob could see her pretty, shiny toes. "Nice, huh?"

She reminded him so much of Maya at that moment, he couldn't help but laugh.

She looked up. Her eyes were such a deep, dark brown he could almost taste melted chocolate. "How was the mud bath experience? Gritty?" she asked.

"Cleansing. You sink into hot mud, which is actually rather heavy when it's caked on your chest, and then you have a mineral bath and a sweat and a shower. It was great."

"You do look pretty relaxed. Maybe we should call Jo and tell her this was a brilliant idea."

"Maybe," Rob said, stepping closer to where she was sitting. Kate, whose hair was twisted up off her shoulders in a way he'd never seen her wear it before, looked up. "Or we could do what our mothers probably had in mind from the moment we met."

Her eyes sparked with a mischievous glint. "And what would that be? Sex? I don't think so. Maybe Jo is different, but I guarantee you Yetta has never once said, 'Run off to Mesquite and make mad passionate love with a man you're not married to.'"

This kind of frankness from a woman who rarely shared her most private thoughts left him struggling to keep up. "But—"

She looked at him expectantly. When nothing came out of his mouth, she smiled and said, "You're usually more articulate."

"And you're usually not this open."

"Ah…well, that's because you've never been around me after a massage and pedicure. You haven't complimented me on my toes. Aren't they pretty?"

She placed her foot solidly against his belly, stopping him from getting any closer. "The girl tried to talk me into a French nail. I said, 'Nope.' Hot pink or nothing."

His gaze went from her toes to her face. "They're dazzling. You're dazzling."

She flopped back, her gaze fixed on the ceiling. "No. I just wanted a change. I'm tired of being mad all the time.

While I was facedown on the table, I decided the only way to be happy again is if I forgive Ian." She paused, then went on. "We both made mistakes, and poor Maya got caught in the middle."

Rob pulled over the desk chair and scooted close enough to see her face. "Divorces are never pleasant. So much blame and finger-pointing. Most people don't like admitting they shared some of the fault."

"During my massage, I was thinking about my dad. His first stroke came as such a shock to everyone—he was our rock—we all felt so vulnerable. My family needed me. Maya was still nursing. Grace and I were negotiating the lease on our building." She tossed her hands up. "I think by not paying enough attention to my husband and our marriage, I gave Ian just enough rope to hang himself."

When Rob failed to say anything, Kate pushed up onto her elbows to look at him. The expression on his face made her add, "Don't get me wrong. I'm not saying the embezzlement was my fault. Ian blew it. He gambled and lost. And it's not like he didn't know the risk he was taking. I made it very clear the importance I put on trust when he asked me to marry him."

Rob leaned over and took her bare foot in his hand. His touch was gentle but firm. He ran the tip of his finger over her newly polished toenail.

Forgiving Ian wasn't the only decision she'd made while on the massage table.

"Do you believe in luck?" she asked.

"I'm here with you. I'd call that incredibly lucky." His hand tightened around her ankle and he pressed the sole of her foot to the center of his chest. She swore she could feel the pounding of his heart beat in time with hers.

She pushed aside her few remaining qualms. She deserved a life that included passion and tenderness. And Rob was the first man since Ian who made her want both. "What do you say to giving that kissing thing another try?"

She didn't have to ask twice.

Chapter Eleven

Rob had visualized his seduction of Kate much differently. For one thing, he'd imagined that she would be shy and need coaxing. He pictured her as hesitant, maybe even slightly repressed.

He quickly discovered he was completely wrong.

"Did I tell you you're a great kisser?" she asked as she nibbled a trail of wet, playful bites along his jaw.

He'd joined her on the bed and they faced each other, side by side with a small, polite gap between them. They were both still fully dressed. He even had his shoes on.

"And I love the smell of your skin," she said, running her fingers along the open collar of his golf shirt.

Rob couldn't stop himself from touching her hair, exploring the texture of the curls he'd always longed to touch. "I like the way you kiss, too," he said, watching the way her eyes closed when he clenched his hand. "Which probably explains why I spend way too much time thinking about kissing you."

She looked at him through narrowed eyes. "Kissing is a nice warm-up, but do you know what I've missed the most since my divorce? Actually, even before Ian went to jail, because we'd been so wrapped up in our separate lives we rarely crossed paths."

He shook his head.

"Skin. Hot, sweaty skin on skin. Isn't that weird? I used to dream about being in a group orgy with anonymous people. Only I was invisible. I could see them, but I couldn't feel. I'd wake up aroused and breathless but totally frustrated." She frowned. "Does that make me kinky?"

"I'm not a psychologist, but I was engaged to one. Which makes me an authority, of course."

She chuckled. A low sexy sound that made his resistance crumble. "Of course. So, tell me." She reached between them and pulled his shirt free from the waistband of his Dockers.

Her nails lightly skimmed his ribs sending a delicious shiver through him. "And in my esteemed opinion—"

"Self-esteemed."

"Naturally." He tapped her nose playfully. "I'd say you were suffering from epidermal deprivation."

She splayed her hand flat on his belly. He could read the laughter in her eyes but she said, "That sounds serious."

"Hmm…" He was slipping under her spell. Only someone with superhuman powers could resist this bewitching woman with her intoxicating smell and captivating touch. "Could prove fatal," he said, his voice a gruff croak.

Her fingertips dipped below his belt line.

"Oh, no!" she cried with mock horror. "What do you prescribe?"

His breath caught in the back of his throat. "The only cure is immediate removal of all clothing, then C.P.R." He rolled over so he had her half-pinned beneath him. He quickly unbuttoned her pretty sleeveless blouse. Her bra was white cotton. Simple. Demure.

"C.P.R.? The mouth-to-mouth kind?"

"That, too. But I meant close…personal…relations." He slipped the fabric from her shoulders. "Requires liberal touching. And feeling."

She looked at him a moment, then suddenly started laughing. Holding her belly, she wriggled with mirth that seemed to come from the bottom of her toes.

Rob moved enough to kick off his shoes. He tugged his shirt over his head then looked at her. "Quiet, woman, this is a serious matter. We're obviously very close to losing you. Here, take my hand."

Once she was sitting upright, he unhooked the front closure bra and pushed the material aside then pulled her into his arms. "This calls for heat and friction. A life is at stake."

Kate couldn't agree more. For too long, she'd been merely existing, going through the motions, but she hadn't really been living—except where Maya was concerned. But, important as being a mother was, she wanted more. Being with Rob, here and now, was about the woman inside her, the person with real needs that had been ignored too long.

"So, why are we wasting time talking?"

They took care of the necessary precautions because they'd both grown up in a time when precautions were standard. Once the condom was in place, they were free to focus on feeling. Rob seemed to divine her needs even before she could express them. His hands were strong and gentle, bold but never pushy. He asked questions. She answered honestly.

"Do you like this?"

"Yes, but I like this more."

He welcomed her touch—her lips—on every part of his

body. His lean beautiful body. She'd halfway expected to compare him to Ian. How could she not? But that didn't happen. Not even when she held his penis in her hand. Yes, the two men were different, but that was all her mind registered before the urge to put her mouth where her hand was took precedence.

"Now, Kate?" he called out, his voice raspy with need. "Please tell me you're ready."

"Yes," she whispered. "Yes."

Their naked bodies entwined as close as sweat and skin allowed. They seemed perfectly attuned to each other's rhythm. Her climax was better than any she could recall from dreams…or from her marriage.

Heart racing and still panting like a sprinter, she closed her eyes and whispered, "Thank you."

His low chuckle reverberated though her, too, since they were still wrapped in each others arms. "If you're thanking me for saving your life, you're welcome, but I should confess that the thanks are mutual. You saved me, too."

"I did?"

"Oh, yeah. I was painfully close to succumbing to a bad case of M.S.B."

Something told her she was going to regret asking, but she did anyway. "What's that?"

When he whispered the answer in her ear, she burst out laughing. *Massive sperm build-up.* Damn. A man who made her laugh and made her feel like she never felt before. The combination could only mean one thing: she'd found her perfect mate.

FIVE HOURS LATER, Rob reached across the elegant black linen tablecloth to take her hand. After an afternoon of making love, they'd both agreed dining out was essential. A chance to act like grown-ups instead of teenagers.

"What do you think of this place?"

"It's nice."

"But it's not Romantique."

She gave his fingers a squeeze, then reached for her napkin. Kate wasn't big on public displays of affection, he'd noticed. "That's the best thing it has going for it. I don't have to cook."

"Being a chef must make dining out a rather surreal experience. Can you eat without critiquing?"

She opened her menu. "Absolutely," she said. Then, peeking over the top of the four-page tome she added, "Unless it's awful."

"I'm sure it won't be as fabulous as your cooking, but I have to admit I'm starved."

"Well, we did have quite a workout." Her toes touched his pant leg and skimmed downward until they reached his bare ankle. He'd forgotten to pack dress socks. She'd offered to run to the gift shop for him since all she had left to do to be ready was put on her dress, but they'd wound up making love again, instead.

And his body was ready again just from that one simple touch. How? he wondered. His ex-girlfriend had insisted men reached their sexual peak in their teens while women Kate's age were just starting to come into theirs.

He reached for the wine list. "White or red?"

They compromised and ordered champagne.

Kate lifted her glass. "To brilliant men who know C.P.R."

Her wink was nearly his undoing. Damn. He was in love. Plain and simple. Only there was nothing simple about it. Kate's life was in Las Vegas. Her daughter had warmed to Rob a tiny bit during swim lessons, but he knew that Maya still hoped Ian would move in with them.

Plus, his footing in his job was iffy at best. He thought he'd been sent here to make order out of chaos, but it was becoming increasingly obvious that his real role was executioner. If he didn't fire one of the two lawyers earmarked for a pink slip, he'd be free to return to the Bay area. Unemployed, but free.

The crystal chime—and gulp that followed—took the edge off his nerves, but he couldn't help thinking the better toast would have been: damned if you do, damned if you don't. He promised himself he'd bring up the subject of the future after dinner. Well after dinner. Like, around breakfast.

KATE SLIPPED OUT of the room, closing the door behind her with the tiniest of clicks. Rob was sleeping soundly— as were most of the hotel guests, she figured. The clock beside their bed read three-nineteen when she'd woken up suddenly, completely.

She'd lain still for a few minutes, listening to the man beside her. She loved the little sounds he made. She loved his warmth. Being able to slide her toe a few inches to the right and feel his presence. Such a simple act, but one she'd missed more than she realized.

And with that realization came some big questions. Was Rob the one? Would they be able to make a relationship work? A thousand variables crashed through her mind leaving her breathless and tense. She was afraid her worries might somehow leak into his dreams, and he looked so peaceful and happy she didn't want to ruin his much-needed sleep. After all, they'd worked off their meal in stunning fashion.

So, as quietly as possible, she'd dressed in the bathroom, grabbed her purse and left. This was Nevada. Casinos in Nevada never closed.

A pervasive hum from Slots Row, accompanied by the sound effects from the various games, greeted her the moment she stepped off the elevator. She skirted the table games, deciding she didn't want to play anything that required too much brain power. She'd picked up a guest card earlier and sat down to try her luck at a machine called Lobstermania.

Larry the Lobster Fisherman was surprisingly good to her. She was up about thirty dollars when the realization struck her: she was happy. Smiling like an idiot. Madly in love happy.

A sudden infusion of tears made her blink. "You're a fool," she muttered under her breath.

Although no one was nearby, she heard a voice say, *"No, you're a winner."*

A shiver passed through her as she looked around. She was alone. And the voice she'd heard was too familiar to be a fluke of the overheard public address system. It belonged to her father.

She pressed the button to play another game. The flashing lights raced up and down, crossways and diagonal. Lines locked and Larry's song started to play. Another win. She was fifty bucks ahead.

"Come on, Kate. You know what to do when you're on a roll."

The voice in her head was getting annoying. And loud. She ran her hand over her face then glanced at her watch. She'd been playing for over an hour. She was tired, delusional. I need to go to bed, she thought.

"Or switch to craps."

She jumped to her feet and cashed out her points. Talking to the spirit world—or hearing her dead father's voice—was Grace's thing, not hers. Grace and Ernst had had a special rapport. She was the baby and their father's little angel. Alex was first-born, the golden child. Liz and Yetta shared an interest in herbs and healing. Only Kate didn't have a niche. She'd spent a great deal of her life calling herself the invisible child.

She was headed to the bar for a cola when she "felt" a hand on her shoulder. She turned to look and saw two craps tables open. Fewer than a dozen people were playing.

The only time Kate had ever felt really confident in her ability to shoot dice was when her father was at her side. Then they'd challenge each other, bet on long shots and laugh riotously when they paid off. The last time they'd played together had been a few months before his stroke.

She swallowed the lump in her throat. "I can't."

"You can't win if you don't play."

She'd heard Ernst say that a hundred times. Her father had loved to gamble and so had Kate. But that had been long ago. Before her life had turned upside down. Losers only stood to lose more, she'd figured.

But she'd won tonight, hadn't she? And she didn't mean just at the slot machine.

With a confidence she hadn't felt for a long time, Kate changed directions and walked to the craps table.

"New shooter coming out," the croupier said, passing her a selection of dice.

She picked two. Her lucky ones. And she started throwing. She didn't stop until she felt a hand on her shoulder. A real hand. She blinked. "Rob. Oh, my gosh, is it morning?"

He looked sleepy around the edges but fully cogent. "Early. Seven-thirty." He glanced at the table. "Are all those chips yours?"

She looked down. "Uh-huh. I couldn't sleep so I thought I'd play a little." She felt embarrassed but exhilarated, too. "I used to gamble with my dad. He taught me. Is something wrong?"

He nodded. "Yeah. We need to go."

She didn't understand, but she didn't argue. The serious look in his eyes indicated urgency. She left the croupier a sizable tip then gathered up her winnings. Rob led the way to the lobby area across from the registration desk and made her sit down.

Her stomach in knots, she asked, "What's going on?"

He sat down on the low table directly opposite her. "Ian has Maya."

"What?"

"Your mother called about fifteen minutes ago. She said he dropped by unexpectedly when she was making breakfast for Maya and her two friends who spent the night. Said he wanted to talk to you. She asked him to come back later when you were home, but he came in anyway."

"That sounds like Ian," Kate muttered.

"Maya and her friends were eating pancakes. I guess one of them had had a bad night and wanted her mommy, which was why they were up so early. Yetta walked the little girl to the front door. When she returned to the kitchen, Ian and Maya were gone."

"He took her? But he doesn't have a car."

"Maybe he stole one. I don't know. Your mom was pretty upset. I packed our stuff, settled our bill and asked the bell captain to get our car. It should be here in a minute.

If you want to cash in your chips, I'll grab us a couple of doughnuts to go."

Kate stumbled to her feet, her mind disoriented. Rob nudged her in the right direction. Maya was gone? The concept was so huge it didn't quite fit in her head.

The cashier gave her hundred-dollar bills, which Kate stuffed carelessly in her purse. Her adrenaline was starting to pump. She needed to get home. Now.

Rob was standing by the door. He handed her a soda and a small white sack. "Food?" she mumbled, her stomach turning at the thought.

"You'll need it," he said, taking her elbow. "The car's packed. Let's go."

She didn't argue. Nor did she open the sack. Her stomach was too knotted. She couldn't stop thinking about Maya. Was her baby afraid? Worried? Ian wouldn't hurt her. She was confident of that, but what if he tried to keep her? Kate couldn't bear the thought.

Chapter Twelve

Getting out of Mesquite was simple. Getting Kate to talk to him wasn't.

This sudden crisis had waylaid their meaningful, morning-after talk. Rob understood, although when the phone rang, he'd been disappointed to wake up and find Kate gone. His mind had raced with questions. Did she regret what had happened between them? Was she trying to forget their time together?

He'd never know now because her focus was entirely—and rightly so—on her daughter. But he wanted to help. He felt he could be there for both of them, if Kate would let him in.

Her cell phone jingled.

She'd been trying to reach her mother ever since they sat down in the car, but the line had been busy. "Mom? Have you found her? Maybe he took her for a walk. Or—"

Rob's grip on the steering wheel intensified.

He couldn't get much from the one-sided conversation, but he was so attuned to Kate that he sensed the news wasn't good.

"Well, we're on our way back. Call me as soon as you hear something, okay?"

He heard her voice crack and reached out to touch her knee. "She'll be fine, Kate. And we'll get her back. Believe that."

"I shouldn't have gone with you. This wouldn't have happened if I hadn't been thinking about myself. My own needs. I'm a terrible mother."

"This isn't about you, Kate. It's about Maya and a man who is obviously missing a few genes that normal people have. A father who cared about his child wouldn't steal her from her mother and the only home she's ever known just because he was feeling shut out."

She sniffled quietly.

In a softer tone, he added, "We can't undo last night. And personally, I wouldn't if I could. Men like Ian don't need an excuse to hurt people. He probably saw an opportunity and ran with it."

Kate knew he was right. And his calm demeanor and steady hand on the wheel helped her regain some control over her imagination. She took a sip of her soda. Sweet and bubbly. After a bite of doughnut, she said, "You're right. He is an opportunist. And he knew where Mom kept the keys to her car. He probably timed it so she was at the front door while he was putting Maya in her car seat. When Mom walked back to the kitchen, he would have pulled out and driven away."

She could see the whole thing as clearly as if it were on TV.

"He's in your mom's car?"

She nodded.

"Then we have an advantage. We already know the make, model and license plate number." He handed Kate his phone. "Here. Go to my address book and find Zeke's number. If your mother hasn't already called him, he'll be a great resource. After that, I want you to call every member of the Dads Group."

"Why?" she asked, setting her cup in the plastic holder.

"Publicity. The more people who know about this, the faster we find him. Our own personal Amber Alert."

When they pulled into the compound half an hour later—after making record time, she'd already talked to a dozen people. Word was going out in every direction. Cousins. Friends. Friends of friends. Everyone was on the lookout for Yetta's very ordinary-looking Lincoln.

She jumped out of Rob's car the instant it came to a stop and ran inside, her legs wobbly, hands shaking. "Mom?"

"Kate," a familiar voice called.

"Oh, my God. Grace," Kate exclaimed, tears filling her eyes. "How? When? Why didn't you tell me you were coming?"

The two embraced fiercely. Kate knew she'd missed her sister, she just didn't realize how much until now.

"Totally spur-of-the-minute. I took the red-eye. Nikolai looked at me over dinner last night and said, 'Your sister needs you.'" She made a wide-eyed "who knew" gesture that Kate had no trouble interpreting. Women weren't the only gifted seers in the family, it appeared. "So, he called the airport. They had a seat and here I am."

Kate squeezed her sister. "I owe him one. I'm so glad you're here. Have we heard anything yet? Where's Mom?"

"She went with Zeke to file a missing person's report. Alex is at her house, trying to call in some substitute teachers. Liz is at Gregor's talking to poor little Gemilla. She and Maya were together when Mom walked the other little girl—I can't remember her name—to the door."

Rob suddenly appeared at the screen door, Kate's over-night bag in hand. "Knock, knock. Hi Grace. Nice to see you. I didn't know you were coming."

Kate opened the door for him.

"Where do you want this?"

Kate shrugged. Panic was returning, along with a feeling of guilt. If only she hadn't been off having sex with— "Just drop it anywhere. Is there anyone else I should call? Maybe we could hire a helicopter. I won a bunch of money last night." She pushed her purse into Grace's hands. "Over a thousand, I think. Dad was there."

Rob set down the bag and cleared his throat, as if un-comfortable with the revelation that the woman he'd spent the better part of the night with saw ghosts. "Can I use the bathroom?"

Grace gave him directions, then took Kate's hand and led her to the table. "Tell me what happened."

We spent the night making wild, passionate love. "Rob and I had massages. We ate dinner and drank champagne. It was late. We decided to stay over."

"So, you and Dad gambled together. Cool. Was that before or after you and Rob made love?"

"After."

When Kate realized she'd been tricked into revealing more than she'd intended, she brought up both hands as if to strangle someone, but Grace's laugh snuffed the fuse to her anger. "That's wonderful. Really. Rob's great. I have a good feeling about him. And I'm so happy you recon-nected with Dad. Mom always said you were your father's daughter."

"She did? I don't remember that."

Grace sat down opposite her. "Well, she did. I was

jealous, of course. I was supposedly daddy's girl, but you two did share a bond—kinda like Mom and Liz."

Kate might have discussed her strange experience further but Rob returned, cell phone in hand. "I just got a call from Mac."

"Who?"

"Zeke's new partner. The guy at swimming class with the two-month-old baby."

"Oh. Yeah. What did he say?"

"They think they've spotted the car."

Kate jumped to her feet. "Where? Is Maya still with him? Is she okay?"

Rob reacted without thinking. He walked to her and put his arms around her. "That's all I know. He was relaying what he heard from one of Enzo's tow-truck drivers."

When the call came, Rob's first reaction had been one of wonder. *Wow, this networking thing really works.* He'd never been a part of that type of team. He'd been a bookworm in school and hadn't played in group sports. He'd never needed a lot of friends. But meeting this group of men—the Dads Group—had proven a revelation. He liked them. And it appeared that they cared about him and the people he cared about.

Kate didn't pull away until the door opened and Alex walked in, followed by Yetta and Zeke.

"Hey, you two made good time," Alex said.

Kate ran to her mother, who looked shaken. "Are you okay, Mom? Rob said they might have spotted them. Come sit down."

His respect for Kate went up a notch. She obviously didn't blame her mother.

"I'm so sorry, Katherine. I don't know how this happened. He looked so worn out and defeated. It must have been an act. Just to throw me off my guard. Oh, honey, I let you down again, didn't I?"

Rob wasn't sure what that meant, but he knew the best way to keep morale up was to stay busy. "Um, ladies, I should probably apologize in advance, but when I was rallying the troops, I sorta told people to head over here. I figured we'd set up some kind of command post. Maybe coffee. A few snacks or something…" he hinted.

Grace popped to her feet. "Good idea. Liz has a great tea that helps combat stress. I'll run to Gregor's and see if she has any with her. Mom, Kate, you can make sandwiches. Rob will run to the store since this was his idea." Her wink hold him she understood—and approved of— what he was doing. But would her highly independent sister appreciate his butting in?

KATE LOOKED AROUND. Rob had just taken off for the store. She was alone with her sisters. Yetta and Zeke were outside talking beside his unmarked police car. Kate had noticed the way her mother gravitated toward the silver-haired detective. She wanted to talk about this change in their mother's life with her sisters but now was not the time.

Grace, who was chopping ripe olives for bruschetta, glanced up. "So, this thing between you and Rob is serious, huh?"

"I like him."

Grace elbowed Alex. "She spent the night with him."

"In Mesquite?" Alex asked. "Really? Am I always the last to know everything?"

"I didn't…we didn't…plan it. Jo gave us a gift certificate. Two massages. Dinner. And a room. We'd planned to get a second room if we decided to stay over. The hotel was fully booked."

Grace gave Alex a droll look. "The old no-room-at-the-inn trick. I didn't know that still worked."

Kate shook her head. "Shut up. My little girl is some-where in the desert with a crazy person who is going to be a dead crazy person when I get my hands on him, and you're cracking jokes." She pounded her fist into the stiff dough she was getting ready to roll out.

Alex opened another can of olives and handed it to Grace. To Kate, she said, "I know you're angry. And afraid. But we will find them and Maya will come home safely. What you have to do is decide how to handle this. Are you going to retreat back behind the barricade of work and motherhood where you've been hiding since Ian hurt you, or are you going to refuse to give him that kind of power over you this time?"

Kate stopped kneading to look at her. "What do you mean?"

"After Mark and I broke up, I was really mad for a long time. It warped every aspect of my life, including my health. I passed up a couple of really nice men who wanted to date me because I was so consumed by anger I didn't have room for love. Don't let that happen to you, okay?" She wiped her hands on a towel and started to leave. "I've got some sun-dried tomatoes at my house. I'll be right back."

Kate watched her go, a little stunned. Alex wasn't usually that open about her feelings, especially where her ex-fiancé was concerned.

Grace seemed surprised as well. "She has a point, you know. You're starting a new relationship. One with obvious potential. Personally, I think Ian guessed that you were with Rob and he did this just to get back at you. If you let him ruin things, he'll have won."

Grace's comment remained on Kate's mind an hour later. Rob had returned with a dozen bags of groceries. More family members had shown up with food, too. Alex had herded the children into the backyard. The party atmosphere might have driven Kate mad if she hadn't reminded herself that this was the Rom way.

She stood in the doorway, listening to threads of the many conversations without really hearing a word. Two little girls ducked in and out of Maya's playhouse. A crushing pressure on Kate's chest made it hard to breathe. She wondered if she might be having a heart attack.

Rob suddenly materialized at her side. "You look like someone who needs a breath of fresh—okay, smoggy—air. The sky is light tan, not brown yet, so we should be safe."

He took her hand and led her out the front door.

"Why haven't we heard anything?" she cried.

"We will. Zeke said they're being cautious since nobody wants a high-speed chase."

She'd seen enough of those on TV to picture the outcome. And the image increased the pressure on her chest.

"The longer this goes on, the more afraid Maya will be. She might not have been alarmed when they first took off. He is her dad and he can be very charming when he wants to be, but she's not stupid. She'll know this is wrong. She's crying, Rob. I can feel it."

He pulled her close. His support was something she could get used to, but this wasn't his problem. She pulled back. "Why are you still here? Don't you have to fire someone?"

He'd mentioned his employee dilemma yesterday. His compassion and sensitivity had impressed her.

"I called my secretary and told her the flu was worse."

"Did she believe you?"

"Probably not. I was in the supermarket when I phoned."

"Will she lie for you if the big bosses call?"

"Probably not."

"Rob," she cried, stepping away. "You're risking your livelihood for me. I can't let you do that."

"It's already done. Besides, I'd be useless at work because I'd be worrying about you and Maya."

She paced a short distance away. "Rob, about last night…"

He took a step that placed him in her path. "Last night was amazing. You're amazing. And what's happening now is not related."

"But it is," she insisted. "If—"

"Stop right there, Kate. No recriminations or mea culpa allowed. If you blame our being together for what happened, then Ian wins. He accomplished what he set out to do."

"That's what Grace said, but do you honestly want this kind of craziness in your life? Run, now, while you can."

He chucked her chin with his knuckle. "That's just it, love. I can't. But I do think my presence here is a distraction. People remember me from MaryAnn's hearing. They keep asking if I'm here as your lawyer. I don't want to lie, but I don't think this is the right time to broadcast our relationship, either. So, I'm going to run over to the restaurant and fill Mom in. She probably hasn't heard about what's happened and I know she'll be upset."

Kate groaned. "I completely forgot about Jo. And ask how her doctor's appointment went." She paled suddenly. "Oh, my God. Romantique. It hasn't crossed my mind all day. Who'll cook tonight if Maya isn't back? Your mom can't pull a double. Not after the way she's been feeling. We'll have to close."

Rob shook her shoulders gently. "So what? You put up a sign that says closed for family emergency. Your business will survive, just like it did after a month of bad publicity. Let Mom figure it out. You just concentrate on Maya getting back home safely. Because she will be here. Soon."

She wanted to believe him, but it was becoming more difficult as each minute passed to remain optimistic. "Go to your office after you tell Jo. I want you to, Rob. I don't want to be responsible for anything else going wrong, like you losing your job. Promise me you'll go. I'll call if… when…we hear something."

He started to argue, but Kate took him by the arm and led him to his car. "I need you to do that for me, Rob. Seriously. Go."

And he left.

GRACE AMBUSHED KATE before she could find a secluded spot to hide. "Come to my trailer. We can keep each other company."

The tiny, 1950s-era trailer that had been Grace's home before she moved to Detroit to be with Nick was located in the far back corner of their parents' lot. Partially hidden by dense foliage and a sun canopy, it was the perfect hideout. Luckily, Grace seemed content to talk about her love life. Which kept Kate from falling to pieces.

"Nikolai is amazing," Grace said, her tone filled with wonder. "I wake up every morning wondering what I did to deserve such happiness."

Kate was pleased for her sister. She'd witnessed Grace's heartbreak when her first serious boyfriend, Shawn

Bascomb, cheated on her. Kate had been working at a resort in Colorado when Grace was finishing up college nearby. They'd roomed together for a few months before Grace moved in with Shawn. A gorgeous ski instructor in the winter. A gorgeous raft guide in the summer. He was also a liar. Just like Ian.

"Grace, do you think Alex is right? Can love and hate coexist in the same heart?"

"Maybe for a while," Grace answered. "If Ian hadn't abducted Maya, I think you might have found a way to get along—for Maya's sake."

"What if he's filling her head with nonsense about me and our divorce? Or, worse—pretending we'd be together if not for me. And Rob. She's already not too crazy about Rob. This could ruin any chance he might have of winning her over."

"Would you consider getting back with Ian if Rob weren't in the picture?"

"No. Never."

"You're sure?"

"Absolutely. Grace, you know what his scam cost me. My house. Car. Trust account. Maya's college fund. But I finally got everyone paid back, even Mom. The last few years haven't been easy, but at least I can hold my head up in public."

"I know, Kate. You covered his losses. I respect that, but that doesn't mean you deserve any share of the guilt. You didn't know he was embezzling his clients' money."

"But I should have, Grace."

"How? You're not an investment counselor."

"No, but I'm not stupid, either. I knew—deep down— that we were living beyond our means. Even though Ian insisted he was making money hand over fist, I should have been suspicious. I took business classes in culinary school. I can balance a checkbook. I should have taken a long hard look at our records, but I didn't."

"You were busy. For heaven's sake, you had a baby. And then Dad's…stroke happened. And we opened Romantique. Nobody blames you for anything."

"Maybe they should. I wasn't a good wife. I was so preoccupied I didn't even realize my husband was having an affair." Her voice broke.

"Oh, Kate, you can't blame yourself for that, too."

But I do.

"Stop that. Right now. We need to exorcise this demon."

Grace walked to the stereo and put in a CD. Kate recognized the artist. Rob Thomas, a singer who'd left his successful group Matchbox 20 to go solo. Maya knew all the words to this song by heart. Kate's eyes filled with tears.

"Okay, now," Grace said, pulling Kate to her feet. "Isn't this how we did it when you broke the news that Shawn had been sleeping around the whole time he and I were together? You said, 'Men like him don't deserve women like us.' Then we turned up the music and danced. Because we're gypsy princesses and frogs abound. Even the best of us can be fooled from time to time."

Grace closed her eyes, lifted her arms overhead and started to dance. Kate watched unmoving, but the music was infectious. And the look on her sister's face was one she knew well. When she and her sisters had danced for their father, they'd always felt cherished, safe and adored. And they'd known they were princesses who deserved to live happily ever after.

Ernst had called them the Sisters of the Silver Dollar. He'd reach into his deep, deep pockets and make the coins he always carried jingle in rhythm to the music. When they'd take their bows, he'd toss them coins and applaud. "My beautiful princesses. May the men you marry be worthy of you."

Kate started to move. Not because she felt like dancing but because it was the only way to block the sudden, gut-wrenching fear that the man she'd married might never come back with their daughter.

Chapter Thirteen

Rob needed his mother's help and he knew where to find her. Romantique. Jo met him at the back door since the restaurant didn't open for another hour.

"Maya is missing. Ian took her."

Her grin faded. "Oh, my. When? This morning?"

He quickly filled her in then asked her advice. "I know we're going to get her back. I don't doubt it for a minute. And I know she's going to be a little traumatized—especially if they arrest Ian and bring her home in a police car. So, I thought maybe I should have something for her. Do you have any ideas what to buy? I didn't want to ask Kate. She has too much to think about. One more thing might push her over the edge."

He gave his mother credit for not asking personal questions about their Mesquite trip. She offered three or four ideas, and then gave him the best suggestion, "Why don't you call someone from that dads group of yours?"

"Brilliant." He hugged her and started to dash away, but paused. "Wait. How did your doctor appointment go?"

She made a wobbly sign with her hand. "More tests, of

course. But the lady doc is pretty cool. She said she'd call me with the results."

Rob wasn't sure that was all to the story, but he didn't have time to probe. He had to make some calls.

IT WAS NEARLY TWO O'CLOCK in the afternoon when they got word that Ian was in custody. Maya was safe. Kate burst into tears after handing the phone to Grace. A cheer echoed through the house and neighborhood.

Kate looked around for Rob, but he still wasn't back. He'd phoned half a dozen times to check on her and had apologized profusely for his absence, explaining that he'd wound up going to his office after all and had been swamped with some sort of legal triage.

She wandered from room to room, mostly trying to avoid conversations with extended family members who'd dropped by to see if they could help. She'd pleaded with Zeke to take her with him when he went to pick up Maya, but he'd been in Boulder City when the call came. Kate had agreed that the quickest way to get her daughter home was the best.

She walked into the living room and found Liz curled up on the sofa. Her eyelids looked purplish. She appeared exhausted. "Hey, sis, are you okay?"

Liz yawned and sat up. "Too many sleepless nights catching up with me. I think I'll take a shower. Do you have a T-shirt or something I can borrow?"

"Of course. My closet is your closet." Kate held out a hand to help her stand.

Liz popped lightly to her feet. She put on a pair of functional but, in Kate's opinion, highly unattractive, clogs and started to leave. "Um, Liz, someone asked if I thought

Ian's illness might have played a factor in why he did this. What do you think?"

"I have no idea. The couple of times I saw Ian he looked pretty sick. And weak. Frankly, I was shocked when I heard about this. It sounds like an act of desperation to me."

"Can Maya get it?"

"Hep C?" Liz shook her head. "Not through casual contact. It's not like a cold."

"Alex thinks Ian took Maya because he somehow found out about Rob and me. Do you think I was wrong to go to Mesquite with Rob?"

Liz took a deep breath and let it out. "I'd never judge you, Kate. I don't have the right."

Kate heard a quiver in her sister's voice. She almost asked what the problem was, but Liz wasn't one to share personal information—not with Kate, anyway. Alex might know what was going on with Liz, but Alex was at the Hippo at the moment.

"When you saw him on Saturday, did he talk about the two of you getting back together?" Liz asked.

"He mentioned it. I told him no way."

"Well, maybe that contributed to a sense of hopelessness. Perhaps he felt like had nothing to lose, and when opportunity arose…."

Kate agreed. Ian was impulsive—spontaneous, he'd called it when they were married. What would happen now? she wondered. Would he go back to jail? Or would he be given a second…no, wait, a third chance to screw up her life?

ROB SAT DOWN at his desk. He hadn't planned to come into the office, but his secretary had called in a panic shortly after he'd left his mother at Romantique. Three of the senior partners were on their way to Vegas for a surprise visit.

Or inquisition, Rob thought.

The normally quiet, almost comatose office suddenly seemed to vibrate with a low hum. Desperation mixed with fear, he decided.

Ever since Rob had taken over the leadership position at Ames, Beeker and Constantine, Las Vegas, he'd been quietly evaluating the lawyers working under him. He'd drawn conclusions—some favorable, some not so positive. What surprised him was how quickly and much he'd come to care for the people in this office.

He unlocked his desk drawer and took out the two file folders he'd been studying yesterday before his mother suggested his and Kate's spur-of-the-moment trip to Mesquite. Was that really just twenty-four hours ago, he marveled?

So much had changed. His feelings for Kate had jelled. He was in love. But new relationships were tricky. So many things could go wrong. And pivotal to his and Kate's future was location. He needed to be here. Which meant he had to convince his bosses that he was in for the long haul and thoroughly committed to making this office a success. If that meant cutting someone who wasn't pulling his or her own weight, then, damn it, that's what he'd do.

Would he fire Kwen? Or April? Those were his choices. Single father of three or sole provider and caregiver of a mother who was suffering from Alzheimer's? Both were extremely capable lawyers, compassionate litigators and genuinely likable people, but neither seemed to have the time and energy required to do their best for their clients— or, from the partners' point of view, the capacity to generate billable hours.

"Damn," he muttered.

To put off the "kill" a moment longer, he turned on his computer to check his e-mail. The first message he clicked on had an attachment. The short note explained that Adam had sent photos of his honeymoon. "Five days in paradise is not enough, dammit," Adam wrote. "Hope all is well there. Best to your mom."

Mom. Despite her insistence of the contrary, Rob knew his mother was worried about her health. So many tests. Nothing conclusive. A longtime smoker with a cough? It didn't take a specialist to think lung cancer.

He pushed the thought away.

"Photos. Cool," he murmured. There were seven individual shots. He double-clicked on the one named cheers.jpeg. A colorful image of Adam and Haley in swimsuits snuggled together in a blue-and-white striped cabana on a sugar sand beach. They were toasting each other with drinks served in coconut shells. Corny but kinda fun.

"You look happy, Dad. Really truly happy," he said, clicking on the second icon.

Most of the photos were of Haley. She really was gorgeous, and her bright personality seemed to emote through the image on his screen. The only shot of Adam alone showed him standing beside a five-foot-long fish that he'd apparently caught. Rob guessed that Haley had taken the picture because Adam was grinning in a way that said, "You're the reason I'm here."

He closed the file, which his father had titled: Dreams come true. Rob frowned. Was his father's dream to go deep-sea fishing? Marry his soul mate? Or become a successful author?

Before he could click on the final shot, the phone rang. *Kate? Had they found Maya? Please God...*

"Rob, this is Bart Gravenstein from The Bay And More Realty. I've got good news, buddy. I found a buyer for your condo. It's a sweet deal, but the people want to move in ASAP. Is there anyway you can fly up here and sign the papers tomorrow or the next day?"

His real-estate agent. The property was the last string tying Rob to the life he'd left behind. His safety net, of sorts. "Hi, Bart. Things are a little hectic at the moment. I'll check my schedule and get back to you."

They talked a while longer. The throbbing in Rob's head started to feel like a time bomb. He grabbed the phone to punch in the numbers to Kate's cell phone but changed his mind at the last minute. She'd promised to call the moment she heard something about Maya. Instead, he tried Gregor's number.

"Hey, man, I was just thinking about you. I wanted to thank you for the job referral. My new job is great, and the company's human resources department is so in touch with the way people's lives really are, it's amazing. I mean, it's only like my fifth day and I called this morning and told them what was happening with Maya and how upset Gemilla was and they said, 'Stay home with your little girl. We have job-share people who are set up to fill in at a moment's notice.' Can you believe it?"

"Um...no. That is amazing."

"I agree, but the big boss has this philosophy that employees can't give a hundred percent if half of their heart is somewhere else. Makes sense, doesn't it? So, anyway, what can I do for you, buddy?"

Rob looked at the folders on his desk and started to

smile. "I think you might have just done it, but the reason I called was to ask your advice. I'd like to get Maya something as a coming-home present. Something that might cheer her up and maybe distract her a bit. Any suggestions?"

Gregor left the phone for a minute to consult an "expert." Gemilla.

"A video would be nice. Or anything Nemo-ish, like a new fish for her aquarium. Personally, I've been thinking about getting the kids a puppy. Our dog died last year and life was so screwy we didn't even try to replace her. But, I decided to wait until MaryAnn gets home. Taking care of a new pup might be more than she can handle on top of everything else, you know. So, I wouldn't go that route unless I cleared it with Kate, if I were you."

Rob thanked him for the advice then turned off his computer and made two more calls. Job-sharing? Why not? Instead of firing one of them, he gave them both the opportunity to work part-time. This would save the company one salary and keep two excellent lawyers on staff. And when they were ready, they could expand their hours.

If the big bosses didn't like his plan? Well, he could always turn down the offer on his condo and go home. Right?

He wished.

"THEY'LL BE HERE in ten minutes," Alex said, rushing into the kitchen, portable phone in hand. "Maya's fine. She's asking for her mother, but she's not hurt or anything."

Kate managed to control her tears this time, but Grace pushed a tissue into her hand anyway. "She's safe. I knew she would be."

"M…me, too. Deep down. But what if she's been traumatized by this? She barely knows Ian, and Alex and Mom and I have stressed over and over about not getting into cars with strangers. She might think she did something wr... wrong."

Grace patted her back. "You'll make her understand that this wasn't her fault."

Kate wasn't sure she was up to the task. "A part of me wants to pack a bag and leave, Grace. Start a new life somewhere where he can't find us. If we disappeared, I'd never have to worry about this happening again."

"I know, Kate. I know. But running away isn't the answer. I hate to say this. I know how you feel about Mom's prophecy, but you really can't avoid the past, sis. Ian is here. He'll probably have to go back to jail after this, but he'll be out eventually and you'll have to face him again. If Maya doesn't want to see him, it has to be her choice."

Kate couldn't bring herself to agree, even though she recognized the truth in her sister's words.

"Let's go freshen up. You look a little distraught."

I am distraught. My daughter has been missing for seven hours. And the man I think I'm in love with isn't here.

"Wait. I promised Rob I'd call." She used her cell phone because Alex was phoning other family members to give them the good news.

When he didn't answer his cell phone, she tried the office number. The receptionist answered. She put Kate through to Rob's secretary. "I'm sorry. Mr. Brighten is in a meeting at the moment. Would you care to leave your number?"

"Please tell him Kate called. Maya is on her way home." Then she hung up. She wished he was here with her, but maybe this was for the best. Maya would need Kate's full attention for some time to come.

ROB KEPT THE MEETING short and sweet. He didn't have time to answer a lot of questions, partly because he was winging this and partly because he was still waiting for Kate's call. His secretary had been given strict orders to interrupt the meeting as soon as the call came from the Radonovic compound.

"Gentlemen, you have two choices: cut and run or hunker down for the duration. If you want to give up the inroads this office has made in the Las Vegas market, then the first is your obvious choice. A bad one, in my opinion, but that's for you to decide. The second is going to require some creative thinking—some reaching into those parts of our brains that don't get used much—the human side."

He tried to keep his tone light, but only a few faces actually showed any sign of getting his joke. He pushed on. "Before you is a very rough sketch of my plan. The figures are tentative, but the bottom line is: you'll still make money off this branch. Not a lot to start out, but you won't be in the red, either."

He checked his watch. Again. Why hadn't Kate called?

"Are we keeping you from something?" a deep voice asked.

Rob looked across the conference table at Jordon Ames, his near-miss father-in-law. Haughty. Powerful. Unapproachable. That was how Rob had always viewed him. In the past, Rob had dreaded any contact with the man, at work or on a social basis. Now, he just didn't care.

"My friend's daughter was abducted by her father this morning. Our office bungled the original custody hearing. In fact, one of the two lawyers up for dismissal handled the case. Rather poorly. But I take full responsibility for that since I assigned her to the case and didn't follow through."

"Could we be sued?"

"Possibly, but I arranged for new representation with a lawyer who specializes in family law, so I don't think that will be a problem."

Serena's father whispered something to his neighbor, then winked knowingly at Rob. Did the man know Rob was seeing Kate? Did the creep think Rob was dating Kate just to avoid being sued?

He stood up. "Gentlemen, you have the information you need to decide on the fate of this office. The black-and-white information. But if you want to make informed decisions, I suggest you walk into the hallway and talk to the staff. When I first got here, they seemed to share a sense of floating at sea, adrift and unaccountable. Now, I think you'll see they're committed to being part of a whole. I'm sorry I can't stick around, but I've got important personal business."

He couldn't believe his brass. He'd never walked out of a meeting before in his life. He hurried to his office. His secretary wasn't at her desk. A temp he didn't recognize was in her place. "Where's Jill?"

"She wasn't feeling well. Bad sushi she thinks."

Rob got a sick feeling low in his gut—and he hadn't eaten since the doughnut he shared with Kate on the road. "Did I get any calls when I was in the meeting?"

She looked down. "Um…yes. One. Someone named Kate said to tell you Maya was home. Does that make sense?"

It did. But his not being available probably wouldn't. Not to Kate.

Chapter Fourteen

"Mommy."

Kate had never heard a sweeter, more welcome sound in her life. She was out the door the second the unmarked patrol car rolled into the cul-de-sac. She'd seen that car before. It belonged to Zeke, who had brought her mother home hours earlier then disappeared.

Zeke's partner, the stocky bodybuilder type who came to the swimming lessons with his baby, got out of the passenger seat and opened the rear door. A woman in street clothes stood up, first, then held out her hand to another passenger. Maya.

Kate's knees nearly gave out when she saw her daughter, but somehow she managed to pick her up. "Maya. Oh, baby, I'm so glad to see you. Are you okay?"

Maya wrapped her arms tightly around Kate's neck and buried her face against her shoulder. Her little body shuddered with sobs. Kate did her best to comfort her, rubbing her back until the weeping eased.

"Where did your daddy take you, honey?"

Maya's thin arm lifted as she pointed. Kate realized the foolishness of her question. Four-year olds didn't know directions or maps. "Are you hungry? Thirsty?" *Scarred for life?*

"They were in a café just finishing lunch when a uniformed officer approached them," Zeke said, standing a few steps to one side. "According to the arresting officer, Grant didn't offer any kind of resistance and Maya seemed fine, although she put up a bit of a squawk over going in the patrol car because her mother taught her not to get in a car with strangers."

Kate smiled through her tears. "She did, did she? I'm proud that you remembered, sweetheart."

Maya lifted her chin. "Daddy told me it was okay to go with those policemen. He said they'd take me home because he had other business to do and couldn't take me to the zoo like he wanted."

"The zoo?"

She nodded seriously. "This morning when we left he said we were going to go somewhere that he liked a lot when he was a little boy and he'd never gotten a chance to show me. The zoo. A really big one with lots of animals." She started rattling off the many species.

Kate looked at Zeke. "Which zoo?"

He shrugged and shook his head. "They were in Quartzsite. Make a right turn and you're headed to San Diego."

Kate pictured a map in her head. "Or keep going straight and you're in Mexico," she said softly.

Zeke nodded.

The rest of the family, who'd waited till she'd had some time alone with her daughter, suddenly surged around them. Kate felt safe and loved, but there was one person missing. Rob. And she felt that, too.

"MAYA'S TAKING A NAP. All tuckered out," Yetta told him, when Rob finally reached the Radonovic house after what seemed like a fool's quest. He'd had to go to three pet stores before he found one with a decent selection of fish.

Stupidly, he held up his purchase: four individual plastic Baggies filled with water. "I wanted to get her something," he said.

Yetta smiled. "She'll be pleased."

He looked around. "Is Kate here?"

"No. She and her lawyer were meeting with someone to discuss what to do about Ian. Zeke tried to explain it to me, but frankly, I was too upset to follow. I felt as though I failed them both, you know."

Rob did know. Too well.

He made a gesture with one of the bags. "What should I do with these little fellows? The guy at the pet store said they shouldn't stay in these bags too long."

Yetta motioned for him to follow her. She carefully opened a door and walked into a darkened room. It took a minute for his eyes to adjust. When they did, he spotted the artificial brightness of the tropical aquarium. And a few feet away was Maya's bed with the little girl curled up beneath a frilly pink spread.

His heart compressed from the pressure on his chest. She looked like a curly-haired angel. Defenseless and fragile. Anger surged from some primal spot deep inside him. If he could have gotten his hands around Ian's throat…

"Let go," a voice whispered.

Rob blinked. Yetta's hands were covering his. The water in the clear bags was sloshing from side to side. He let out a long harsh breath.

"She's an amazingly resilient soul," Yetta said softly.

"Her mother was afraid this experience might scar her, but I think my granddaughter is able to discern a person's true motives better than most adults can. Her father didn't mean to hurt her or scare her. He simply got lost."

Lost?

Rob didn't actually ask the question until after they'd released the fish into the tank. He'd listened to the pet store clerk's explicit directions on how to acclimate fish to a new environment, but his patience was long gone. He untied the twist ties and dumped them in. If they made it, great. If not, well, this wouldn't be his first bad move of the day.

"What did you mean when you said Ian got lost?" he asked Yetta once they were seated at the kitchen table. She'd offered him coffee, but he'd turned it down. His stomach was a knot of nerves.

"Ian's mother was Romani. She was very beautiful and very troubled. When things turned sour, she'd take her son and leave. By bus, car, thumb—whatever means was convenient. Ian's central point of his inner compass got mixed up, cross-wired. When he's in one place for too long, he starts thinking he has to leave, and some unconscious force takes over. He does things to precipitate the need for a move."

Rob sat back in the chair and considered what she said. It made sense, but… "Does that excuse him?"

"For taking Maya? Heavens, no. I don't believe he planned to take Maya this morning, but he's an opportunist. When he found out Kate was gone, he acted out of spite."

"Why?"

"Because she was with you. A clear signal that she'd started to rebuild her life—one that didn't include him."

"How could he have known she was with me? Hell, I didn't even know last night was going to happen until it did."

Yetta gave an inward smile that made him shiver. "Ian is a very clever man. Maybe he had somebody spying on Kate—looking for something to use in their custody battle."

Damn. Not once had Rob checked to see if anyone was following them. Heck, he was so infatuated with Kate, the guy could have tailgated him and Rob wouldn't have noticed.

"But surely he didn't think he could get away with kidnapping Maya."

Yetta took a sip from the cup she was holding. "I doubt if he thought past the taking. That's how he is—impulsive. But as I told Katherine, even if they put him back in jail, he's not going to disappear. And now that Maya's older and they've established a relationship, it will be impossible for Kate to ignore him the way she's done in the past."

Rob agreed. The last time he and Maya talked, the little girl had been adamant about Ian's role as her daddy. If Maya had her way, there wouldn't be room for any other man in her life, not for a long, long time.

"I DIDN'T DO IT on purpose, Katie. I just acted. You weren't there. Maya was. And I thought if I took a drive in the desert I'd be able to think clearly. You know that's what I used to do. Remember?"

Kate was sitting across the table from her ex-husband in some kind of interrogation room. She had the uncomfortable feeling there might be someone observing them, although she didn't see anything that looked like a two-way mirror on the wall. Ian was wearing street clothes—denim jeans, a lilac polo shirt that she never would have bought for him and expensive-looking sneakers.

They were alone. Their respective lawyers were elsewhere, probably hammering out some kind of plea bargain with the police or D.A. She didn't know or care.

"So, I was gone and you thought, 'Hey, it's a nice day for a drive. I'll just steal my ex-mother-in-law's car and take my daughter for a little road trip'—even though it's against the law, the provisions of your parole and our custody agreement."

His chin dropped to his chest. "I didn't really stop to think. That's pretty obvious, isn't it?"

She didn't answer.

He looked up. "I had a dream last night. I saw you in bed with another guy. You told him you loved him. I kept shouting, 'No. No. You can't love him. You're my wife.'"

Kate felt her face heat up. Had he guessed where she'd been and with whom or was this some kind of Rom mind game? "But I'm not your wife, Ian," she said firmly. "We're divorced."

"That's just paperwork, Katie. We said vows."

"Which *you* broke."

"I made some really lousy decisions and took risks that didn't work out the way I thought they would, but I never stopped loving you."

She crossed her arms. "Really? And where was the keep-yourself-solely-unto-each-other part when you ran off to Mexico with the blond bimbette?"

He took a deep breath and let it out. "I didn't cheat on you."

She snorted skeptically. "Tell that to the woman you were arrested with."

"Her name is Cara. Her brother owed me money. A lot of money. He was one of the reasons I got caught short when the auditors came down on me. He was afraid I was going to use my Mafia connections to put a hit on him if he didn't pay up."

"What Mafia connections?"

He grinned. "Exactly. I didn't have any, but he didn't know that. So, he begged me to think of some other kind of payback. I told him I needed a woman to play the part of my mistress."

Kate blew out a breath of frustration. "This is pathetic, Ian. Did you spend the last two years thinking this up? I've never heard such a crock. I'm leaving."

He reached out with his hand, but stopped short of actually touching her arm. "Katie, please. You have to listen. This is the truth. Ask my lawyer, she'll tell you."

"She's your lawyer. She's paid to believe you."

"Then ask Cara. She's married now and living in Boulder City. She visited me a couple of times in jail. She's a good person. She just wanted to help her brother."

Kate heard a sincerity that couldn't be denied. "Why would you do such a thing?"

"I figured getting away was a long shot, but when you're desperate you'll try anything. If I would have made it across the border, I'd have contacted you as soon as it was safe for you and Maya to join me."

"Life on the run," she said. Did he really believe she'd have taken an infant across the border to live on money he'd stolen from her family? "There's a great way to raise a child."

He grimaced. "You're right. I knew that, too, but I panicked. Everything was crashing down around me. I couldn't tell you the truth, so I lied. To protect you."

Something in his tone made her stifle her automatic response. Ian had always insisted that his role in the family was to keep his wife and daughter safe. He'd been neurotic about alarm systems, air bags in cars and child-protective locks.

"So running away was your way of protecting us?"

"Yes. It was the best I could do. And just in case I got caught, I figured I needed something to keep you from wasting any more time and money on me."

A lump formed in Kate's throat making it impossible to ask what needed to be asked.

"Cara was a front. A prop. The police let her go after questioning, but by then you'd already assumed the worst. Like I knew you would. You saw her and said, 'Hang the bastard.'"

"Not in so many words," she said softly.

"I know you, Katie. I know how much value you place on trust and integrity. I didn't know how long I'd be in jail, but I didn't want you and Maya wasting time worrying about me, visiting me."

"So you set me up to hate you?"

He nodded.

"Well, congratulations. It worked. I do."

"No, you wish you could. But you don't."

Kate wanted to deny the allegation, but her emotions were too jumbled. She hung on to anger. It was much safer than sympathy. "It doesn't matter whether or not you actually slept with that woman, Ian. If you think what you did somehow makes you noble, you're sadly mistaken. You destroyed the life we'd built together and shattered any illusion I held dear about love and trust. I know you're Maya's father. There's nothing I can do to change that, but if I have my way, you will never spend time alone with her again. Do you understand?"

He didn't say a word, but Kate could see the answer in his eyes. He believed her.

"Now, I have to go. I still have a business to run, and thanks to you, a traumatized daughter to worry about. I hope they toss you back in jail and throw away the key."

"You don't mean that, Katie."

"Oh, believe me, Ian. I do. I sincerely do."

Chapter Fifteen

The minute Kate escaped from the meeting with her lawyer, she called Jo.

"Good news, sweetie," Jo said. "We finally caught a break."

"What kind of break and how much is it going to cost?"

Her partner laughed. "Oh, quit being so cynical. This is a good thing. I just hired an old friend to cook tonight. He's wonderful. We worked together for a couple of years. He and his wife split and he's sort of between jobs. He pitched in during lunch and I think he's going to be perfect. Nothing long-term. Just a few days to give you time to regroup and be with Maya."

Kate's brain struggled to process the information. She'd thought seriously about closing the restaurant for the night because she'd had practically no sleep the night before and was emotionally drained. "Are you sure?"

"Hey, this is my place, too, remember? I wouldn't let just anyone stand at this stove."

"You're right. I'm sorry I…I'm a little wiped out."

Jo made a sympathetic sound. "I know, dear. Rob told me. He's pretty upset, too. And then this thing at work came up." *Thing at work?* "I know it's killing him not to be with you, but a person can't be two places at once, right?"

Kate didn't know what to say. She hadn't talked to Rob since he left, except for voice messages on their cell phones. She was alone. Like always. That's all she knew for sure.

"Listen, Jo, how 'bout I ask Grace to hostess tonight? That way if this new guy has any questions, she can help."

"Great idea. Anything to keep you at home with your little girl. Now, I gotta run. We still have to nail down tonight's specials. Talk to you later." She hung up.

After calling her sister, who wasn't going back to Detroit until Monday, Kate took her time driving home. She'd checked in with her mother and learned that Maya was still napping. That was good. Maya was happy at Yetta's. Content. Living in Kate's childhood home was convenient. But one thought that had jelled in Kate's mind over the course of the day was: Maya and I need a place of our own.

She didn't blame her mother for letting Maya out of her sight. Ian could have weaseled his way past even the most vigilant babysitter.

But even if this situation hadn't happened, Kate knew it was time to leave. She'd taken advantage of her mother's generosity long enough. Grace would loan her the money if Kate asked. She just hoped her mother would understand.

"Mom?" she called, walking into the kitchen.

No one answered. She dropped her purse on the table and dashed down the hall to the bedrooms.

Yetta was sitting on Maya's bed, reading a book.

"Hi, Mommy. I got a new book from Daddy."

"Really? You had time to go shopping while you were off on your adventure?" Kate asked, tilting her chin to read the cover. The title had the word *jokes* in it.

"We bought it when we got gas."

"Oh."

"Zeke brought it by, along with Maya's sweater," her mother said. "I guess they'd gotten overlooked in my car. Enzo is making arrangements to return that to me later."

"Wanna hear a joke, Mommy?"

"Sure, but then Grandma and I have to talk."

"What's a three-letter word for mousetrap?"

Kate's mind was too numb to think. "I don't know. What's a three-letter word for mousetrap?"

Her daughter's brown eyes twinkled with mischief. "C-a-t."

Kate laughed, but her emotions surged. She had to blink fast to keep her tears inside. Her little girl—the child she and Ian had produced—was growing up so fast. She was smart and funny and kind and wonderful. And Kate knew she would do whatever it took to make sure nobody hurt her or crushed her amazing spirit.

"That's great. I love it. We can read some more later. I'm not going to work tonight. I figured we'd just hang out and watch movies. Does that sound good?"

Maya nodded, but she also looked at her grandmother, as if needing Yetta's okay.

"I'll go make a fresh pot of coffee," Yetta said. "Why don't you introduce your mother to your new fish, Maya? The ones Rob gave you."

"Rob? When was he here?"

"About an hour ago. Maya was asleep. He had to run home and get dressed for some fancy dinner his bosses were dragging him to. He didn't seem very happy about it."

Once Yetta had left the room, Kate sat down at the foot

of the bed. Her gaze was drawn to the fish swimming in the bright clear water of the aquarium.

There were a couple of pretty ones she didn't recognize.

"Grandma said this black one's name is Molly, only I think he's a he not a she because he's so mean to the other fish."

"Not all males are mean, Maya."

Maya moved to the far side of the aquarium so Kate couldn't see her clearly.

"You know some very nice men, like Gregor and Great-uncle Claude and Zeke and…Rob."

Maya tapped on the glass, sending the fish toward the safety of an artificial rock formation. She didn't say anything.

"Maya, I need to be sure that you understand that what happened today wasn't your fault. Your daddy made a mistake today but he didn't mean to hurt you."

"He said you won't let him live with us, Mommy. Why?"

"Because it just wouldn't work out. I've changed."

"Can't you change back?"

Kate shook her head sadly. "No. I'm sorry, honey. I can't."

"Why not?"

"Well…you like being four, right?"

Maya nodded.

"Would you ever want to be two again?"

"No. I'm not a baby anymore."

You're my baby. "There you go. You've moved on and that's how I feel about your dad. I can't ever live with him again."

"Does that mean we'll always live with Grandma?"

"No. In fact, you and I are going to start planning for the day we move into our own place. Probably an apartment to start out, but eventually, we'll have a house."

"Will it have a swimming pool?"

"Maybe."

"Will Rob come there and teach swimming lessons?"

Leave it to her daughter to ask the tough questions. "I don't know, honey. He's a pretty busy guy."

"Won't Grandma be sad if we leave?"

"You know, I think she's been happy to have us living with her because she was lonely after Grandpa died. But, maybe, if she doesn't have us to worry about she'll go out more."

"Like on a date?" Maya asked, her eyes growing wide. "With kissing and stuff?"

"Maybe."

"Mommy, if we move, why can't we take Daddy with us? He's all alone, you know."

"Sweetheart, Mommy and Daddy are never going to live together again," Kate said firmly. "I'm sorry, but that's just the way it is."

Maya's lips turned down and tears welled up in her eyes. "You're mean. Daddy says he loves us and wants to move home but you won't let him. You're too busy being Rob's girlfriend."

Kate knew that kind of logic didn't come naturally to a four-year-old. Just as she'd feared, Ian had crafted a story that made him the martyr. "I know your father loves you very much. He's missed out on watching you grow up and he probably wishes he could make for up that, but I have to do what I think is best for both us. And living with your father isn't good for me. This has nothing to do with Rob."

Maya peeked around the corner of the fish tank. Her heart-shaped face looked drawn, worried. "I like this gold one Rob bought me. She's pretty. Her fins look like feathers."

Kate moved to her knees and crept closer. "She's beautiful. Does she have a name?"

Maya pressed her nose to the glass. "I dunno. Will he come back? So I can ask him?"

He? "Rob?"

The little girl nodded.

I dunno. "S…sure." Although at the moment she wasn't certain of anything. "But since he gave them to you, they're yours to name. Or, maybe if you concentrate real hard, they'll tell you their fish names. Can you do that?" ·

Maya brightened noticeably. "Uh-huh. Auntie Alex says I'm good with animals. That's why we're going to get a doggie soon."

"We who?"

Maya didn't answer. She seemed intensely focused on her mission—to talk to the fish.

"I…um, I'll be in the kitchen. Grandma and I need to talk."

Kate watched her daughter a moment longer, then left. Surely understanding the language of fish was a no more impossible task than understanding why some men were mean.

"ROB WANTED YOU to call him," Yetta said, after Kate was seated a few minutes later. She'd detoured to her room to change into sweats.

"I tried his number a little while ago and it said no service. Maybe he turned it off."

Kate tried to keep her tone even. She didn't want anyone to know how hurt she'd been that he'd disappeared in her hour of need. True, she'd practically ordered him to leave, but she'd expected him to return at some point. Surely he'd known how upsetting this had been for her. His devotion to his work seemed a pretty lousy recommendation for a boyfriend.

"He told me what happened. The big bosses came to town for a surprise meeting. They were threatening to close the whole operation, but Rob persuaded them to give the office another chance." Yetta smiled. "According to his mother, Rob saved sixteen jobs, including his own."

"Really? He didn't mention any of that in his message."

Yetta's smile disappeared. "You're mad at him, aren't you?"

"No."

"Yes, you are."

Kate was too tired to argue. "I could have used him around today. That's all."

"Does that mean you two are officially a couple?"

"Huh?"

"Well, usually it takes more than one date for someone to feel comfortable hanging around in the middle of a family crisis. If you wanted him here the whole time, then you must be pretty sure he's the one."

Kate's cup nearly slipped from her fingers. "I...he...we haven't really had time to talk about how we feel. I guess I was a little hurt that he went to work, but you're right. He had every right to."

Her mother stepped closer and patted Kate's shoulder. "I was just making a point, dear. People sometimes make hasty decisions in times of crisis that they later regret."

Kate felt a stab of guilt. *Like making up my mind to move?*

"Rob is a good man, Kate. I know you see that, but you've been through a lot lately. No one would blame you if you were a bit gun-shy when it comes to love."

Love? Kate wasn't sure she even knew what the word

meant, but she didn't have time to think about it for long. The man in question suddenly appeared at the kitchen door. Dressed in a tux.

"Rob? My gosh, where are you going?"

He stepped inside and took a deep breath. His hair looked slightly damp. Kate was positive she'd never seen anyone more handsome. Even the frazzled look in his eye was sexy.

"Dinner. At some five-star place. On the wharf."

Her heart thudded hard against the wall of her chest.

"Wh...what wharf? There's no wharf in Las Vegas."

He ran a hand through his hair. She recognized the gesture of frustration. "I know," he said. "The partners are in town. They're flying back to San Francisco tonight. The corporate jet. That's why I wasn't here. Had to put on the dog and pony show. Now, they're hauling me back with them for some meeting tomorrow."

"Why?"

He looked down—embarrassed or reluctant to say? "It's not a consensus. My would-have-been father-in-law, whom I'm pretty sure orchestrated my being sent to Vegas in the first place, can't bring himself to admit that I'm not the screw-up he wants everyone to think I am, but two of the partners want me to come back."

"To San Francisco?"

"Uh-huh. They said they need my energy and grit." He smiled. "I think that means I was so frantic to get in touch with you, I walked out of a meeting. People don't usually do that to these guys."

"I called your office. Your secretary said—"

"I know. Sorry about that. That woman was a temp. My regular admin. went home with a stomachache."

He reached out and touched the side of her face with his

fingertips. "This really wasn't how I saw this day happening. I wasn't here with you, and I'm really sorry about that. At least Maya's home safe and sound, right?"

Kate nodded. "Pretty much. She's a little confused and her trust in men rivals mine, but…" She tried to keep her tone light. "When will you be back?"

"A day or two. But what's really crazy is I got a call this morning from the Realtor who's had my condo listed ever since Serena and I broke up. Talk about weird timing. He has a buyer. With cash. I have to give them an answer by Friday."

"Wow. That's fast."

"I know. Yesterday, I would have jumped at the offer, but, now…well, I won't know until I hear the partners' terms. But I think they're going to ask me to take over our Walnut Creek branch. This is huge. I'm a little shellshocked. One minute I'm certain they're here to fire me, then next I'm some kind of wunderkind."

Kate didn't know what to say. "Why? I mean, you are amazing, but what changed their minds?"

He paced a few steps away, his brows drawn. "I'm not sure exactly. The cynical side of my mind thinks it's because of you."

"Me? Why me?"

"I told them how April bungled your custody hearing and I hooked you up with another lawyer who specializes in family law. They liked the way I handled the matter. Not trying to sweep it under the table. My almost-father-in-law tried to suggest that I started dating you so you wouldn't sue us. Which is ridiculous, of course. But that's the kind of thing he would have done. And probably did at some point in his career. He's as ethical as a—" He stopped midsentence when he looked at Kate.

Her mouth had dropped open; her eyes expressed dismay. "Kate? You're not buying that. No way."

"Your dad's wedding? Was that a bribe?"

Rob heard the words and her tone—pure hurt. "No. Of course not. I just wanted to help. My God, Kate, this is nuts. Why would you think that?"

She gave a bitter laugh. "Historically, the men I've cared for the most are handsome, glib and pathetically short on principles. Why should you be any different?"

"Because I am. I haven't lied to you. This—us—what happened last night has nothing to do with your case. The partners might see it that way, but that's because their lives are tweaked. You know me. I'm not like that."

"Do I? Rob, what I know is we have very little in common. You hate Vegas and can't wait to leave it. My business, my family, my life is here. Despite the fact that you're amazingly good with kids, you claim to not want children. I have one, in case you didn't notice."

"Dammit, Kate, you're twisting things to make me look like the bad guy here. Your ex ran off with Maya today, not me. I'm sorry I wasn't here to help, but I had fifteen people—and their families—counting on me to save their jobs. My bosses want to reward that. Period."

"You're right. I'm overreacting. Probably because I'm emotionally shot at the moment. You need to go to San Francisco and figure out what you want to do with your life. I already know what I want to do with mine. I want to make Romantique a huge success, take care of my daughter without worrying that someone from my past is going to snatch her away from me and, last but not least, buy a place of our own because a woman my age shouldn't be living at home with her mother."

Rob didn't know what to say.

"This is a lot to process, Rob. My brain isn't completely over what happened to Maya. I'll wish you good luck, then we'll see what happens."

He looked at her and frowned. "I'm coming back, Kate. I am. We'll talk then. I promise. Okay?"

Kate didn't have a chance to answer. His phone rang. He looked at the number and groaned. Impulsively, she put her arms around him and squeezed tightly, hoping she didn't mess up his tuxedo too badly. "Sure. Grace is planning a little pool party to thank all the volunteers who helped us get Maya home safely. If you get back in time, I hope you'll come."

He took her face in his hands. "That I can't promise, but I will if at all possible." Then he kissed her, hard and fast. "I…" He paused, obviously reconsidering whatever he'd started to say. "I'll miss you. Tell Maya I'm glad she's okay and I hope she likes her fish."

"You can tell her yourself. She's in her room…no. Forget I said that. I don't want you to get a speeding ticket. Go."

Her smile wasn't the same one he'd seen this morning when he tapped her on the shoulder at the craps table. This one said friend, not lover. But they weren't a couple, he reminded himself. They'd made love. That didn't automatically imply a lifelong commitment, did it?

Rob replayed their conversation in his head as he drove to the airport. His gut told him he'd blown it. He hadn't said any of the things he should have said. Like what last night meant to him. Or how much he adored Maya and wanted to do whatever it took to make her like him. Or the most important words of all, I love you.

He pounded his heel on the steering wheel. His glib

tongue had failed him. Why? Was it because he didn't really want to commit to her? Before today, he had assumed he'd be living in Nevada for the next several years. Now, it seemed he had a choice.

Or did he?

Las Vegas meant Kate and Maya. And his mother. And a group of people who now appreciated him because he'd managed to buy them another year with the firm and saved two careers in the process. And the Dads Group. His little swimmers.

But was any of that worth the kind of emotional risk that went with marriage? Serena, the woman he'd almost married, had claimed he was a screwed-up emotional mess who wouldn't know commitment if it bit him on the ass. What if she was right? Was he really the right guy for Kate? Could he possibly be trusted to give her and Maya the life they deserved?

He just didn't know.

Chapter Sixteen

The next morning, Kate stumbled out of bed too early. She'd suffered through a restless night—one chase after another. First, she'd spent hours searching for Maya, only to find her home in bed. Then, she'd followed Rob across a bridge that kept getting narrower and shakier. She'd awoken just before she stepped into a pool of black water.

"Good morning, dear," Yetta said, entering the kitchen as Kate popped the top on a cola. Her mother was carrying a bouquet of cut flowers, including roses.

"You have rose bushes?" Kate exclaimed. "Where?"

"At the cemetery. Grace planted them on either side of your father's headstone. Your sister and I went for a visit this morning. She's at Alexandra's now."

"Oh."

"How'd you sleep?" her mother asked.

"Crummy." She followed Yetta to the sink and watched as she clipped the stems to a uniform length. Kate picked up one dark pink bud and held it to her nose. "It doesn't smell."

"Many of the newer varieties were bred for beauty only. They don't need to attract bees because they're not pollinated the old-fashioned way."

"Hmm. You and Grace didn't happen to talk about dating, did you? As in, you and some attractive older man."

Her mother fumbled with the utility shears.

"Someone like Zeke Martini?"

Yetta sighed weightily. "I've raised a gaggle of gossips."

"We love you, Mom. We want you to be happy. None of us would be upset if you started seeing him. Or someone else. You're too young to live the rest of your life without love."

"Ezekiel is an interesting man, but not my type."

"Oh, really. Why is that?"

"He's a solitary person. A loner. He wouldn't know what to do with all my kids and their…"

"Problems," Kate supplied.

"Issues." Her mother smiled. "But I enjoy having coffee with him now and then."

"Having coffee, huh? Is that old-person speak for making out?"

Her mother gave her a look Kate remembered all too well from childhood. "Katherine, if I were you, I'd figure out my own love life before I meddled in someone else's."

The advice was blunt, but the tone was gentle. Inviting. "I wish I could, Mom. There's a part of me that feels ready to move forward—shake off the weights that have kept me down. But I swear those shackles are attached by Velcro. I just get one side open and the other falls back on itself."

"I can picture that. Maya on one hand, Ian on the other."

She finished arranging the flowers then sat down and motioned for Kate to join her at the table. "What's really on your mind, dear?"

Kate swallowed the lump in her throat. "Mom, I'm

afraid. A part of me is already in love with Rob, but another part points to Ian and says, 'Look. You blew it once. What if you make the same mistake again?'"

"If you want to talk mistakes, why not start with mine. When you came to me and said you were pregnant, I immediately heard my mother's voice. Lord, how she drummed a litany of shame and recriminations into my head about what would happen if I ever 'got in trouble.' That's what we called being pregnant out of wedlock back then. I convinced myself that any husband—even one like Ian—was better than no husband. I couldn't have been more wrong, could I?"

Neither spoke for several minutes. Kate could tell this confession had cost her mother. "I didn't have to follow your advice, Mom. I made up my own mind. And for a while, I think we all believed I'd made the right choice. Ian put on a good show."

"Not all men are deceivers."

"Maybe not, but they all have their own agendas, Rob included. He's back in the Bay area and who knows what will come out of his meetings? Maybe a chance to move home. And, maybe that would be best for both of us. The timing is all wrong. He's—"

Her mother interrupted her. "He will be here on Saturday," she said, her tone indisputable.

Saturday. The thank-you party for everyone who'd helped bring Maya home. Kate didn't argue with her mother. Yetta had a fifty-fifty chance of being right, but even if Rob showed up, he could just be coming to tell her he was leaving for good.

ROB WAS SURPRISED by how strange it felt to be back in the Bay area. And by how bad the traffic was. As he sat in his

rental car on a virtual parking lot called Highway 101—
eight lanes going nowhere fast—he had time to think about
what the past two days had meant to him.

A new job offer was on the table. More money. Company perks. The fast track to partner.

It had become clear very fast that his ex-fiancée's father
was not happy about this offer. Jordon Ames had ambushed
Rob in the parking lot after their fancy dinner to dispel any
illusion Rob might have been under about the ax being
buried between them.

"You're not a man of your word," the older man had
said, gripping Rob's elbow in an iron clasp. "You make
promises you don't keep and break hearts that don't
deserve to be broken. Your father is a philandering prick
posing as an educator, and you know what they say, the
apple doesn't fall far from the tree."

Rob had tried to shake off his words. He'd carried on with
the interviews and meetings as scheduled. By asking the
right questions, he learned that the company had suffered
some embarrassing harassment allegations that had gone
public shortly after he'd moved to Las Vegas. A media firm
had been consulted to try to spruce up the law firm's image.
Rob's rather modest, but truly compassionate, efforts on
behalf of his employees fit seamlessly into their agenda.
And all Rob had to do to benefit from this providential set
of circumstances was sign on the dotted line.

Same with his condo. Given the housing market, he
stood to make a tidy sum, which would serve him well if
he wanted to re-invest in Vegas real estate but if he planned
to move back here, he'd be better off keeping it.

So, he called his father for advice. Predictably, Adam
called for a tee time.

A horn alerted him that traffic was moving. Forty minutes later, he was at Amberlein. Rob and his dad had golfed at the private course many times in the past. This would be their first round since his father's wedding, though.

"Does Haley golf, Dad? She could have joined us."

"She's not feeling too well at the moment."

"I'm sorry to hear that. Too much honeymoon fun?"

His father didn't reply. Instead, he drove a high, solid tee shot right up the fairway. "Nice," Rob said, watching it land. "You're going to annihilate me if you keep that up."

By the time they reached the eighth hole, Rob was down by six strokes.

Adam sank a four-foot putt then looked up. "So, when are you going to spill your guts?"

Rob kept his head down as he addressed the ball. "I'm being offered the promotion of a lifetime." He followed through—or thought he did. The ball missed the cup by a foot.

"And this is a bad thing because…?"

Rob tapped the ball into the hole then walked to the cart. "It would mean moving back here. Which I thought I was prepared to do in a heartbeat, but there are complications. Mom's not well, for one thing."

"I know. I talked to her a couple of days ago. But she's finally seeing a doctor about the symptoms, so this can't be what you're upset about."

"Dad, do you believe that adage about the fruit not falling far from the tree?"

His father had just started to get into the cart but straightened abruptly. "I beg your pardon?"

Rob's stomach was in knots. "When you and Mom were married, you had a certain reputation. You—"

Adam cut him off. "Now, wait a second, that was a long

time ago. I'll admit your mother and I didn't have the most conventional marriage, but—"

"I knew about your special students, Dad. The Brighten Scholarship was a standard joke on campus. Only young beautiful women need apply. The name of the recipient always made its way back to me. And Mom," he added.

Adam sat down, heavily, his hands gripping the steering wheel. He hung his head. "I didn't know that, son. Maybe I did and didn't want to admit it."

Rob waited, unsure of what to say.

Adam looked up. "Rob, I won't lie to you. I was a conceited, self-important fool. I tried to pretend that what I was doing benefited both parties, but I knew it was a lie. I haven't actually had a special 'friend' for the last ten years. I hope you believe that."

He did. He wasn't sure why.

"I'm sorry you had to deal with those rumors, Rob, but it's the past. Why are you asking me about this today?"

"Because I've found somebody who means a lot to me, and I'm afraid I might disappoint her. What if I don't have what it takes to stick it out through thick and thin? You and Mom didn't. I'm your son."

Adam put his hand on Rob's shoulder. "You're also yourself. You're the guy who read the *Chronicles of Narnia* every night for six months until you finished it. At age eleven. You've never walked away from anything in your life."

"Except my engagement."

"Ah, well, some might say that was an act of survival. Pure and simple." Adam glanced over his shoulder. Rob turned and saw another group of golfers approaching. "Let's go, son. We only have one hole left, then we'll have a cold one and talk about this some more."

Twenty minutes later they were seated across from each other in the cool, classy bar. "Rob, you've never asked for my advice—particularly in the romance department, but I assume that's what you're doing, now. I watched your engagement to Serena the way people on board the *Titanic* saw the iceberg hit. Her father orchestrated that match, and she's too much of a daddy's girl to say no. You saved yourself—and that intense young woman—a lot of grief, in my opinion."

Rob remained silent, trying to process the frank words.

"As for what went wrong in my marriage to your mother, all I can say is we married young and for all the wrong reasons. We gave it our best shot and were pretty damn lucky in most respects. We have a great son and we still like each other. But it wasn't until I met Haley that I really understood what love is all about."

"Can you explain it to me, Dad? I thought I was in love with Serena, but the more she talked about the wedding, the more I felt like a dog on a chain…that was getting shorter and shorter."

"That's not love. That's power. Love is wanting more for the other person than for yourself. Like the way you arranged for my wedding to be held at Kate's. I'm not complaining. Haley and I couldn't have asked for more, but I know why you booked it there. To help Kate out. And I'm not surprised. Because the minute your mother suggested that you were interested in Kate, I recognized the truth."

"What truth?"

"That you're in love with her. Takes one to know one. A person in love, that is."

Rob didn't argue the point. He did love Kate. She never left his mind. But was love enough? He didn't ask because he knew this was a question only he could answer.

Rob took another sip of beer.

"By the way," his father added, "Haley's pregnant."

The gulp went sideways and started out his nose. "What?"

"She knew it at the wedding but she made me promise not to say anything. It's her first time and people have told her all kinds of first pregnancy horror stories."

"Pregnant?" he sputtered.

"We had an ultrasound before we left for Tahiti, and we're pretty sure she's having a girl. We're going to name her Daisy after Haley's grandmother. Haley thinks her middle name should be Josephine. Daisy Jo. But I'm not sure your mother would be all that pleased. What do you think?"

Rob swallowed hard and wiped the moisture from his eyes. "I don't know. She might be honored."

Adam smiled. "So, if you take this promotion you mentioned, is there a chance your new sister and your step-daughter might wind up being neighbors?"

"You mean Maya? No, Dad, I'm afraid not. Kate's business is in Vegas. Her family is there. Even if Mom's health problems turn out to be nothing, Kate couldn't just leave. That's not her style."

"Well, it's not yours, either. So, I guess that means if I want our kids to be close, I'll have to buy a second place in the desert. Actually, Haley and I talked about it at the wedding. As soon as she's feeling up to traveling again, we'll fly over for the weekend. Sound like a plan?"

Rob laughed. How like his dad to embrace the big picture and conveniently ignore the missing pieces. Like the fact that Kate and Rob had had sex, but neither had used the *L* word. And there was still Maya to woo over to his side. She wanted a life that included her real father. If Rob could convince Kate to marry him, he'd probably be one daddy too many.

Chapter Seventeen

"You look beautiful, Katie. You didn't have to get all dressed up just to see me."

Kate quickly sat down across from Ian. Six pairs of prisoners and guests shared the same table, each separated by a shoulder-high barricade of pressed wood. Ian was dressed in dark pants and a bright orange shirt. His hair, which had begun to grow out, was brutally short again. His complexion was sallow.

"How are you feeling? You don't look so good."

"The food they feed you in here isn't the best. People with Hep C do better with lots of fresh vegetables and fruit. But it won't kill me."

"That's good to know."

He didn't ask why she was dolled up. She wouldn't have had an answer if he did. She and Jo had had a long, serious talk the night before. Among other things, her new partner had mentioned that Rob was coming back today. Kate hadn't asked if he planned to attend the swim party but she'd put on a sundress and styled her hair, just in case.

"So, Katie girl, what's up? I know that look. It's the I've-made-a-decision-and-to-hell-with-everyone-else look."

"Is that what I do? Really? I've always thought of my-self as kind of a pushover. I usually go with the flow, while other people make decisions around me. Grace decided she wanted to open a restaurant, next thing you know we're partners." She tossed up her hands. "You're the one who decided we needed to get married."

"Well, you were pregnant."

Her cheeks heated up. She'd been on every kind of birth control known to man, but somehow she and Ian had created a baby. They hadn't planned Maya, but she'd im-mediately made their other plans seem unimportant.

"True, but we had options. We could have lived together for a while. It's not as if either of us was worried about what people said."

"Speak for yourself. I was scared spitless of your dad and the Gypsy mafia. I'd heard stories. How was I sup-posed to know they were all made up?"

She shook her head and sighed. "Daddy was a sweet-heart. All he ever wanted for me and my sisters was for us to be happy and secure. That's what the money in our trust funds was all about."

The mention of money seemed to drop the temperature in the room. Kate's trust fund had been transferred to a joint account that Ian immediately reinvested into diversified stock holdings. The first year under his management, the fund had doubled. But after that his reports to Kate became few and far between. Whenever she tried to pin him down on the balance, he had a long, convoluted explanation that usually included a speech on being in the market for the long haul. In the end, there'd barely been enough to repay half his client list.

"Kate, I'm going to make it up to you. Every penny."

She looked down. "That's a lot of pennies, Ian."

"I know that, but I'm a whiz, remember. I can make money in my sleep. I just had a run of bad luck before."

She took a deep breath. "Ian, you're smart and clever and you do know numbers. But you don't just take risks, you seek them out. The way some people feel compelled to jump out of airplanes or ride bulls or any of the myriad methods thrill-seekers have of getting that rush.

"For you, it was buying and selling stock. But like any gambler, you are never content with the win."

"Were, Kate. Past tense. I learned my lesson. My God, talk about humility. I was brought home in chains and leg irons. Do you think I don't carry the memory of the look on your face when you saw me get out of that van every day of my life?"

"Maybe. But will it be enough to keep you from putting your daughter's college fund on the line—if I ever recoup enough to set one up? I don't know. And I can't risk it. Not again."

"Katie," he said, reaching between them to touch her arm. His touch was warm and familiar, but not the touch she wanted.

"We can work this out. Let me come home after I get out and once I find a job, I'll have my paycheck direct deposited into an account that you control. You can handle all the money. You can give me an allowance and I—"

She brushed his hand away. "I'm not ready to pass out allowances, Ian. That's what a mother does when her child is old enough. I have enough to do keeping my daughter happy and my business afloat."

"She's my daughter, too, Kate."

"I know that. And I've made a decision. She needs her dad

in her life. I'd like for us to set up some kind of visitation schedule once you're on your feet. I talked to your attorney who said you're interested in relocating to Reno. I can understand why. A fresh start might be just what you need."

She saw his lips form the words as he silently repeated, "Visitation. Will your legal eagle boyfriend draw up the agreement?"

Her shoulders stiffened. "Don't, Ian. Rob isn't to blame for any of this. You made your choices a long time ago and there's no way to go back. This is what's in my heart. I'll always care for you, but the love we shared is gone."

He looked tormented. "I killed it, didn't I?"

"We both made mistakes. All I know is you can't erase the past—and I wouldn't even if I could. We had some great times, but I can't go down the same road again. I'm sorry."

He sat back and closed his eyes. "That sounds like something your mother would say. Prophetic."

She nodded to herself. *Maybe I'm finally getting the hang of this Romani fortune-teller thing.* Now, if only she had a crystal ball to look in to see what Rob was thinking.

"Kate."

She blinked, bringing her thoughts back to reality. "Hmm?"

"If you talked to my lawyer, then she told you about Rafe's offer, right?"

She nodded. Ian's old friend and mentor, Rafe Borba, apparently had heard about Maya's abduction and put two and two together. He'd offered to help Ian out with a job and a place to live once Ian had his parole violation straightened out.

"He's got a bunch of properties in Reno. He told me he needed me to run things while he travels. He's trying to make up for sitting on his butt for too long." He smiled. "Believe me, I know the feeling."

Kate did, too. "The furthest I've been from Vegas in two years is Mesquite. We're quite a pair, aren't we? Gypsy moths with their wings clipped."

He appeared startled by the comment. "Gypsy moths. That's what I called us the day we met. Do you remember?" He blinked suddenly as if something had gotten in his eye. "You took quite a risk giving me your number."

Kate felt a sudden easing of the band around her chest. She had indeed taken a risk. One that had paid off handsomely for a while. "Not really. I recognized you immediately. We were kindred spirits, both looking for a place to land."

She shrugged. "This is my place, Ian. I belong here. And don't plan to leave, but if you think Reno will be better for you, then I'll do whatever I can to make sure Maya gets to visit you whenever possible…as long as you swear you'll never try to run off with her again."

"I promise, Katie. On Maya's life, I promise." He let out a shaky breath.

Neither spoke for a few seconds, then Ian commented, "That's really generous of you, Katie. I guess you can afford to be generous since you're in love."

He made it sound like a done deal.

"I have to go. My sisters are throwing a thank-you party for all the volunteers who pitched in to find Maya. Even my future brother-in-law is flying for in it." She didn't stand up right away. She felt as if this was goodbye, even though she knew she'd see him again once he got settled.

"Will the Sisters of the Silver Dollar dance?" he asked, his tone wistful.

"I don't know. We haven't danced together since Dad died. But maybe it's time to start liv…dancing again."

AFTER THE RELATIVE CHILL of the Bay area, Rob welcomed the heat of the desert. To his surprise, Vegas actually felt more like home than "home" had. The interior of his car was nearing meltdown when he got into it, but he put the top down anyway—and rolled up the windows and turned on the air-conditioning full blast. He wanted to feel the sun and breathe the dry desert air.

Haley had given him a new CD which he blasted at boom-box levels as he drove to Yetta's. He'd called his mother before getting onto the plane and she'd informed him that Kate was taking the day off because of the party. Jo planned to oversee the lunch shift then drop by later in the afternoon. "I probably won't stay, though. My doctor gave me some medicine for my cough and it really knocks me out," she'd added.

There was a defeated quality in his mother's tone that didn't sound like Jo. He planned to investigate that next. After he talked to Kate. And Maya.

Haley had asked him not to share the news about the baby until she told Jo. While she and Jo got along well, this was a life-altering event and Jo had enough on her mind at the moment with her health issues and new partnership.

Rob was certain his mother would be happy for her ex, although she'd probably have a few things to say privately about his parenting skills. But Rob couldn't complain. Not really. His father was human, flawed and imperfect. But that didn't mean he couldn't learn from his mistakes and be a better husband to Haley and a better father to Daisy.

"I hope," he murmured.

He turned down the volume as he swung into the cul-de-sac. Yetta's house sat straight ahead; Kate's car was in the garage beside her mother's. A few other vehicles were parked on the street. Was the party already going? Damn. He'd hoped to arrive ahead of the other guests.

He quickly parked and walked to the door.

A face appeared at about thigh level in the side window. Maya. He leaned down and said loudly, "Hi. Can I come in?"

Her frown told him she wasn't wild about the idea.

"I have a present for you."

She looked skeptical. "What is it? One of the new fish died. Grandma helped me bury it at the cemetery where my grandpa lives."

"I'm sorry. I have the receipt. Maybe we can get another one to replace it. Is the black fish behaving himself?"

"The other fish don't like him, but he hasn't eaten any of them."

"That's good, isn't it?"

She nodded, and a second later the door opened.

The first voice he heard upon entering the foyer was Yetta's. "Hello, Rob. How was your trip to California?"

"Good. Fast. But I got to see my dad and Haley, so that was nice."

"I had a dream about them the other night. They were strolling on a moonlit beach. They seemed very happy."

Rob smiled and nodded. "Hey, you really are psychic. They just got back from Tahiti and they're in absolute bliss."

The twinkle in her eye made him wonder if she knew the other part of the joy. He almost asked, but Maya distracted him. "You said you brought me a present."

"Maya," her grandmother said, reproachfully. "That was rude."

"It's okay. She's right. I do have a present for her." He whipped the book he was holding behind his back out for them both to see. "You like jokes, right? I even learned a couple. Want to hear one?"

"Um…I don't know. Maybe," Maya said.

She took the book but didn't open it.

Rob wasn't sure what to do next. He looked to Yetta for guidance. She smiled and ushered him inside. "Come in and sit down while Maya remembers her manners."

The living room was simply decorated with eclectic touches—a well-used Persian rug, a beautifully framed copy of "The Kiss" and furniture that ranged from leather to antiques. The blinds were angled down to keep the sun and heat at bay.

"Wow, in all the times I've been here this is the first time I've sat in this room. It's beautiful."

"Thank you," Yetta said. "A repository for our meager treasures."

He walked to the mantle to examine an interesting sword and scabbard. "Is Kate around?"

"No, I'm sorry. She's—"

"With my daddy. My *real* daddy," Maya said, pointedly.

Yetta gave her granddaughter a stern look and said, "Why don't you read a couple of jokes to Rob, Maya, while I call your mother and see what's keeping her. Other guests are starting to arrive, too."

She left so abruptly Rob didn't have time to get nervous— until he looked down and saw Maya staring at him, with those big brown eyes that seemed to gaze right to his core.

He sat down in a convenient navy-blue tweed recliner.

"That was my grampa's chair."

Her tone was so accusatory he started to move.

"But you can sit there. He doesn't live here anymore. He moved to the cemetery."

Rob had no idea what to say. "Um, you're sure he won't care if I sit in his chair?"

"It's okay. He visits sometimes, but he's not here now."

Rob looked around uneasily. "Good. Uh, so, what kind of jokes do you like best?"

"Funny ones."

Of course.

"Knock, knock," she said, catching him off guard.

"Um…who's there?"

"Boo."

"Boo who?"

"You don't have to cry. It's only me."

He laughed. Her expression was so endearing he couldn't help it. "That was funny. You're good."

She didn't smile back. "Your turn."

His stomach clenched the way it did the first time he addressed a new judge. He'd practiced on the plane. How hard could it be to impress a child?

"What do you call a boat shivering on the bottom of the sea?"

Her shoulders rose and fell. "I dunno. What?"

"A nervous wreck."

She didn't even crack a smile.

Feeling more on the spot than he had when he told the partners he preferred to stay in Las Vegas than climb up a rung in the corporate ladder, he blurted out, "I know a secret."

She took a step closer. "What is it?"

He lowered his voice. "I'm going to be a brother."

Her eyes went wide. "I'm going to have an uncle when my Auntie Grace gets married. Who are you going to marry?"

The question made sense, he supposed, from her point of view, but he was quite sure she wouldn't like the answer he was tempted to give her. "My situation is different. My father got married and his wife is going to have a baby. That makes me a brother."

"Oh. Well, my daddy is going to marry my mommy and they're gonna have two babies that come at the same time. That's called twins. Just like Dora the Explorer's mommy."

She sounded so matter-of-fact that Rob had to shake his head to remind himself this was probably—hopefully— more Maya's wish than the truth. Then he remembered something. His mother once told him that the family believed Maya had inherited her grandmother's ability to see into the future. What if she was right?

He heard a voice call out his name. "Rob?"

Kate had entered the house through the kitchen. "Maya and I are in here," he hollered.

Seconds later Kate appeared in the doorway. Breathless and beautiful. He swore he'd never seen her more vivid and alive. Her hair was swept off her neck. She was wearing a sleeveless sundress that skimmed her knees. She looked like a princess.

She looks happy, he thought. His heart did a painful little dive toward his shoes. She'd just come from her ex-husband's company, and she looked as radiant and in love as Haley had when she'd greeted Adam after Rob and his dad returned from golfing.

"Hi, Kate." He stood up. He'd made a mistake by presuming that he could simply show up and expect Kate to be as ready as he was to move forward. He was a fool.

They'd spent one night together. That barely even constituted a date. He couldn't simply propose. "Your daughter was keeping me entertained. What a little jokester!"

Maya's look made him even more nervous. Who was he to think he could ever replace her father?

"Well, I'm glad you're here. Come out back and say hi to everybody. Most of the members of your Dads Group are here." She took his elbow and started leading him toward the back door. "Maya, do you have your swimsuit on under your shorts?"

"Yes, Mommy."

"Good. Be sure to bring me your floaties to put on before you get in the water."

"But Jacob's daddy brought noodles," Maya said. "I can hold on to one of those."

"Maya, you know I want you in either a life vest or arm floaties when you're near the water."

"Oh, Mommy…"

Rob opened the sliding door. He almost added his two cents but didn't want to get in the middle of their argument. A second later, he was surrounded by his eclectic group of friends, including Nathan Barnes, who immediately handed him Gretel. Or was she Lucinda?

Kate was drawn aside by a woman Rob didn't know. She appeared to go willingly. Rob guessed the need to clear the air between them was something he alone felt. Maybe it was his legal mind at work. He routinely convinced people of B when they thought they believed A. If she were still vacillating between him and Ian, Rob needed to sit down with a legal pad and lay out his argument. *"You should pick me over Ian because…"* There were reasons. Good reasons. He just needed a little more time to think of them.

"How 'bout breakfast tomorrow, Rob?" Nathan asked.

Rob hadn't been paying attention to their conversation, so he had no idea how the idea of dining together had come about. "Um, it would have to be early. And I haven't run in a couple of days. Maybe lunch. Later in the week?"

Out of the corner of his eye, Rob saw a flash of color. Orange. The color of Maya's swimsuit. He turned to look over the head of the wiggling child in his arms. She was carrying a tube of hot pink Styrofoam that was at least twice her height. She was laughing and talking to a little girl who appeared a few years older than Maya. A prickling sensation ran down his arms. Something felt wrong. He couldn't explain it.

He spotted Grace's cousin Gregor and motioned him closer. "Hey, Greg, do me a favor. Take this little beauty for a minute. I need to check on something."

He was about twenty feet away from the pool, but there was a milling crowd of adults, including Kate, between him and the spot where he'd last seen Maya. He scanned the area looking for anything orange.

There she was. Sitting on the edge of the pool. Noodle in hand. Nice and safe. But she wasn't wearing the flotation devices her mother had asked her to put on.

He looked at the table where Yetta was sitting with several other adults. Just a few feet from the pool. The half-deflated armbands he recognized as Maya's were on the ground behind her. Had Maya removed them without anyone noticing?

"Maya," he murmured under his breath. "Shame. Shame. I thought I taught you better."

He walked over and scooped up the plastic armbands then turned to the pool. Only a few seconds had transpired, but Maya had disappeared. No orange suit. But the hot pink noodle floated on the water on waves churned up by the five youngsters playing Marco Polo in the deep end.

Rob didn't stop to think. He threw down the floaties and sprang forward, clearing the distance to the pool in three long strides. He paused only long enough to spot her. Underwater. Struggling. Then he dove in, grabbed her arm and pushed to the surface with one adrenaline-charged kick.

Kate was aware of a loud splash behind her but didn't give it any thought until she heard someone cry, "Oh, my God. Maya."

Everything slowed down to strange, impossibly clear images that landed in her brain like raindrops on a windshield. Splat. A man in street clothes erupted from the water with Maya's limp body balanced on his hand like a server with a tray. Splat. He went under—twice—until his feet found purchase. Splat. He surged through the water like an Olympian, carrying her daughter, who was coughing and choking, to safety.

The people standing around her—her sisters and two old friends—moved toward the pool, carrying Kate with them. Her legs were useless. They didn't seem to understand what she wanted them to do.

"Maya," she cried, clawing her way through the crowd.

Rob seemed impervious to anyone else. His sole focus was on Maya. He worked so swiftly Kate barely had time to register what he was doing. Seconds passed. Long, terrifying seconds that felt like minutes. A lifetime. Then Maya started to wail. A harsh, painful, beautiful sound.

Kate fell to her knees beside them and pulled her daughter into her arms. "Maya. Maya. Oh my God, what happened? How did…?" She couldn't complete the question she was so overcome with emotion.

Maya clung to her fiercely, still shuddering with convulsive coughing. She was crying. From fear, not pain, Kate sensed. Someone handed Rob a water bottle and he pressed it gently to her daughter's lips.

"Try a drink for me, sweetie. Your throat is probably sore from throwing up and getting chlorine down your nose."

After taking a sip, Maya turned and buried her face in Kate's chest, sobbing as if she might never stop. Kate clasped her tight and looked at Rob. "What happened? Where are the floaties I put on her? How come nobody—?"

He sat back, easing his legs out from under him. He was fully dressed. Right down to his shoes, which leaked water until he leaned over and took them off. "Boy, if she thought they squeaked before…"

His low chuckle seemed out of place, but Kate could tell he was still coming down from the terrifying experience— her daughter's.

She looked at the pool then back to him, still trying to figure out in her mind what had just happened. "How did you see her? You weren't even close."

He shrugged, the wet fabric of his shirt stuck to his shoulders. "Some sixth sense, I guess. I've only had to pull three kids—four, now—out of the water. There were always people around, but seeing a child on the bottom of the pool just doesn't make sense. Your mind has to get past the horror before you can do something. A lifeguard reacts without thinking."

"Guess that makes him a bona fide hero, huh, sis?" Liz said, handing Rob a towel.

He used it on his face and hair, but not before Kate

spotted his blush. He was a hero. He'd saved Maya twice, although he probably didn't know that his suggestion to spread the word about Maya's abduction through his network of fathers had given them the break they'd needed to find Ian.

Before she could express her thanks, Maya gave a little shudder in her arms. Kate stroked her daughter's wet hair. "Oh, precious, I'm so sorry. I should have been watching closer."

"No," Rob said, moving to his knees. "Maya should have left the floaties on."

His tone was stern. Gruff, even. Maya lifted her head and looked at him. "You took them off, didn't you?"

Her bottom lip started to quiver and tears filled her eyes. "I th…ought I c…ould swim. Gemilla can."

He reached out and gently touched her chin. "I know, sweetie, but Gemilla is older than you. She's taken lessons at the public pool. But…" He smiled with a tenderness that melted Kate's heart. "I'm very proud of the way you held your breath for as long as you could."

"The noodle slipped out of my hand and I was too far away. I tried to kick but I couldn't reach the side and water got up my nose and—"

Kate squeezed her tight, blocking the image she could see all too easily. She buried her face in her daughter's hair, afraid to let go until a hand on her shoulder made her open her eyes. "She's going to be fine, Katherine. Let's get her into dry clothes. I think she's had enough swimming today, don't you?"

Kate let her mother take Maya, who started crying again as soon as she was in her grandmother's arms. She watched them go into the house.

Rob, who'd removed his shoes and socks and looked half-drowned himself, stepped to her side and offered her a hand up. "If it's okay with you, I'd like to have a little talk with the other kids about what just happened. They all need to learn to watch out for each other and not let the little ones near the water if they're not wearing life vests."

"Yes, please," she said. "Maybe the adults should listen, too. I can't believe what just happened."

He put his arms around her and held her until she stopped shaking. "Everything's going to be okay. This was a good lesson for her. She's stubborn, and I think she honestly believed that she could swim. Maybe she'll be more willing to learn now."

"Well, she won't be allowed near the pool without a life vest on until you say so," Kate vowed. "I'd better go check on her."

He nodded. "My bag is still in the car. I'll get changed then do my spiel." He bent down to collect his shoes.

"You're not going to leave, are you?"

"I…um…I don't know. I'd kinda forgotten about the party. We haven't really had a chance to talk and—"

Kate understood. They had a lot to say to each other, but she couldn't abandon her daughter—or her guests. "Please stay. Grace and Nikolai should be here soon. My sisters and I are going to dance." She felt her cheeks heat up. "We haven't practiced. We're probably going to suck, but Grace insists this is something you never forget, like…" She was going to say how to make love but was too embarrassed. She didn't want him to know how much she'd been thinking about their night together. "Riding a bike," she finished, lamely.

"Well, okay. I did want to be here when Mom shows up. She sounded rather blue on the phone. Is there something she's not telling me?"

Kate shook her head. "I don't think so. But you know Jo. There are times I swear she and Maya are related. They're both bullheaded."

She followed him to his car and watched him toss his wet shoes into the trunk. He dug through his suitcase for a change of clothes. Maybe it was seeing the suitcase—a reminder that people come and people go—that made her say, "Um, Rob, I'm going to go check on Maya, but would you do me a favor?"

"Of course. What?"

"Would you let me borrow your truck?"

"Any time."

"This afternoon? After the party?"

"Sure. It's still at Mom's. She can run me over to pick it up after she gets here."

"No. Your mom has been working overtime. She needs a break. I'll go with you. If Maya's feeling okay by then. If not, then maybe tomorrow."

He didn't ask any questions. Which was good. Since Kate had no idea why she needed the truck—only that borrowing it gave her a plausible excuse to spend time with him. Alone.

ROB WENT THROUGH the motions on autopilot. He survived his friends' congratulatory accolades, endured every handshake and pat on the back that came his way and even delivered a lecture that made every parent hug his or her kid tightly.

But inside, he felt numb.

As soon as he could, he escaped to the guest bath-room. Locking the door behind him, he leaned on the counter—just as his knees buckled. A wave of nausea passed over him.

Was this any way for a hero to act? But this hero was also scared spitless. Questions shot through his mind like ricocheting bullets. What if he hadn't looked for her? What if she'd bumped her head on the wall? What if she'd swal-lowed too much water to be resuscitated?

He fought back the taste of bile and squeezed his eyes to keep the tears inside. A light knock on the door shook him out of what he assumed was some kind of post-traumatic shock. "Just a minute."

He hastily ran a faucet and splashed water on his face. Then he opened the door.

And looked down. *Maya.*

"Hi, sweet girl, how are you? Is your throat better?"

She nodded and held out her arms to be picked up. He was happy to oblige, but assumed she wanted to sit on the counter so she could talk to him on the same level. She was wearing a matching short set that had purple butterflies set against a yellow background.

She coughed delicately. "Grandma said that after I thanked you for saving me, I needed to 'pologize for scaring you. She said you looked ten years older when you came out of the pool with me in your arms."

Rob poked his head into the hall to see if Yetta was nearby. No one else was present, although he could hear the sound of voices coming from the backyard.

"Well, she's right," he admitted, stepping back into the room. Her mass of curls had dried in wild disarray that reminded him of her mother. She was going to be a beauty someday, just like Kate. The sudden image of her struggling in the water sliced through him.

He swallowed hard against the constriction in his throat and looked down. "I was just checking for gray hairs. Do you see any?"

Her nose crinkled and she motioned for him to lean closer. Her tiny fingers carefully parted his hair. "Nope. Not yet."

"Good."

He started to straighten but her hands on his shoulders stopped him. "I'm sorry about your shoes." Tears filled her brown eyes. "They really didn't squeak. I just said that because...I don't know why, but I didn't mean it."

He pulled her against him and gently comforted her. His heart was dissolving and he could barely breathe but he managed to say, "It's okay. I didn't like them anyway."

Blinking, she looked up. "Really?"

He nodded. "Hey, I just remembered a joke. Why is six afraid of seven?"

She thought a moment then shook her head. "I dunno. Why?"

"Because seven...eight...nine."

It was too old for her, he realized too late. He didn't know anything about kids. He was retarded. Asinine.

Then suddenly she started to giggle. "Seven ate nine," she repeated softly as her laughter grew. "That's funny. You're funny. I love you, Rob."

"I love you, too, Maya."

She looked at the floor. "I told a fib earlier. Daddy and Mommy aren't going to have two babies and call them twins."

"Oh."

"Mommy said Daddy has to go into grown-up time-out again because he took me without permission. And when he comes back, he might not live here any more. He might go somewhere else."

"Yes, I know. I'm sorry."

She didn't say anything for a minute, then she scooted forward and slipped to her feet. "Wait right there. Don't even move."

No problem. He wasn't sure his legs were working.

She returned a few seconds later, carrying a piece of white construction paper the size of a legal pad. "Here," she said, handing him the artwork. "This is for you. To put on your refrigerator."

"Thank you. It's beautiful," he said, admiring the vivid primary colors.

"These are the people in my family," she said. "Well, not all of them."

Just four, in fact. A stick-figure girl with long brown curls. A mommy figure that actually resembled Kate somehow. And two men. One stood with Kate and Maya. The other was alone on the opposite side of the page, loosely connected by a bright wiggly yellow line.

The solitary figure wore a gaudy green-and-purple tie.

Before he could ask her to decipher the image for him, she said, "I have to go back to the party. My Auntie Grace is coming. 'Bye."

She was gone in a blink. Rob studied the painting a few minutes more, then carefully rolled it up and took it outside to his car.

On his way back to the house, another car pulled into the driveway. Nikolai, whom Rob had met during the Charles Harmon debacle, was behind the wheel. Grace leaned out the passenger window and waved with her usual exuberant style.

"Hey there, Rob, I hear you're a real live hero," she called. "If my sister doesn't marry you, she's an idiot."

And hope, despite his qualms about his place in Maya's painting, blossomed in his heart. With Grace in his corner, maybe he had a chance to convince Kate they truly did belong together.

Chapter Eighteen

"The key is inside. Do you want to wait here or come in?"

Rob's plan to talk to Kate yesterday after the party had been sidelined. First, there'd been the necessary rehashing of his rescue of Maya for the newcomers, Grace and Nikolai, who had heard the short version on the phone but had demanded blow-by-blow details. Then, there'd been food, conversation, a guys-versus-gals game of water polo and more food. Then, dancing.

Amazing dancing.

Rob had been mesmerized when four nymphs in belly-dancer costumes had appeared in the twilight. He'd been sitting with his mother when the music started. He couldn't quite define the sound—part flamenco, part Middle Eastern rhythms. Their costumes shimmered with gold coins and glittering jewels woven into sheer fabric. Bright scarves fluttered as curvaceous hips oscillated in tempo.

While the performance could be rated PG, his desire for one of the dancers was anything but. Evocative images had toyed with him all night, dancing on naked feet through his dreams. He'd awoken cranky and exhausted from chasing an elusive sprite who remained just out of arm's reach.

The same sprite who'd called at nine. "I still need to borrow your truck. Can I come over?"

Now, she was at his door. Dressed in snug black shorts and a wine polo shirt with Romantique appliquéd on the pocket. "I'll come in."

He backed up, nearly stumbling over his suitcase, which he'd dropped inside the entry without bothering to unpack. Today was Sunday. His list of things to do covered two pages—single-space, but he couldn't get his mind in gear. "I should have asked you to bring me a cup of coffee."

"Ahem."

He glanced over his shoulder. "Black. One sugar. I called your mom to ask," she said.

He blinked twice. How had he missed the grande cup from his favorite coffee shop in her outstretched hand? *She must think I'm some kind of head case.* "Perfect."

He walked to the suite's sliding glass door and pushed it open to give some light to the dim, suddenly claustro-phobic-feeling room. The place was just as he'd left it. Neat. Orderly. Impersonal. "Have a seat."

Maya's painting was facedown on the coffee table, right where he'd left it. He'd spent an hour studying the artwork trying to decipher any message she might have intended for him. Ultimately, he'd reminded himself that she was four—and no Picasso.

He slid it to one side as Kate sat down across from him.

"Sorry about yesterday. Things got pretty crazy after Grace and Nick arrived. I didn't have a chance to talk to you much."

Whatever she was drinking came with a straw, so he assumed it wasn't hot. "She looks really happy. And I enjoyed talking to Nick. He's an interesting guy. Sounds like he might get that promotion."

"Speaking of promotions, I'm still waiting to hear about what happened in San Francisco."

"I met with a lot of people, including the Realtor who wanted to sell my condo. He made me an offer I couldn't refuse. I decided to take another look at that house we saw," he said. "I called when I got to town yesterday to see if it was still on the market. It is. I made an appointment to see it again today. I was kinda hoping you and Maya might go with me."

She sat forward. "Excuse me?"

"I thought it had a lot of potential. Open floor plan. Big backyard. If I remember correctly, there was even a kennel area. I liked it, but you know what a terrible shopper I am."

"K…kennel?"

"You like dogs, don't you?"

"Of course, but…you're staying? In Vegas? Your mother said you had a fabulous job offer. The kind nobody in their right mind could turn down."

He took a fortifying gulp of coffee. "Whoever said I was playing with a full deck?"

Her laugh was light. Its echo danced down his spine. Could he live the rest of his life without her laugh? A simple question, when you came right down to it. And the answer was no. He couldn't. No company car, healthy raise and well-padded expense account was worth it. Even the thought of wearing socks and a sweater in the middle of summer couldn't compare to Kate's laugh.

But could he convince Kate he was the man for her? He had the rest of his life to try.

"The truck keys," he said, starting toward his bedroom, where he remembered seeing the extra set. "What did you say you needed the truck for? Not that it's any of my business, but if you're moving something heavy, I'd be glad to help."

Kate followed behind him. "Um...actually, I've been wracking my brain the whole way here trying to come up with a good excuse, but I don't have one."

"Huh?"

"It's not the truck I want. It's you. Damn, that sounds needy, doesn't it?"

"It sounds pretty good to me."

"It does?"

He nodded.

She smiled and shrugged. "I missed you. And things got kinda crazy right before you left. I didn't have a sense of where...where we stood."

"I know. When the partners showed up, my gut response was to protect my people. Believe me, that was a first. Before I moved here, the only person I thought about was me."

"I don't believe that. You're caring and kind and I know perfectly well the reason you booked your dad's wedding at Romantique had nothing to do with protecting your company's butt. You're a good man, Rob, and, frankly, I find that very sexy."

She moved close enough to touch her temple against his so their eyelashes touched in the corners. "And you're a teacher. My first crush was on my fourth-grade teacher, Mr. Walder."

She pressed her lips to the corner of his mouth.

Rob stepped back. "I...wait...um...wait." Then he dashed into the bathroom to brush his teeth. He could hear Kate's chuckle follow after him. He felt stupid and flustered and dangerously aroused. What about his pledge to take things slow? For Kate's sake and Maya's.

When he walked back into the room, Kate was sitting demurely on his rumpled bed. Her right hand was holding his pillow as if she'd just crushed it to her chest to inhale his smell. His mouth went dry.

"Come here, you." The look in her eyes told him everything he needed to know.

He crossed the room in three steps and pulled her into his arms. "I love you, Kate," he said, tossing his agenda to the wind. "I love you more than anyone or anything I've ever known in my life. I can't imagine—"

She didn't let him finish. She looped her arms around his neck and kissed him. Her mouth spelled out the words she didn't say back to him. It was enough. For now.

Neither bothered with finesse while undressing. Clothes flew in different directions. One of her shoes narrowly missed the television set.

"You're sure about this?" he asked.

"Yes, Rob, I'm finally on the right road," she said, kneeling on the bed and drawing him to her.

He wasn't sure what that meant, but he didn't care. All he wanted was to hold her again. He ran his hands down the length of her back, feeling the velvet smoothness of her skin. Then he retraced the path upward to her hair.

"I need this loose and free."

Instead of taking out the ponytail herself, she turned sideways toward him then tilted her head. "Do it for me."

In profile, he saw her small but perfectly shaped breasts. He loved the way they turned up slightly, the nipples perky and pointed. Her belly wasn't as flat as say a model's might be, but this belly was perfect, considering it had once nurtured a baby. Her butt was one of his favorite parts of her body.

After inching the rubber band from her unruly curls, he

brushed the heavy hair aside and started nibbling kisses downward from the base of her neck. His tongue flicked across her shoulder bone.

"You carry such a heavy load on these shoulders." What will it take to let me share it? he wondered, but didn't ask.

She moved against him, her buttocks brushing his erection.

His need jumped up a notch, but he wasn't a greedy lover. He wanted her to share the pleasure. He took her hands and put them on her breasts while his hand trailed down her belly to the triangle of dark curls. She responded with a shaky whimper. Her head went back to rub against his as she moved in harmony to his strokes. When her breathing became fast and broken, he stopped.

She let out a little cry but he caught it with his mouth. "Now. Please."

He moved away far enough to reach the second drawer in his vanity and withdrew a package of condoms. He opened one and sheathed himself. "Whatever you say, princess."

Kate butted him gently with her head until he was on his back. Her hair framed her face as she straddled him. The room was light and filled with green and the scent of human heat and lust.

She lifted up, taking him in. Arching her back, she rocked her hips in rhythmic circles that made him start to pant.

Life had changed since Mesquite and their lovemaking mirrored those changes. Kate seemed less playful, more intense. Rob tried to pour every ounce of emotion that he was feeling into the moment.

They joined together as if suspended in a world of their own making. And it was perfect.

"I love you," she said softly against his chest once their breathing started to return to normal.

"It's about time you said the words. I was starting to feel used," he said, turning his head so she could see he was teasing.

"I didn't want to make another mistake," she admitted.

He knew exactly what she meant. He kissed her, then said, "I know. I'm big on perfection, too. But being afraid to fail is almost worse than failure. As my favorite philosopher once told me, you can't win if you don't play the game."

"Well, I'm in the game now. And, in case nobody warned you, I'm a helluva shark. I like to win."

"What's the bet?"

"Everything."

Then she rolled to her side, taking him with her. "What time is your appointment?"

He froze, mid-nibble, then looked at the bedside clock. His muttered curse told her playtime was over. "Will you go with me?" he asked. "I mean only an idiot would buy a woman a house without getting her okay first, right?"

She lifted up on her elbows. "What?"

His mouth was suddenly dry. "I know this is moving pretty fast, but I'm sick of living in a motel and I have all this cash to reinvest…"

Shut up, already. You're going to blow it. A woman needed hearts and flowers—romance—when a guy proposed to her. He sat up abruptly and turned so his feet were on the floor. He was about to get up when he glanced out the door and spotted Maya's painting on the coffee table.

Forgetting he was naked, he dashed into the living area and picked it up. "Your daughter gave this to me. As a thank-you, I guess. But talk about mixed signals. Can you tell me what it means?"

Kate took the paper from his fingers and spread it on the bed. "Alex told me about this one."

Because he felt raw and exposed, he pulled on a pair of boxers before sitting down beside her. He pointed to the single figure—a guy in the flashy tie, embarrassed by the way his finger trembled.

She must have noticed because she picked up his hand and kissed the tip before putting the index finger back down so it rested on the image of the family group. "This is you," she said with a smile. "The man standing alone is Ian."

"But he's wearing my tie."

She made a face. "God, I hope not. You have way better taste than that."

The little joke broke the tension just enough that he could let out the breath he'd been holding. "I don't get it. I would have thought she pictured me as a guy in a suit."

"I told Maya that Ian was moving because he has a new job waiting for him. In her mind, men who work wear suits. And ties."

"Even gaudy polka-dot ones?"

"Her current favorite colors."

"And is Ian going to be okay with this?"

She shrugged. "I think so. Moving to Reno doesn't mean he's totally out of the picture. That's what this road is about, I'd guess," she said, pointing to the squiggly line her daughter had drawn.

He scratched his head. "Would you prefer he stayed here?"

"No. I'm glad he's going to Reno. The distance is close enough that Maya can visit relatively easily, but not so close that we're in each other's faces all the time."

"You're going to give him generous visitation rights, then?"

She flopped on her back and pulled the loose end of the bedspread over her entire body. "I finally realized that Maya shouldn't have to suffer because I want to punish Ian for cheating on me and ruining my life. I know in my heart he didn't plan to abduct her. He acted on impulse and then couldn't undo what he'd done. He says he loves Maya and wants what's best for her. That's one of the reasons he's leaving."

"It is?"

The covers moved so he knew she was nodding her head. "How so?"

"He knows that I want to be with you. If he's around, Maya will never have a chance to...um..." The last word was too muffled for him to hear.

He tossed the painting over his shoulder and dove under the covers to face her. In their ecru-colored cocoon, he made her meet his eyes. "Maya won't have a chance to do what?"

"Bond. With you."

His throat tightened. "Is that what you want? For your daughter and me to bond?"

"It's the only way we'll ever be a...family."

His wishes were answered, but.... "Kate, what if I'm not...good enough to be Maya's stepfather? My dad didn't set the best example. I can't guarantee—"

She let out a small cry and tears filled her eyes. "You're you, Rob, not your father. Just like Maya isn't me. Or Ian. She's herself. And I know her life would be blessed to have you in it."

He closed his eyes and took a deep breath. The truth was so simple, yet profound. "She's an amazing kid. Head-strong, like her mother, but compassionate, too. I'm head-over-heels crazy about her."

He pulled the covers down and took in a lungful of fresh air. "My dad's pregnant," he said.

Kate looked stunned. "Well, that's not something you hear every day."

He rolled over and half pinned her to the bed, then kissed her nose. "You know what I mean. I'm not supposed to tell Mom. Haley wants to do it in person. I wouldn't be surprised if they flew down next weekend."

She went stiff.

"What's wrong? You know my dad. You like him, right?"

She nodded. "Yes. I even read his book. It made me laugh because it was so tongue-in-cheek. No wonder it's a bestseller. I wish everyone could look at themselves with a bit more humor. No, that's not what I was worried about. It's…um…well, your mom."

"You're afraid she's going to be upset. Why? She adores babies and she and Dad are—" He stopped. The look on her face was so torn he nearly stopped breathing. "What?"

"She made me promise not to tell you."

"Tell me what?"

"That would be telling."

He swore and rolled over to reach for the phone. He quickly punched in his mother's cell number. It rang five times before a familiar voice said, "Leave a message. I'll call you back if I feel like it."

"Mother. This is your son. Your son who doesn't like to be kept out of the loop. Now, I'm going to torture Kate until she tells whatever bloody secret it is she's keeping unless you call me right back."

Kate sat up and crossed her arms. "Hey, I love your mother. I don't like secrets, but if she tells me something and asks me not to mention it, I'm going to respect her wishes. Even if that means you don't—"

He smiled at her. "Kate, Mom knows I'm kidding. I respect and appreciate your loyalty toward her. My feelings for you aren't going to disappear just because you're keeping her confidence. Now, we'd better get moving."

Kate smiled suddenly. Loyal. Of course, she murmured under her breath as she reached for her clothes. "Now I know why I needed your truck. I have to buy you a house-warming present."

"I haven't bought the place yet."

She stopped dressing long enough to kiss him. "My Gypsy sense tells me you will."

He didn't really have time to argue. He had to meet the real estate agent in forty minutes and it was probably a thirty-minute drive across town.

As he shoved his feet into his sandals, he looked at Kate, who was tucking in her shirt and made a decision. Although this wasn't the romantic moment he'd planned, he walked into the bathroom where his travel bag sat open beside the sink. A small tube that had once carried a popular painkiller was tucked inside. He quickly returned to where Kate was sitting and went down on one knee. "This is for you," he said, presenting her with the tube.

"I don't have a headache, but thanks anyway."

"Look inside."

She unscrewed the top and held it to the light so she could see inside. Her brows knitted. "What...?" Impatiently, she turned the container upside down and a ring fell onto her lap. A large diamond ring in an antique setting.

"It was my grandmother's. I had the stone appraised before I asked Serena to marry me. The jeweler called it rare, almost perfect." He took a breath and let it out. "I guess I should have known then that she and I weren't meant for each other because I couldn't bring myself to give it to her."

He looked at Kate and added, "You can pick out a new setting. Something more fashionable."

Her unplanned intake of air got caught in the middle of a swallow and suddenly she couldn't breathe. Tears flooded her eyes. Her mouth opened and closed but no sound came out.

"Kate?" Rob said in concern. "Breathe, honey. You hate it?"

She shook her head.

"You like it?"

She nodded, with passion.

"Then, you'll marry me?"

Kate didn't answer right away. She felt a rush of emotions too complicated to identify independently, but she knew the predominant one was love. She was just about to say yes when his cell phone rang. He picked up the little silver phone. "Hi, Mom," he said. "I'm a little busy. I'll call you—"

Kate braced for what she knew would be a blow. Jo had shared her secret with Kate, but only on the vow that she wouldn't tell Rob. "I don't want him changing his plans for me," she'd insisted. "He has to live his life. He can't be expected to hover around his dying mother. Not when she brought this on herself."

Kate had argued that cancer—if that's what the surgeon found when he took a biopsy of her lung tissue—wasn't something handed out in retribution. Yes, Jo had been a lifelong smoker, but they both knew people who smoked who didn't wind up with lung cancer.

"Yes, she's here. Looking quite lovely, actually. But she's holding Grandma Brighten's engagement ring and won't put it on her finger. I'm not sure what that's about. Do you want to talk some sense into her? Convince her not to pass up a sterling catch like your son?"

Laughing at whatever his mother said in reply, he handed her the phone. "I'm going to finish dressing," he said softly. "We really do have an agenda."

Then he pressed a quick kiss to her lips and went into the bathroom.

"Jo?"

"Kate?"

"He asked me to marry him."

"I told you he was mad about you."

Kate smiled. "You and Mother should open a fortune-telling shop together."

Jo laughed, until a cough cut her off.

"Jo, he needs to know about the results of your X rays. He's talking about buying a house. That means he's staying in Vegas, so you don't need to worry that he's giving up San Francisco because you're ill."

"But, darling girl, this is a happy time for you both. I don't want to be the downer in your life."

Kate jumped to her feet. "Stop playing the martyr, Josephine. Talk to your son or I will."

Chapter Nineteen

Rob looked in the mirror and smiled. She hadn't said yes, exactly, but she hadn't said no, either. He picked up a brush, but before he could get one stroke through his hair, the door opened and Kate handed him the phone. "Talk to her. I'll be outside."

"Mom?"

"Son. You do know that Kate is rather pushy, don't you?"

"Only with people she loves."

After a few seconds, Jo said, "Yes. I guess that's true. Okay, then, I'll tell you what I know—which isn't much. There are a couple of spots on my lungs. Showed up in the last bunch of X rays. I'm seeing an oncologist on Monday. He'll decide if we run more tests or do a biopsy."

Rob froze. The information didn't fit into his brain right at first. Cancer? His mother? No. Of course it was possible, but…no. "What time on Monday? I'll take you."

"See? I knew you'd do this—change your whole life to try to help. That's why I didn't tell you sooner. There's nothing you can do, son."

"You're wrong, Mother. I can hold your hand and take notes and do research about your options. I can and will be there for you. If you thought otherwise, you don't know me very well."

She sighed. "I do know you. That's why I swore Kate to secrecy. I didn't want to turn your life upside down. Or postpone your wedding."

"She hasn't actually said yes, Mom. Heck, we haven't even been out on a real date yet," he added, with a chuckle. The thought had occurred to him on the plane. He needed to woo his new fiancée and was looking forward to it.

"So, where are you?"

"At the coffee shop on Sunrise."

"Stay put. Kate and I will pick you up in ten minutes. I'm going to buy a house, then Kate has a stop to make. When we're done there, we're all going to go back to Yetta's and discuss this matter, okay?"

He didn't give her time to argue. His mother could be stubborn, but so could he.

KATE PACED from the sports car to the truck and back. *I bet I've spent half my life pacing.* She still carried Rob's ring. She wanted to slip it on her finger but couldn't. Not until she talked to her daughter. How would Maya take this news? So much change, so fast. Too fast?

"Are you ready? We're picking up Mom on the way. I don't think she should be alone to stew about things."

She followed him to the pickup truck and climbed into the passenger seat. "How's she feeling?"

"I didn't ask. If I know her, she's writing her obituary."

The thought made Kate's heart ache. She adored Jo. They made a great team. She couldn't imagine having a more perfect mother-in-law.

"Um…Rob…I…" She played with the ring, turning it

nervously. "I can't…we can't…do this. Not right away. I think I should break the news to Maya after she's had time to adjust to Ian leaving."

"But I thought you said she accepted the fact that I was part of your lives now. She made that picture."

"I know. And I think she'll be happy once she has time to assimilate all the changes, but you're still…new."

Rob took a deep breath. He didn't want to do anything that would jeopardize his chance to establish a strong relationship with his future stepdaughter.

"No problem. We'll wait until you think the time is right. Same with our wedding date. I'm prepared to be flexible—as long as it's sometime this month."

"What?" she squawked.

He winked. "Just testing." Looking over his shoulder as they backed up, he said, "Next month, then."

She tugged on her shoulder belt to get some extra room and leaned across the console between them. "You're crazy, but in a good way. Are you going to tell me what happened in San Francisco?"

He filled her in on the meetings, the PR people and why he turned down the "offer of a lifetime." "I had an epiphany. Isn't that a cool word? Dad and I did our golfing thing, but this time we actually talked. About life. Love. The mistakes parents make. I finally realized that I would make mistakes as a parent. Not necessarily the same ones my parents made because I'm not them. But nobody is perfect and that's okay."

Her hand was warm and comforting on his thigh. Her smell made him feel content, complete. "I'm glad to hear you say that because we both know that I'm a mess. And talk about a bad parent, I nearly lost my daughter twice in one week."

"Not true. You said yourself Ian acted on impulse. He would have come back sooner or later and Maya was never in any real danger. And what happened at the pool was probably a good thing."

She sat back. "How do you figure?"

"You know that Maya had been acting very cocky around the pool. I think she'll be more respectful in the future. And the other kids will learn from her close call."

Kate didn't speak for a few minutes. "You never cease to surprise me—especially when it comes to kids. When Maya first met you, she said you didn't like children. She's usually very astute about people."

"She was probably right. At the time."

"What?"

"When I first got to town, my office was in chaos. My senior staff member is a guy that everyone likes. He's a gem, but his personal life is a mess. His wife had just left him with their three kids. He brought the little demons to work with him half the time. To be fair, those kids had just had their world turned upside down, but a law office isn't a day care center."

"And because you're a compassionate guy, you tried to help him and the kids and got burnt out."

"Something like that."

"So, what did you do?"

"Organized a job-sharing situation. Another colleague needed time to care for her elderly mother. Now they work in tandem with their combined client list and do some of the work from home."

"Sounds like a perfect solution."

He touched the blinker. "We'll see. So, where are we going after we buy the house?"

She gave him a saucy grin. "To buy you a dog."

Rob turned so sharply, he bounced over the curb. "A what?"

ROB STOOD as far back from the chain link pen as possible. He hadn't been able to convince Kate that buying a dog before he closed escrow was a bad idea. To his surprise, his mother had jumped on the bandwagon and even volunteered to dog-sit until Rob moved into his new home.

The smell and noise coming from the various pens was overwhelming.

"Do they all bark?" he asked the clerk who was accompanying them. He had to shout to be heard.

"Not all," the woman, a Kathy Bates lookalike, said. "Poppy—over there against the back wall—is very quiet. We don't know much about her background. Part Jack Russell and beagle, maybe with a little whippet or minigreyhound in the mix."

Rob stepped closer so he could put one eye up to the fence. "She's bigger than the rest."

The clerk—Rosie, he saw her name embroidered on her smock—nodded. "We had her in with the larger dogs but she was miserable. She's a bit timid and one or two of the more aggressive ones picked on her."

"Nice coloring," his mother said.

Rob gave the animal a second look. A short coat that was mostly white with soft, irregular brown blotches, like a pinto pony. Her nose was dainty and very black. All four feet were white. "Poppy," he called.

Her ears perked up and she looked at him. He whistled softly. All the dogs—except Poppy—rushed the fence, yipping and pushing each other in anticipation of a treat or petting. His gaze remained fixed on the elegant little dog on the far side of the pen. She stood up with great dignity and slowly walked toward him.

Jo knelt beside the pen and put her fingers through the holes. Poppy sniffed politely a few seconds, then let out a little moan that seemed to say, "Thank God you're finally here."

Rob looked at Kate who had a funny look on her face. When their gazes met, she nodded, then put her hand on his mother's shoulder and said, "It looks like love at first sight, Jo."

To Rob she said, "I'm sorry. I think I got it wrong."

"Huh?"

"I thought we were supposed to come here today to buy *you* a dog, but it looks like this pooch is totally stuck on Jo. And vice versa."

Completely baffled, Rob put his hands on his hips. "What are you talking about?"

"Mom woke me up this morning and told me I needed to take you to buy a dog. She hasn't been that specific about one of her visions in months. Usually she talks about dreams that don't really make any sense. But she was definite about this. She practically pushed me out the door."

He still didn't get it. "But she couldn't have known Mom would call and we'd pick her up. That just isn't possible."

Jo, who rose stiffly, let out the first laugh Rob had heard since he'd returned. She put her hand on his arm and gave it a strong squeeze. "Yetta's visions don't always make sense to the rest of us, son. But if you're wise, you don't argue with her. Some things simply were meant to be."

"I SIGNED the final papers today," Rob said, sliding a large silver key across the tablecloth between them. "We own a house."

Kate was sitting across from Rob at a table near the door to the kitchen. Two weeks had passed since his proposal. A hectic, scattered time fraught with fear—they still didn't have a definitive diagnosis on Jo's condition—and private joy. She'd shared the news of their engagement with her mother and Jo, but no one else. Her first concern was Maya. She didn't want to rush the child into a change she wasn't ready for.

"You own a house," Kate repeated. "How did you manage to make it happen so fast? Banks take forever to process loans."

"Agreed. But the people who bought my condo paid cash. I put every bit into the new house, which made me a very attractive buyer, let me tell you. I had mortgage companies fighting over me. I went with the one who could close the deal the fastest." He beamed, triumphant. "There are a few loose ends to tie up, but, basically, it's a done deal. No phone or Internet service, but the power and water work."

"Congratulations. That's wonderful."

She meant it. She just wished she had the energy to sound more enthused. Tonight had been the first Friday since the E. coli rumor that every table had been filled for all three seatings. She was thrilled, but exhausted—both physically and emotionally.

Their new fill-in chef, although extremely talented, was a flake. Kate had had to come in early to cover the lunch shift for Jo, whose latest doctor's appointment had run late. Jo still hadn't returned when Rob called and asked to see Kate. She'd jokingly told him the only way to make sure that would happen was to make a reservation at Romantique. Which he had.

This was the first chance she'd had to sit down in six hours. And she wished she was anyplace but here.

He cocked his head, questioningly. "What's wrong?"

"Nothing. I'm just tired. My new cook's ex-wife is in town. She's some major bad news. Makes Ian look like a saint."

"Speaking of which, I heard his petition for a new parole hearing was granted. The letter you sent on his behalf must have helped."

She tried to smile.

"Kate," he said, taking her hand. "Are you okay?"

No, she wanted to cry. She wanted him to hold her and tell her everything was going to be fine. But she couldn't say anything. Not yet. Not until he'd talked to Jo.

"It was a rough night. I'm going back in and make sure my crew isn't poisoning someone. Your mom is upstairs. Why don't you go check on her?"

He gave her a funny look. Apparently her attempt at blasé wasn't too successful. "Something's wrong. Tell me."

"I'm just pooped. Too many late nights in your arms, I guess." She tried to make it sound like a joke, but, in truth, she wondered if the best thing that ever happened to her was actually going to be the death of her. Going to Rob's after work was the one bonus in her life, but that usually meant she wound up with two or three hours of sleep followed by a predawn dash to her mother's so she'd be in her bed when Maya got up.

He leaned across the table and kissed her. "All the more reason to get married soon." He ran the back of his fingers down her cheek. "This is Vegas, baby. We could hit the drive-through chapel tonight."

Kate was tempted—so very tempted, but she couldn't do that to Maya. She was trying to lay the groundwork to insure this transition went smoothly. She ignored his suggestion. "Are you still planning to take Maya to the Ethel M chocolate factory tomorrow?"

He made a face. "I don't know if that's a good idea. I'm afraid it might be too old for her. The machines are all behind glass. I checked it out the other day. It's interesting, but—" A mischievous sparkle appeared in his eyes. "What if we show Maya the new house? Very casual. A backyard picnic. Mom can bring Poppy over."

Before she could answer, a head popped out of the kitchen and a panicky voice called, "Kate? We need you."

She heaved a sigh as she pushed to her feet. "Duty calls."

"How come Mom's not pitching in?"

She scurried toward the door without answering but paused to point toward the second story. "She's upstairs. Go talk to her."

He frowned and finished off the last of his wine. Something was up. He'd tried Jo earlier and she'd nearly bitten his head off. Probably because of all the run-around she'd been getting from her doctors, he figured.

"Mom?" he called a minute later when he reached the second-floor office space.

She was sitting in Kate's chair, facing the wall, her legs resting on the two-drawer filing cabinet. Typically, she would have been smoking but since this was a no-smoking office, he expected to find her chewing the eraser off a pencil.

She twirled about so fast, her feet hit the floor with a

loud snap. No pencil in hand. Instead, a tissue, which she used to dab at her eyes and nose.

His mother crying? That never happened.

Rob hurried across the room. "What is it? What's going on?"

"Nothing. I'm okay."

"Mom." He walked around the desk so they were only inches apart and sat down on top of the papers that were scattered about. He didn't glance down at them.

"I…um, I just got off the phone with your father."

"Oh. Oh," he exclaimed with a smile. "He told you about Daisy."

Her expression was one of utter bafflement. "Who's Daisy?"

Rob swallowed. *Oops.* "He didn't tell you? He and Haley are expecting. It's a girl. They're going to name her Daisy Josephine."

Fresh tears welled up in her eyes. "Oh, my. He didn't say. That's wonderful. I'm so h-happy for them."

Her voice broke and she started to cry.

Rob's fear level spiked. He reached out and put his hand on her shoulder. "Mom, what's wrong? Tell me."

"I got a call from my primary care doctor this afternoon. Even after all these tests they're not sure if I have cancer or not. And I feel so damn lousy, I just want it to be over."

"Mom."

"Your father thinks I should get a second opinion at Stanford."

"Mom, that's a great idea."

"I don't know, son. A good friend of mine died of colon cancer. The treatment…well, it wasn't pleasant. And in the end, it failed."

Rob tried to grasp what she was saying. "You mean you might not try anything?"

"Maybe."

Rob fought the panic gnawing at the edges of his control. If she were his client, approaching him to establish a living will, he would have listened without judging, but this was his mother. "Mom, you can't *not* fight. I'm not ready to give you up. Kate and I are getting married. We need you. Even Dad is going to need you once the baby comes. What does Haley know about babies?"

Her watery smile was more indulgent than convinced.

"And Poppy needs you."

Jo's brows drew together. "You planned that, didn't you? You and Kate—and Yetta. That's why you took me to the shelter with you."

They looked at each other and smiled. His mother stood up. She put her arms around him and hugged him fiercely. "You're right, son. I can't leave now." She patted his back firmly as if sealing her decision. "Poppy needs me."

He swallowed against the tightness in his throat. "Me, too. Can I take you home?"

"What about Kate?"

"I'm sure she'll understand."

Jo threaded her arm through his. "Well, even if she doesn't, the poor girl needs a good night's sleep."

Chapter Twenty

"Hurry, Mommy, it's hot on my feet."

"I told you to wear your flip-flops," Kate grumbled, grabbing a stack of towels from the back seat of the car. They'd driven her mother's sedan since hers was leaking oil and she didn't want to leave a spot on Rob's pristine cement.

Somehow, between the time she left the restaurant last night and woke up this morning, Rob's plan for a laid-back picnic had been expanded. The casual visit now included a catered brunch. She had no idea how he'd pulled that off.

"Are my floaties in the bag?" Maya asked her grandmother who was collecting their totes from the trunk.

"Yes, indeed. And your new ladybug water toy."

"Her what?" Kate had been so distracted lately, she sometimes felt as though she were walking through dense fog without a clue about what was going on around her.

She was definitely ready for a little R&R, she thought as she took her daughter's hand and led the way to the front door. The impressive two-story columns provided a welcome escape from the sun.

Maya pushed the doorbell.

Kate was poking in her bag to make sure she'd packed

the sunscreen when she heard a little yip. She looked over the top of her sunglasses at her daughter. "Jo and Poppy must be here."

Maya clapped. "Oh, good. I love Poppy."

A quick thud of footsteps on tile told her Rob was hurrying to meet them. He threw open the door a second later and swept her into his arms. "You're here," he cried. After hugging Kate, he bent low to give Maya a quick squeeze then did the same with Yetta. "I'm so glad you all could make it. Are Liz and Alex coming?"

Kate tucked her shades in her bag. "Yeah. But Liz said she had to do something first."

He took their bags in one hand then made an expansive gesture with the other. "Come in. Mom's in the kitchen with Poppy. We don't have any furniture yet," he said, seemingly for Maya's benefit. "But we do have food."

Kate paused to look around. Her last visit had been in the company of a Realtor who was determined to make the sale. Kate had done her best to appear uninvolved, but inside she'd been dizzy with excitement. Rob was buying this house with every intention of sharing it with her and her daughter. She could have burst with joy, if she'd let herself believe the dream might actually come true.

Rob started toward the kitchen, but Maya dashed past him, calling, "Here, Poppy. Here, Poppy."

He looked at Kate. "You realize of course that she's going to need a dog of her own once you move in, right?"

Kate looked over her shoulder at her mother. Yetta knew about Rob's proposal, but they hadn't talked logistics.

Yetta smiled and nudged Kate into the brightly lit kitchen. "Maya's wanted a dog for a long time. What a good idea, Rob."

"A dog is also work. Feeding, brushing, walks, shots, lessons, poop to clean up. Who's going to do that? Maya is too young, which means—"

"Somebody else would have to pitch in," Rob inserted. "Someone like me."

Kate had heard that line before. Ian brought home a puppy once. Sunny. A beautiful golden retriever that Kate had grown to love with all her heart. She'd wound up doing every chore that Ian had vowed would be his responsibility. And when he disappeared and Kate came to the realization that she couldn't humanely move a large dog into her mother's small backyard and care for a toddler and work sixty hours a week, she'd been forced to find a new home for the animal she loved.

Kate suddenly burst into tears.

Rob whispered something to Yetta then took Kate in his arms and waltzed her backwards into the living room. In the privacy of the bay window that she'd fallen in love with the first time she walked into the house, he said, "Kate, love. Tell me what's going on. You don't want a dog? No problem. I thought a pet might be good for Maya. Make her feel like this was really her home, but there's no rush."

He rocked her gently and offered the hem of his shirt to wipe her tears. "It's not that. I was thinking about the last dog I owned. Ian brought her home when I was eight months pregnant. He said he wanted the baby and Sunny—that was the dog's name—to grow up together. He promised to take care of her, but before long he was never home."

Rob groaned. "You had to take care of it."

"I didn't mind, really. She was a sweetheart and I loved her. But after I sold the house, I c-couldn't take her with us. Mom's yard is small. She was a big dog. She needed room to run." Her tears started again. He held her tight.

"Oh, honey, I'm so sorry. Maybe, when you're ready, we could adopt a golden. I've always heard they're a wonderful breed."

She wiped her eyes and smiled. She couldn't help it. He sounded so earnest and sincere. "I'm sorry, too. I overreacted. I don't know what's wrong with me. I hadn't thought about Sunny in a long time. Not even when we picked out Poppy."

He touched his knuckle under her chin and made her look at him. "Are you okay? Really? We can cancel this little bash. No big deal."

Her heart swelled with all the feelings she had for this man. "I'll be fine. Just let me freshen up then I'll meet you outside."

"It's a date. I'd better go make sure Maya's got her life vest on." He gave her a quick kiss then left. "I love you."

Kate lingered, watching him through the window. He did love her. She knew it. And she loved him. Which meant the life she'd been living had to change. She was sick and tired of straddling two worlds. What was she waiting for? A sign that her destiny was finally here?

Maybe.

Yetta was sitting at the counter stirring a glass of iced tea when Kate walked in. "Mom, we need to talk."

"I know."

"I love you and I can never thank you for what you've done for me and Maya, but—"

Yetta interrupted her. "Katherine, you're my daughter. There isn't anything in the world that I wouldn't do for you. And the same for Maya. She kept my heart beating when it would have stopped. The sparkle in her eyes reminds me so much of your father that I was slowly able to see that he lives on in each of us. You both helped me heal. That might not have been possible if you hadn't needed me."

Emotion made it hard to speak. "I haven't been that easy to live with, lately."

"Because you're thinking with your head, not listening with your heart. You're afraid of making an impulsive decision, like the one that brought Ian into our lives, but, darling girl, he led you to the path you're now on. If not for him, you might never have met Rob."

Kate needed a moment to digest that truth. She sat on a stool that had apparently come with the house. Was what her mother said the truth? Had the rough road she'd traveled recently been an unavoidable detour to her destiny? She sighed and rested her chin on her hand. "Mom, I need to marry Rob and move."

"Katherine, I've enjoyed having you and Maya with me, but, frankly, I couldn't agree more."

"Really? You're not just saying that to make me feel better about deserting you?" She was teasing and her mother responded with a smile.

Yetta put her arm around Kate's shoulders. "I'll manage. Somehow."

Kate returned the hug, then stood up. "I'd better check on Maya."

"Katherine?"

She stopped and looked at her mother. "Yes?"

"Perhaps it's time to put on that pretty ring you keep hidden under your shirt."

Kate reached up and touched her treasure. She unsnapped the clasp and let the ring tumbled into her palm.

Smiling, she looked up and said, "Thanks, Mom."

"MAYA, SWEETIE, can you come here? I need to talk to you." Rob looked at his mother, who was sitting in a lawn chair, fidgeting nervously. A nicotine craving, he bet. "You, too, Mom. This is important."

Poppy, who never left Jo's side, seemed comfortable around Maya as long as the little girl was sitting quietly. Maya squeezed in next to Jo and gently petted the dog.

"Maya, I have a problem. Mom might be going away for a while and Poppy will have to stay with me."

"Going? Where?" Her voice sounded alarmed.

"To California. But just for a little while."

"Why can't Poppy go, too?"

"She doesn't like to fly," Jo said.

Maya gave the dog a serious look. "Oh."

"Anyway, if Poppy moves in here while Mom is gone, I thought maybe you could help me out. Play with her. Brush her. Make sure I don't forget to feed her. Stuff like that."

"Me?"

He nodded.

"Where will Poppy sleep?"

He looked at Jo. "That's a good question. I'm not sure. On my bed, I guess. Once I get one."

Maya petted the little dog. "She could sleep with me."

Rob wasn't sure what to make of that suggestion. He looked at his mother, who had a funny smile on her face. Before he could pursue the point, Kate joined them. "This looks like an important powwow. Did I miss anything?"

Maya looked at her mother and asked, "Mommy, are you going to marry Rob?"

Rob nearly choked on his frozen daiquiri. Kate's skin tone paled. "Well…um, yes. Eventually, but we didn't want to rush you. You've been through a lot lately and—"

Maya interrupted. "But if I lived here, then Poppy could sleep with me when Jo's gone."

Rob looked at his fiancée. "Indisputable logic. She could be a lawyer when she grows up."

Kate cleared her throat. This wasn't the way she'd pictured this conversation. "Sweetheart, I love Rob. He gave me this beautiful ring. See?" She held up her hand and heard Rob's sharp intake of breath. She sensed his surprise—and pleasure. "And I want to marry him. But you're our first concern. Poppy will be fine here without you."

Maya studied the pretty diamond a minute then looked up. "But, Mommy, Rob needs us, too."

Kate didn't know what to say. Her daughter's insight amazed her.

"You're right, Maya. I do need you. This house is going to feel pretty empty until you and your mom are living here. I'd marry you both tomorrow if we could arrange it," he said, taking Kate's hand. He brought her fingers to his lips and tenderly kissed the ring.

Maya frowned. "No. That doesn't work for me. I have school tomorrow. We're doing art."

Rob chuckled softly. The sound echoed through Kate's heart. They were doing this. They were talking marriage with her daughter. There was going to be a wedding.

The part of her who knew that rushing into things was a mistake said, "I love you, Maya. You're the best. And I promise to include you in all the decisions about when and how to make this happen, okay?"

Maya looked at Rob. "Okay, but I still think Poppy should sleep with me when Jo's gone."

Rob burst out laughing. "I agree. Let's go ask your grandmother if she minds. It's her house, right?"

Once Rob and Maya had left in search of Yetta, Kate

looked at her future mother-in-law and said, "Wow. That went better than I thought it would."

Jo smiled serenely. "Your daughter is the oldest four-year-old I've ever met."

Kate agreed. Which meant they would need to be very careful what they said about Jo's illness.

"You know, Kate, Rob doesn't want the kind of wedding his father had. You're both too busy for all of that nonsense. What if you held it here? Small and simple. A white tent. An evening affair to avoid the heat. Just family and close friends," Jo said, making a sweeping motion to encompass the backyard.

Kate looked around. She could almost envision it. "When?" she wondered, idly.

"What about late June or early July?" Jo asked. "That should give me time to get this doctoring business straightened out. We ought to know by then if I'm going to make it, right?"

Kate's heart plunged to her feet. She reached across the table to touch Jo's arm. "Of course you're going to make it."

Jo chuckled softly. "You sound a lot like my son at times. But not to worry. I've never passed up a chance to bake a wedding cake. The one I have in mind is three layers and adorned with foil-wrapped chocolate coins."

Kate went to her and hugged her—Poppy and all. "I love you, Jo. I'm so blessed to have you—and your son—in my life."

She might have said more, but at that moment, the French doors opened and her mother stepped outside followed by Liz and Alex. And Ian.

Chapter Twenty-One

Rob was making a fresh batch of freezer drinks when he heard someone enter the kitchen. Kate, he hoped. They had been entertaining her family for three hours and had yet to talk about their wedding.

He topped off the last of the glasses and turned around. Ian.

The man looked surprisingly well. He was dressed in Bermuda shorts with a Hawaiian print shirt and sandals. So new they still had creases from being folded on a shelf. "Ah, good, someone to help me carry these outside," Rob said.

Ian didn't smile. Instead, he walked to the side-by-side refrigerator. He pointed at the painting Rob had tacked up right after Ginny, his Realtor, handed him the key to the front door.

"She's got talent," Ian said. He laughed a bit self-consciously. "I suppose every proud papa says that about his child, but I mean it. She sees the world in a special way and isn't afraid to put that out there."

"You're right. She's an amazing little girl," Rob said.

"She's my little girl."

Rob didn't say anything.

"But I don't deserve any credit for the way she's turned out. When she was a baby, I was too busy working to spend time with her. I always figured I'd make up for it when she was older."

Ian pointed at the solitary figure in the drawing. "She made her choice."

Rob had no idea what to say. That could just as easily have been him, standing alone in a hideous green tie. And he knew he'd feel just as lousy as Ian obviously did.

Compassion made him cross the room and hand Ian the drink he'd poured before he added the booze to the mix. "Here. A virgin daiquiri. Liz said alcohol aggravates your condition."

Ian took it, then glanced up. "Thanks. You're being a good sport about me just showing up like this. I was as surprised as anybody when my attorney handed me my release papers. I have forty-eight hours to report to my parole officer in Reno."

"I'd heard it was going to be soon. Do you have a ride?"

Ian nodded. "Yeah, an old friend. The guy who's putting me to work. He'll be getting to town in a couple of hours. Liz said she'd take me home in time to meet him. Alex convinced me that saying goodbye in person would be best for Maya."

"I agree. I'm glad you're here."

Ian gave Rob a smile that seemed tinged with sadness. "I'm glad Katie found you. I think you'll be good for each other."

"Thanks."

"Daddy," a little girl's voice called. "Where are you?"

A second later, Maya appeared. She was wearing her

swimsuit—a Dora the Explorer one-piece and pink flip-flops. Her slightly wet shoes made a squeaky sound crossing the tile.

"There you are. Auntie Liz wanted me to make sure you remembered to take your pills."

Ian patted his pocket. "I just did, sweetheart. Thank you for reminding me." He glanced at Rob and said, "We were just talking about your picture. It's really good. Will you make one for me to take with me when I move?"

"Sure." She walked to where they were standing and held out her arms to be picked up. Ian obliged. When level with Rob, she said, "I'll make you one that has me and Mommy and Rob and Jo and Poppy in it. So you won't forget where we are."

Ian nodded gravely. "That would be great, honey."

"We'll keep this one here because it shows the road from us to you. When we drive to see you, we gotta sing. Like Dorothy." She looked at Rob. "I told Mommy I needed ruby slippers and she said she didn't think so. Can you buy me some?"

Rob knew he was being manipulated, but the little charmer was almost impossible to resist when she gave him that sweet innocent look.

"Maya Katherine Grant. Are you begging Rob when I specifically told you no ruby slippers?" Kate barked, hurrying to where they were standing.

"But Mommy. How else will I find Daddy after he moves?" Tears brimmed, threatening to spill over her little cheeks.

"A map," Rob said. "I'll teach you how to read a map. There are big roads and little roads and towns with funny names, like Pahrump."

She didn't look as though she believed him until Ian spoke, "Rob's right, baby doll. I went there once. A long time ago. The guy who owned the bar had a pet buffalo named Bill."

"Bill?" Maya repeated.

"Buffalo Bill," Rob and Ian said together, chuckling. They toasted their glasses together, in a total guy gesture that meant something neither could probably put into words.

Maya wiggled to be put down. "I gotta go show Auntie Liz my new room. It's empty, but Mommy says we're going to move all my stuff and dec-o-rate it real pretty," she said, stressing each syllable of the word. "Wanna see it, too, Daddy?"

After they were gone, Kate put her arms around Rob and said, "I should warn you, Maya will take you for all you're worth, if you don't watch it."

He grinned and looked at his painting. A mommy, a daddy, and a little girl. Together. A family. He'd gladly pay whatever price Maya extracted. He couldn't wait.

KATE WAS HONESTLY surprised by how well the afternoon was going—until Liz announced it was time for Ian to leave. Then Maya, who obviously needed a nap, threw a tantrum. Yetta volunteered to take her home for a rest.

"We'll catch a ride with Liz," she said. "That way you and Rob can talk about wedding plans."

She squeezed Kate's hand, which now sported the sparkling engagement ring, and added, "Just remember. The—"

Kate stopped her. "Please, not another prophecy."

"I was going to say, the starter on my car is a little sticky. You have to wiggle the steering wheel a couple of times before you can turn the key."

Kate felt her face flush. "Oh."

Her mother hugged her. "It's okay, dear heart. Your road has been a tough one, but I'm absolutely positive things will be less rocky from now on."

Kate wanted to believe her, but nagging fears remained. Was this the right move? Maybe she and Rob should just live together for a while. Shouldn't they postpone any wedding plans until after Jo's health issues were cleared up?

"You're Romani, Katherine. Never forget that."

Kate blinked. She wasn't sure her mother had spoken the words. Or her father.

Yetta smiled serenely, then kissed Rob who was carrying leftover watermelon into the kitchen, where Jo was cleaning up.

The two women exchanged a quiet word then Jo shook her head and said, "Well, I'd better push off, too. I'm going online to see if there are any yoga classes in my area."

"Yoga?" Kate asked.

"Liz suggested it. Said it might help with my cravings, plus, I told her a bit of medical history. You know, I had rheumatic fever when I was a child. She said yoga might help me build up lung strength and help with stress."

Rob looked at Kate. "Sounds like a good idea."

"I told Yetta she should go with me. She said she's had lung problems since infancy. Maybe we'll both live to be a hundred."

Kate liked the sound of that. She gave her mother-in-law-to-be a big hug. "I love you, my friend. Your son is amazing. You did good, Jo."

"Thank you. I hope you know how much I adore your daughter, your mother, your sisters and, above all, you."

They hugged until Poppy protested from too much affection. "Can you believe this dog? It's almost as if she's always been a part of my life. She's absolutely perfect. How could anyone have let her go?"

"Sometimes circumstances dictate what we do," Kate said, thinking of Sunny.

"And sometimes," Jo said, kissing her pooch on the head, "we just luck out."

"I CAN'T STAY."

"Why not? We're almost legal."

"I promised Maya I'd tuck her in. She may seem okay, but I think she's still upset about her dad leaving."

He nodded. "I know. And I also know how tired you are. Have you thought about going to the doctor? This thing with Mom has me a little freaked out."

Kate shrugged. "I'll ask Liz for some herbal tea. She made me promise to stop drinking soda, you know. My body is probably going through the same kind of withdrawal that Jo's is."

"Ah," he said. "That might be it. But you promise not to doze off during our wedding, right?"

She kissed him. "I promise. Besides, did it ever occur to you that all the exercise I get at night with you might be the culprit?"

He nuzzled her neck. "To be honest. I was hoping you might be pregnant."

Kate laughed and shook her head. "No. Not possible. We've been careful." Of course, she and Ian had been careful, too. She tried counting backward in her head. "I don't think it's possible."

Rob sighed. "Wishful thinking on my part. But, you do want more kids, don't you?"

"Yes. I loved being pregnant. My body felt strong and blessed and fruitful." She shook her head. "You're talking to a woman who feeds people for a living. What does that tell you?"

"That you're a giver. And as such you have to be careful not to give away too much because then there might be nothing left for yourself." His protective tone warmed her. "But, I promise you, Kate, I'll never let that happen. I'm the keeper of laws, and the number one law in this house will be: protect the queen."

She grinned. "My sisters and I grew up thinking we were princesses. Grace is going to be very upset when she learns that I've been promoted to queen."

"Too bad. You are my queen and I love you with all my heart and then some."

"What's the 'then some'?"

His eyebrows waggled suggestively. "Come upstairs and let me show you. I don't have a bed yet, but I think we can make do."

Kate laughed and took his hand because she knew without a doubt that she'd finally found the right road— her destiny, and she would walk each step, arm in arm, with the man she was born to love.

* * * * *

Be sure to watch for Liz's story,
the next title in Debra Salonen's intriguing
Sisters of the Silver Dollar miniseries.
BRINGING BABY HOME
will be available in August 2006
wherever Harlequin books are sold.

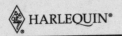

HARLEQUIN®

American ROMANCE®

To Wed,
or
Not To Wed

**A new series about love, relationships
and the road to the altar**

THE MAN
SHE'LL MARRY
by Ann Roth

Cinnamon Smith's attraction to
Nick Mahoney is purely physical—
or so she thinks. From the moment
she meets him, Cinnamon can't seem
to get him out of her mind, even though
Nick is miles from her idea of the
right man for her. But finding love—
and the right man to marry—
rarely happens as we expect!

Available June, whereever books are sold.

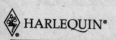

® HARLEQUIN®

American ROMANCE®

A THREE-BOOK SERIES BY

Kaitlyn Rice

Heartland Sisters

To the folks in Augusta, Kansas, the three sisters
were the Blume girls—a little pitiable, a bit mysterious
and different enough to be feared.

The three sisters may have received an odd upbringing,
but there's nothing odd about the affection, esteem
and support they have for one another, no matter
what the crises that come their way.

THE THIRD DAUGHTER'S WISH

When Josie Blume starts to search for the father she's
never known, she's trying to lay some family ghosts to rest.
Other surprises are in store on her journey back into time—
and one of them is rediscovering Gabe Thomas, a man who
shares not only her past and present but her future, too.

Available June 2006

Also look for:

THE LATE BLOOMER'S BABY
Available October 2005

THE RUNAWAY BRIDESMAID
Available February 2006

Available wherever Harlequin books are sold.

SPECIAL PRICE!

This riveting new saga begins with

In the Dark

by national bestselling author

JUDITH ARNOLD

The party at Hotel Marchand is in full swing when the lights suddenly go out. What does head of security Mac Jensen do first? He's torn between two jobs—protecting the guests at the hotel and keeping the woman he loves safe.

A woman to protect. A hotel to secure. And no idea who's determined to harm them.

On Sale June 2006

HOTEL MARCHAND

Four sisters.
A family legacy.
And someone is out to destroy it.

A captivating new limited
continuity, launching June 2006

The most beautiful hotel in New Orleans,
and someone is out to destroy it. But mystery,
danger and some surprising family revelations
and discoveries won't stop the Marchand sisters
from protecting their birthright…
and finding love along the way.